Beach Town

Ann Roberts

Bella
BOOKS

2008

Author's Note:
Ocean Beach, California, is a real beach town. I have taken many lib-
erties with its history, certain locations and events, all in the name of
fiction. I do so as a tribute to this wonderful place, and I mean no offense
to the town or its residents.

Bella Books, Inc.
P.O. Box 10543
Tallahassee, FL 32302

Printed in the United States of America on acid-free paper
First Edition

Editor: Christi Cassidy
Cover designer: Stephanie Solomon-Lopez

ISBN-10: 1-59493-132-1
ISBN-13: 978-1-59493-132-1

Acknowledgments

I owe a big thanks to Christi Cassidy, who teaches me so much each time she works with me on a project. Also, without the continued support of Linda Hill and everyone at Bella Books, these words would just continue to be scribbles in my notebook.

I loved writing this story because it combined some of my favorite things—the ocean, dogs and a character based on my own son. I have spent much of my adult life visiting beach towns on both coasts. Each has a distinct culture and no two are the same.

I am indebted to the beaches and towns of Ocean, Laguna, Pacific, Mission, Yachats, Virginia, Kill Devil Hill (a.k.a. Kittyhawk) and Cocoa.

Thanks for the memories.

About the Author

Ann Roberts is rather certain she grew up in Arizona because her parents' car died before they could reach the California coast. She continues to bake in the Phoenix heat with her partner, her son and two dogs—Wylie, the relaxed Ridgeback, and Babe, the neurotic beagle.

She is the author of *Paid in Full*, *Furthest from the Gate* and *Brilliant*.

Chapter One
Jonah Israel

It was all in the packaging.

Jonah Israel's mother had taught him that lesson. Gloria Israel could expertly display the smallest trifle and convince her sons that it was grand and exceptional. She was a psychological magician who implemented a mental sleight of hand, persuading the five boys that their lives were rich. Growing up in Hell's Kitchen, there was plenty of nothing, and finding the silver lining was never obvious and, at times, totally illusory.

His childhood was a flurry of energy toward survival, beginning when he was ten years old and could work alongside his four older brothers at the dock to support his family. Their father had died from hypothermia when he was eight, leaving his mother with all of them. His memories of wantonness resulted in one philosophy: money may not buy happiness, but it can rent it for a lifetime. This appreciation for wealth most often manifested itself at mealtime, and once he climbed out of poverty, he vowed to enjoy the finest restaurants around the world, sampling every delicacy possible. The langouste belle-aurore was one he always craved in Paris at the L'Ambroisie, while the chateaubriand at MEGU's in New York was exquisite.

Such dinners were a far cry from the meals of his childhood. Each day his mother served a bowl of broth in the morning and another in the evening, accompanied by a small hunk of bread on a chipped plate. During the day he survived on the kindness of a fisherman's wife, who made sure he and his brothers each had a tuna sandwich for lunch. It certainly wasn't enough sustenance for a growing boy who spent his leisure time hauling fish out of the harbor. Yet he never felt he went hungry because his mother employed an artful deception at mealtime, which emerged as the basis for his other life philosophy: it was all in the packaging.

As Gloria set the bowls full of broth down on the table each night, she would recount an elaborate story about a client who had come into the talent agency where she worked as a secretary.

"Boys, today I met the most amazing man. His name was Mischa Romakov, a juggler, but he used to be a professional sword-swallower—until someone stole his voice." Jonah's eyes bulged with interest, and his mother motioned for them to keep eating as she told the story.

"How did he lose his voice?" his brother Benjamin asked.

"That's exactly what I wondered. And he told me his sad tale of woe that happened twenty years before. He'd worked in a Moscow circus, where he was the star attraction. People came from all over the countryside to see him swallow the longest and sharpest swords. One night a beautiful young girl attended the performance, and she was so amazed that she waited to meet him after the show. When Mischa saw her, he fell in love instantly. For many nights after, Ivana, for that was the girl's name, came to the performances, waiting for her true love to defy death and plunge the long steel blade down his gullet. This went on for two weeks as Ivana and Mischa fell deeper in love. However, unbeknownst to Mischa—"

"What's unbeknownst?" Jonah interrupted.

"It means he didn't know," his oldest brother, Jacob, quickly explained.

"Yes," Gloria said. "What Mischa didn't know was that Ivana was already promised to another, an evil man named Rudolph. When he found out that she was seeing Mischa, he went into a rage and wanted revenge. He snuck into the performance, and after Mischa had swallowed the sharpest sword, and while the audience was applauding wildly, Rudolph jumped onto the stage and twisted the blade while it was still submerged in his throat." Gloria paused while they gasped in horror. She motioned for them to finish their meals as she completed the tale. "The police quickly led Rudolph away, but there was blood everywhere and the damage was done. Mischa's throat was cut to ribbons, and although he lived, and learned to speak again, he could no longer swallow swords. That was when he became a juggler."

"What about Ivana?" Jonah asked hopefully.

Gloria sighed heavily. "Ivana had no interest in a juggler. It wasn't exciting enough. She never saw him again after that night. Isn't that a terrible tragedy?"

They all agreed that Mischa was robbed of his happiness. They cleared the table, Jonah musing that he was grateful he hadn't lost his voice, so distracted that he never thought to complain that the broth was cold and the chunk of bread was insufficient.

It was all in the packaging.

Jonah had created movie and television stars for nearly twenty-five years, since 1969 when he'd pitched an idea to a TV executive for a show about high school teachers—*Room 222.* Although he didn't get any acknowledgment, he gained credibility and people started taking his calls. His incredible intuition ensured his name was mentioned often in Hollywood, and he had established himself as the top agent in L.A.

His gift was taking the most untalented, illiterate and inept morons and turning them into marketable celebrities. At times it was almost boring because it was so predictable. On those days he would turn it into a game. One night on a dare from a drinking buddy, he dragged a total hick from absolutely nowhere West Virginia into the neon lights of Hollywood. The fact that the kid crashed and burned after only two years was his own doing. Chomping on Valiums and downing Jack Daniels nonstop tended to ruin a career and end a life.

Such consequences were the price the climbers—as he liked to call potential celebrities—risked for a chance at stardom. And the secret fact that was whispered among the best agents and talent scouts, unbeknownst to the general public and the climbers themselves, was that their destinies were predetermined by people like him.

Talent had nothing to do with success. Some of the most gifted actors would forever languish in off-Broadway roles or B-movies, never acquiring a home in Beverly Hills or a standing table at the Russian Tea Room. They would drink in the haphazard praise given in a ten-line review in the *New York Times* or be satisfied with the hushed murmurs of their name by small audiences as they departed a dying theater. Such accolades were fleeting and notoriety extinguished quickly without the proper packaging. It was all in the packaging.

He could reach back in his memory and remember the eight-by-ten headshots he had piled into the nowhere category. There was a variety of reasons the names would never see bold-faced print in a magazine or receive thunderous applause as they walked onto the stage of a late-night talk show. At his most capricious moment, he would send a potential star packing on a whim if he didn't like the lilt of a person's voice, or if the climber was rumored to have slandered him. Those climbers found their headshots at the bottom of his trash can.

In his most scientific moments he could analyze star potential from reviewing the roles listed on a résumé and studying the smile of a black-and-white glossy. He called it the Mona Lisa Rule. Some agents noticed the eyes and believed all of the "windows to the soul" crap, but he knew the smile revealed the true nature of a person. A tentative smile lacked confidence, endurance and a thick skin, while a broad smile could project great aplomb but also naïveté, a quality that would be devoured by unscrupulous producers and studio heads. He found these clients demanded much of his time as he babysat their decision-making. It was like watching a toddler around water.

The smile he desired was casual. It happened without practice or encouragement. That was the smile of self-assurance, intelligence and promise—the promise of money. Because in the end, that was all that mattered. It ensured that he would never see another meal like the ones from his childhood. His job was to make stars, and most of the time it was his choice. A coin could be flipped and the result would matter to no one except the lucky climber and his family. Any attractive blonde could giggle and jiggle through the next must-see comedy, and there were plenty of buff, tough beefcakes who could play the sidekick in a suspense blockbuster.

It was all in the packaging.

Only once every few years did a guaranteed return drop on his desk. These were the prospects that ensured his retirement, and he would seek out these climbers and nurture them with the loving effort of a concerned grandfather, because it was their talent that was unique, not their dream. He orchestrated every part of their life—where to eat and with whom, when to throw a fit and how to gain the attention of the paparazzi, who really were every celebrity's lifeline. No press equaled zero print time, and if you weren't in the gossip columns or featured on entertainment programs, you'd better be one of the guaranteed returns, because there was no other formula for success.

His brightest and most promising star was Kira Drake. From the moment he saw her, he knew she would leap above her contemporaries and grab hold of fame with a tightened fist. He'd been enjoying a leisurely rack of lamb dinner at a popular L.A. eatery with one of his girlfriends while his wife was out of town. Kira sat across the room with her parents and a second-rate agent. He immediately studied her face, its heart shape, full lips, radiant blue eyes and picturesque smile. She smiled as she would on a magazine cover, but it was done with the greatest of ease as she passed the salt to the agent.

She laughed nervously at everything the agent said, working hard to impress him. Jonah noted her eyes often drifted to her mother, who also laughed along, but the father remained tentative, studious. He guessed Dad would be the obstacle, the person to persuade—if he decided to steal the beautiful ingénue from his substandard competition.

He was not above such acts, and he rationalized that it was in the climber's best interest. A second-rate agent would never take a client beyond commercials or bit TV roles. Their names would never flash before the credits rolled nor would they command salaries in the six figures. When he absconded with someone else's client, he was doing the climber a favor and changing a life.

He watched the other table until they stood to leave, ignoring his girlfriend and her mundane stories about life as a production assistant on *Murphy Brown*. Of course the agent ran to retrieve his car and, as Jonah had hoped, Mom and the ingénue headed to the ladies' room. He grunted an excuse to the girlfriend and lay in wait outside the lavatory hallway until the pair emerged.

"Excuse me, miss," he said. Kira's bright eyes widened, not in fear, but at the possibility of opportunity. He liked that. "My name is Jonah Israel." He did not bother to explain himself further, for if neither mother nor daughter knew his name, then the girl was not worthy to be his client.

The mother instantly stuck out her hand, proffering an introduction in a proper British accent. "Mr. Israel, I'm Francesca Drake and this is my daughter, Kira. It's a pleasure and an honor to meet you." She shook his hand furiously and squeezed it before letting go.

Kira offered an enthusiastic hello and a handshake, one that would warm the prickliest talk-show host or interviewer. He estimated that she was probably no more than twenty-one, the perfect age to rise to the top.

"It's a pleasure to meet you," he said, reaching for his card. "I won't interrupt your evening, but I would be interested in talking to both of you about Kira's future. Call me for a meeting. We'll do lunch."

Francesca Drake practically snatched the card from his fingers and blushed at her own rudeness. "Oh, we'll call you, Mr. Israel. I believe Kira has much untapped potential, and frankly, I don't think Mr. Hornstein will ever maximize her talent."

He smiled patiently until she concluded her speech, appreciating her sincerity but cynical of familial praise. Stage parents were the worst to assess ability. There was no such thing as objective parents, and he was most wary of the ones who said they were not.

Francesca Drake had indeed brought Kira in the next day, and after some legal wrangling with Harry Hornstein, who recognized his limitations, she was sold to him like chattel—for a profit of her first movie role. Within six months Hornstein was paid off as she landed a small part in a successful independent film.

Four years later she received stellar reviews for the roles she accepted, and Academy Award buzz surrounded her latest performance in *The Autumn Months*. The fact that she was British only added to her credibility, since it was the Brits who could really act—or at least that was the continual stereotype perpetuated by a belief that all British people were somehow related to William Shakespeare. Jonah knew it was only a matter of time before she reached the apex of stardom, making him wealthier in the process, thus distancing him even further from his Hell's Kitchen roots. They would all benefit as long as she followed his directions explicitly.

It was all in the packaging.

Chapter Two

Maureen "Mo" McFadden

Mo McFadden stood in her favorite spot—inside her restaurant, the Ocean Beach Pier Café. As the name implied, her eatery sat suspended over the Pacific Ocean at the end of the longest pier on the West Coast, facing her favorite beach town in the world, Ocean Beach. Nestled in the Point Loma area, OB was a mere ten-minute drive to the San Diego airport and practically around the corner from Sea World. She was afforded a fabulous view on the occasions when Sea World staged fireworks.

Although she shared a 1950s Spanish bungalow with her daughters and her mother on Narragansett Boulevard, she considered the pier her home, and according to the city charter, it was. Her father had bought the rights to build the pier after World War II. By the 1960s, when it was evident OB would take off as a beach town, the city filed a lawsuit to seize the pier from

Seamus McFadden. They underestimated the stubborn, uneducated Irish immigrant, who eventually won the five-year lawsuit but paid the price with his health. When her father died of a sudden heart attack the year after his legal victory, she blamed the city and closed the pier. After the huge iron gates shut out the many fishermen who enjoyed a daily haul of mackerel, they stormed city hall and demanded OB make redress with the woman who had lost her father—a woman who was a young, single mother. Her Italian immigrant husband had stayed around long enough to impregnate her twice and realize that life in a beach town was not for him.

Mo chose to ignore the gossip mongers who whispered behind her back about her scandalous personal life and focused on her business. The city council offered to rent the pier, and she used the profits to build the Ocean Beach Pier Café. Everyone was happy, and the café proved to be a popular hangout for fishermen and tourists alike. It provided a panoramic view of the sea and the town, affording her a sense of security, as though she were engulfed in the arms of the water and Ocean Beach at the same time. She kept it open from sunrise, which she had arbitrarily declared as six in the morning, until sundown, which literally meant when the giant ball of fire dropped below the horizon. Locals knew that in the summer they could count on the café remaining open until at least eight in the evening, but in winter, they knew to hurry up and eat. She shut the doors one half-hour after sundown—no exceptions.

She loved Ocean Beach, a hidden treasure unappreciated by many tourists who preferred Pacific Beach or Mission Beach, where they were surrounded by commercial retail stores and fast-food establishments. OB had refused to sell out to corporate America, rejecting their requests to land a prime spot on Newport Boulevard, the main drag and the heart of the town. She often chuckled at the reactions of unsuspecting tourists the first time they passed the rowdy crowd at the Bullfrog, or waited in line at Hodad's, the premier hamburger joint, or gazed into Ezmerelda's, a shop that displayed colorful bongs in its window. On a Friday night the street was packed with locals and tourists in various states of dress, many having just crawled out of the waves moments before. It wasn't uncommon to see a bagpipe player on one corner and a zydeco band across the street.

She'd heard tourists describe OB as gritty, rough. Everyone was welcomed, whether you were a surfer, a gay runaway or a tourist—you had a place in Ocean Beach. OB was not for the pretentious, just the friendly. First-time tourists quickly assimilated with the OB townspeople, or they forever switched vacation destinations to Mission or Laguna. Such logic was fine with her. It wasn't about the amount of visitors—it was the quality.

Yes, she thought as she gazed out into the Pacific, her life was rich. She couldn't imagine life anywhere else and had spent all of her forty-six years living in OB, rarely trekking across the San Diego county line. She busied herself by tallying the receipts of the morning and humming along to a Celine Dion song. *That woman is so talented*, she thought. The receipts added up to a few hundred dollars, a typical amount for a post-Labor Day morning. She knew the flow of cash would slow now that most of the tourists were gone, and she couldn't help but feel a little anxious when she thought of the upcoming slow winter season.

At the sound of raucous laughter, she turned to find her daughters, Flynn and Megan, bursting into the café, still wet from their morning of surfing. She smiled at her girls, who were as opposite as two children could be, each containing a unique genetic mixture of their Italian and Irish heritages, two cultures that probably never should have crossed, she thought. Flynn, the red-haired spitfire, possessed a lean body made for surfing but received her father's dark coloring. Mo had never seen an olive-skinned redhead, but God must have known Flynn would spend her life outside and couldn't risk the sunburn. She had thought Flynn would turn to an occupation involving the sea, perhaps a marine biologist or a boat captain, but as the girl prepared for her twenty-fifth birthday, she had a year left of veterinary school.

Megan, two years younger than Flynn, had her father's dark hair—when it wasn't some other crazy color—but her mother's soft curves. Megan was far more delicate than Flynn physically, but she was her match intellectually, and her streak of stubbornness often got her into trouble. She had no interest in college and after high school she had apprenticed as a tattoo artist and found her calling. Someday she dreamed of opening her own shop, but Mo couldn't imagine how she would ever afford it. She shook her head every time Megan appeared with new art on some part of her body, wondering what people at her retirement home would think when the girl was eighty.

"Good ride?" she asked as her daughters plopped down at a table.

"Fabulous," Flynn said.

She nodded. It was always wonderful or fabulous. She couldn't remember a day when surfing wasn't the best for Flynn. She noticed Megan kept quiet. "What about you, Meg? Have a good day out?"

Megan shrugged. "It was okay, except Flynn kept dropping in on me."

Flynn gasped. "Me? I don't do that."

"You certainly did. Every time I caught one, I lost it."

The girls' voices escalated in volume, and fortunately it was late enough in the morning so that only a few of the regulars heard their drama. The customers continued to read their newspapers or stare out at the ocean, accustomed to the banter of the colorful McFadden sisters.

"Girls, stop. I need your help." Mo came around the counter and the three of them sat at one of the square tables. She put on her reading glasses, pulled several stapled sheets of paper from her apron and smoothed the papers out on the table.

"What is it?" Megan asked, squinting to read the small print.

"It's a contract," she said. "The movie people want to use the café for a few of their scenes. I'm not sure what I'm signing, and I want you girls to help me decide if I should."

Flynn picked it up and rifled through several pages. "How much are they paying you? That's the bottom line."

Mo took the contract and flipped to the last page, pointing at the written amount, fifty thousand dollars.

Flynn gasped and showed Megan, who squealed with surprise. "You're kidding, right? There's got to be a mistake."

"No mistake. At first I thought it was wrong, too, so I called the attorney listed on the front, and that's what the café is worth to them for a week."

Flynn studied the document. "It says here that you'll have to shut down your business, and they'll also take over the pier. They want to bring in some vans and dressing rooms." She smirked, and Mo could tell that she hated the idea of losing the pier so stars could primp.

"I know it will be an inconvenience, but it's more than I'd ever make in a week. And the locals will understand. It's perfect timing, too. I won't lose much tourist business since they've already cleared out."

Mackerel Manny turned around from the counter where he was enjoying his coffee. "I still say it's selling out."

Mackerel Manny was a regular, an early retiree who spent every day fishing on the OB pier. His face and arms were leathered from the sun, and his tan was a deep brown from years of leaning over the railing, fishing rod in hand. He always wore the same thing—Hawaiian shirt, chino pants, old sneakers and a fishing vest that held all of his lures and, many said, all of his secrets. No one caught more fish than Manny, who sold his catch each day to pay his rent.

"I know you don't care about my opinion, Mo, but I've known you a long time, and you're not a sellout."

She put her hands out in question. "Why is it selling out? It seems to me that it's an opportunity. When will fifty grand ever drop in my lap again?"

"It won't," Flynn said. "Take the deal, Mom. Sorry, Manny."

"I agree," Megan said with a nod.

Manny mumbled to himself and returned to his coffee. Mo sighed deeply and carefully signed her name and initialed at the appropriate places. She put the pen down and sat back in the chair. "Okay, it's done."

Megan picked up the contract and stared at it. "So, what's the name of this flick, anyway?"

"*Beach Town*," she said. "Some romance piece about two people who fall in love in a beach town and then lose each other." She put her hand to her forehead for dramatic effect.

"Who's in it?" Manny asked.

She looked at the cover letter. "Kira Drake and Sanford Wyatt."

Megan made retching noises and stood to leave. "I can't stand that Sanford Wyatt. He's the worst actor in the world. And Kira Drake's not much better. She always comes across as so . . . British. I much prefer anything with Meg Ryan, like *Sleepless in Seattle*."

Flynn rolled her eyes. "Kira Drake *is* British," Flynn said. "I think she's a good actress. I really liked her in *The Autumn Months*."

"You just like the way she looks," Megan teased. With a quick hug to her sister and mother, she disappeared, offering Manny a ride to the meat market. Mo returned to her duties in the café while Flynn poured herself a cup of coffee and sat at the counter.

"Is everything all right, dear?" she asked gently. "Problems with Melissa?"

Melissa was Flynn's on-again, off-again girlfriend, and more recently they were off. Flynn gave a half smile and shrugged. "I don't know, Mom. We didn't see each other much this summer. I was so busy working. I think it's over, but I really don't care."

Mo raised a cynical eyebrow. She knew when Flynn was brushing aside a concern. "Really?"

Flynn nodded adamantly. "Yeah, I'm not upset. I'm more preoccupied than anything else. What if I stink as a veterinarian?"

She smiled at her eldest daughter, so full of life. She didn't know another person with as much stamina and fortitude as Flynn. She touched the red curls that she loved so much and offered her most motherly advice. "My darling, you will do wonderfully well if you are just yourself. Don't be anything you're not. Do your best and you'll be fine. You're Flynn McFadden and that's all you need to remember."

Flynn grinned, kissed her mother on the cheek and barreled out of the café, her energy already moving in another direction. All she ever needed were a few words of encouragement. Mo realized that Flynn required little from anyone, except a momentary reminder of her own abilities, a little cheerleading. Megan was another story, and Mo spent much of her life supporting Megan emotionally. She hoped that the girl would eventually grow up, but it hadn't happened, so as a good parent, she waited—patiently.

She turned her attention back to the contract that sat on the table. She was glad that her daughters approved of the opportunity, but she had made up her mind the first time she read the document. The family needed that money. Although Flynn was paying for the majority of vet school, she still could use financial help, and Megan was always on the brink of poverty. The good part was that they owned everything outright—the huge house on Narragansett, which was probably worth a fortune, the café, worth a larger fortune, and the pier, which was priceless. Yet having assets did not equate to paying bills, making payroll and running a business. Yes, she had her responsibilities, and she hoped the appearance of the movie crew and the fifty thousand dollars would help lift the load from her shoulders.

Chapter Three
Kira Drake

Kira casually glanced at the daily itinerary set before her by Rona, the world's most effective personal assistant. At thirty thousand feet she was far more interested in watching the clouds rather than reading a mundane list of the activities that would consume her day. And after seven movies she didn't really need to read the itinerary to know what Jonah had planned. It was all predictable, designed to overexpose her whenever possible, although he would never suggest she had spent too much time in the limelight. His machinations were clever, and each role she accepted vaulted her into a higher echelon of fame. He always talked about packaging, and she pictured herself as a prize passed around from studio to studio.

This movie *Beach Town* was yet another layer in her stratosphere. It was her first major role in a big-budget film that was already backed by a studio. Previews were currently being generated from the scenes they had filmed on the soundstage in Toronto. Most importantly, she liked the script and felt challenged in the part. Those facts combined pulled her attention away from the window and helped her focus on the page before her.

"So where are we going?" she asked Rona.

"Ocean Beach. It's a little town next to San Diego. Garrison has insisted that we all stay in this *quaint* hotel near the ocean."

"You don't sound thrilled."

Rona rifled through a magazine with a smirk on her face. "Anytime someone describes a place as quaint, I'm always reminded of the rundown flat my grandpop owned in Devonshire." She checked her watch. "We should be landing in about an hour. After we get settled, it's straight to dinner and a PR moment with the mayor." Kira had no comment. "You should get some sleep. You look like crap."

Kira chuckled at her frankness. Rona could say whatever she wanted to her, as they had evolved into best friends over the past five years. Spending nearly twenty-four hours together every single day had that effect. She yawned, knowing Rona was right. She had not slept well in the New York hotel where they had spent the last week doing a photo shoot for her newest endorsement, a perfume line. She had fought endlessly with Jonah over whether she should accept the contract since she hated the scent, but he won the argument as he always did. He was the agent and she was the trained monkey.

Shoving him from her thoughts, she pulled a postcard from her purse and smiled. It was from her parents, who were vacationing in the Bahamas, her anniversary gift to them. A quick note was scribbled in the message box, letting her know they were having fun and had just gone deep-sea fishing. She turned the card over and stared at the picture of a white sandy beach. She imagined herself and a beautiful woman lying together on the shore, rubbing coconut oil over each other.

She sighed and thrust the postcard back in her purse, determined to follow Rona's advice. She reached back into her purse and withdrew her portable cassette player and headphones. She pushed play and R.E.M. blocked out the sounds of the jet engines. She unfastened the hairclip that held her chestnut locks in place and leaned against the first class headrest. She hated having her hair this long but Jonah insisted. He called it her trademark, and it had indeed won her two other contracts with the cosmetics industry, but she wanted desperately to lop off a few inches. She closed her eyes and thought of her flat in London. She had not been home for nearly two months, and Iris, the woman who had slipped in and out of her life quietly, was most assuredly gone. Her mind involuntarily flashed to the last image she had of Iris, lounging in bed, naked. The sheets lay strewn over her legs, hiding her most delicious parts, but Iris's large, perfect breasts jutted out toward Kira, who stood in the doorway, her travel bag in hand.

"Stay a little longer," Iris said, her deep green eyes weakening Kira's willpower. "You won't miss your flight if we just have a quickie."

She pursed her lips in protest, but she dropped the valise on a chair. "Iris, I don't have time to get undressed."

"I know," she whispered in a husky breath full of sex. "But you could be a love and give me a little good-bye gift." She yanked the sheets away and rocked her hips upward, spreading her legs so Kira could see she was wet. And perfect. Sighing softly, Iris licked her French-manicured middle finger and slid it across her glittering clitoris. "Really, darling, you should be doing this for me."

Kira strode to the bed, the place where she had spent the last six hours exchanging pleasure with Iris, her emotions swirling between frustration and arousal. Common sense told her to march out of the flat to the waiting cab, but even the threat of Jonah's wrath couldn't quell her overactive libido, and she fell to her knees, pulling Iris's bum to the edge of the bed. She buried her lips in the soft folds of flesh, and with each flick of her tongue, Iris's moans increased until her screams filled the room.

Before the clock could reach the hour, she was back at the door where she had originally started, and Iris rested in the bed. Kira glanced at her watch, knowing she would be late to the airport. Jonah would be pacing at the gate, furious that he was kept waiting. And he had indeed lectured her for an hour during the flight until he met an attractive brunette who desired his company and willingly joined the Mile High Club with him in the lavatory. Kira had kept silent throughout his rant, lost in the image of Iris writhing in pleasure on the bed.

During their stay in New York, Rona had tried to reach the world-renowned model with no success. Kira was only mildly upset because she couldn't blame her. She was never there. Recently she had bemoaned her lack of a personal life to Jonah, who told her that she could have a relationship in one year and four months, because according to his timetable, that would be when her fame would peak. She could hardly wait.

All of the rooms at the Ocean Beach Hotel faced a lovely courtyard. The movie entourage had filled the place and hired some extra security to keep onlookers and fans away from Kira and her costar, Sanford Wyatt, but she really couldn't see the need for it. None of the locals seemed to care that they were there, and she had not been inundated with autograph hounds or throngs of people swarming around her, invading her personal space. Ocean Beach really was a nice place.

She awoke at six thirty, determined to spend her first morning in OB walking by the ocean. She had a few days to herself before filming, and she almost shouted in glee when she remembered that neither her mother nor Jonah would be standing over her shoulder during the shoot. They were both dealing with other decisions about her career elsewhere, and she would have a few weeks of total freedom.

The hotel was quiet, everyone still asleep from the previous night's activities. Dinner with the mayor had evolved into a huge party at a ritzy San Diego nightspot, filled with city bigwigs dying to rub shoulders with Hollywood folk. She had little stomach for it and longed for the evening to end, but she dutifully smiled, signed autographs and posed for pictures with everyone who asked.

She crossed the courtyard and entered the small lobby where a frizzy-haired college student catnapped on a stool behind the counter. His glasses perched crookedly on his face and he snored lightly. She noticed he'd been reading *The Complete Works of Shakespeare*, which rested on his chest. She coughed and he sprang to life, nearly falling off the stool.

"I'm awake," he said, righting himself and standing before her, the heavy book dropping to the floor with a thud. He adjusted his glasses and pasted a lopsided smile on his sleepy face. "How can I help you?" His voice slurred as though he were coming off a great marijuana buzz.

She suppressed a laugh and returned his smile. "Don't you want to pick up your book? Wouldn't you agree that Shakespeare shouldn't lie on the ground?"

The young man's eyes widened and he retrieved the thick volume immediately. "Sorry, Ms. Drake."

"You don't have to be sorry, and please call me Kira."

He looked as though he'd just been given an expensive gift to covet. "Thanks, Kira." He extended his hand. "I'm London. London Bridges."

She swallowed a chuckle. "That's your real name?"

"I know it's unusual. My parents thought of it."

"I imagined that might be the case."

"They picked it because their name is Bridges and I was conceived in a hotel overlooking the London Bridge in Lake

Havasu, Arizona. Needless to say I was the victim of endless taunting during my school years, and the beloved nursery rhyme forever echoes in my head."

"You could always change your name."

He smiled. "That's an excellent idea."

Since he seemed to dislike discussing his name, she artfully changed the subject. "London, what are you reading?"

He appeared momentarily confused until he remembered the book. "Oh, this is Shakespeare."

Her bemused smile broadened. "Yes, I see that. Which play are you reading?"

"*Midsummer Night's Dream.* It's my favorite. I got to play Puck in my high school production."

"I was in that play, too."

"Were you Puck?"

"Um, no. I was actually Helena."

"Oh, that's a good part."

"I thought so. Listen, London, can you tell me where I might find an excellent cup of coffee?"

"Not here in the lobby."

"Okay, but do you have any other recommendations?"

"Well, the best coffee in the whole town is at the OB Café down on the pier."

"Thanks. And by the way, you might want to conceal your bong a little more effectively." She pointed to the front pocket of his cargo shorts and the end of the glass bong that stuck out prominently.

"Oh, thanks, Ms. Drake, I mean Kira." He withdrew the bong and tucked it into a large side pocket. "You won't tell anyone, will you?"

"Of course not. It's our secret."

He sighed in relief. "You're the best. I really loved you in . . ." He struggled to remember the name of the movie while she waited patiently for her adoring fan. "It was the one where you played that girl who lived on a farm . . ."

"*The Farm Girl?*"

He nodded. "Yeah. That was it. I loved that movie."

"I'm glad you enjoyed it." She stepped toward the door, offering him a small wave of her hand. "Well, have a good day."

"You too, Ms. Drake. And thanks for the idea about changing my name. I'm going to get right on that."

She watched as he jumped off his stool and headed out the back door and down Newport Boulevard. She glanced at the abandoned lobby and wondered if she should find a manager and inform him about London's departure, but she had no idea who to contact this early in the morning. She sighed heavily and headed down to the beach, toward the pier. She found herself laughing about the interesting conversation with London Bridges. She climbed the two flights of stairs to the pier and strolled past the morning fishermen, noticing the heavy smell of fish that surrounded her. She turned up her nose at the sight of the squid and gutted mackerel that littered the railing and noticed a handsome middle-aged man standing off to the side, wearing a bright Hawaiian shirt and a fishing vest. Three tackle boxes and two enormous poles surrounded him, and his four buckets were already full. He pulled in another wiggling mackerel, quickly removing the hook before adding it to his catch.

He noticed her watching and flashed a friendly smile. "Good morning."

"Morning. You've got quite a lot there."

He peered in the buckets and shook his head. "Actually I'm a little off my quota."

She laughed in surprise. "Well, how many do you usually catch?"

He thought about it as he attached more bait to his free line. "Oh, I'm usually about fifty by now, so I'm guessing I'm down by ten or twelve. They're just not biting as well on the squid today."

She smiled pleasantly, unable to add anything to the conversation. She'd never held a pole in her life, and she wouldn't know what to do.

He eyed her with amusement. "You're one of the movie people, aren't you? You're that British actress."

She nodded and remembered her manners. She bravely stuck out her hand, hoping the man wouldn't take it. "I'm Kira Drake."

"I'm Manny, the fisherman. Excuse me for not returning a greeting properly, but I'm covered in fish guts. It's nice to meet you, Kira, the actress. I hear you're shutting down the pier tomorrow."

She shook her head. "I don't know anything about that. I'm sorry, though."

His eyes narrowed and she imagined that he would lose some of his livelihood if the pier weren't available for fishing. She'd make a point of mentioning the situation to the film's assistant producer. She continued to watch him until a bright flash caught her eye. She looked up the pier and noticed a figure clad in a black wet suit with yellow trim holding a surfboard. She watched as the surfboard flew over the railing and landed in the ocean. Almost as swiftly, before another wave could heave itself forward, the surfer pulled herself up onto the railing into a perfect dive, her body arching forward with confidence and grace. Her fingers stretched toward the moving waves, as if longing to embrace the ocean. Kira watched her slice the water and retrieve the board. She paddled away from the pier until she found the spot she wanted. A few waves rolled by, and she pushed her board over them, waiting for the right moment. When the sea churned up a massive wall of water, she started paddling until she and the wave came together. She rode with great ease, practically landing on the shore. Kira could only imagine the exhilaration.

When she stood, Kira got a good look at her body. Her dark skin contrasted to the curly red hair that cascaded over the wetsuit. The woman had definite sex appeal, and she couldn't take her eyes away.

"Do you surf?"

"No," she said. "I wish I did. It looks like a lot of fun."

He motioned to the female surfer. "You should talk to Flynn. She could give you lessons."

"Flynn?"

"That's Flynn McFadden. She's kind of a wonder kid around here. Her mother owns the café."

She glanced at the small white and blue building that seemed to float over the water, the place with the coffee London Bridges had recommended. She moved next to Manny and gazed at Flynn, who was now paddling back out to meet the waves. "Manny, what else can you tell me about Flynn?"

He paused before he answered, and she could tell he was studying her, assessing her motives and deciding how much to share with a stranger. "Well, she's about twenty-five. She lives with her mother, sister and grandmother. Studying to be a vet."

Kira was impressed. "Really?"

"Uh-huh. She's got a year left. A really sharp girl."

They both smiled at the description and looked out as Flynn paddled back into the sea. "Thanks, Manny. It was a pleasure to meet you."

He bowed. "Likewise. I look forward to seeing you another time, Kira. And by the way, I loved you in *The Autumn Months*."

She blushed at the compliment. "Thank you again." She worked her way down the pier, passing men, women and children, all of them holding their poles with leisurely patience as they toiled to fill their buckets. None were as successful as Manny, but they all seemed to enjoy the quiet solitude of the ocean and the excitement that came when their rod suddenly bowed into the sea and a fish pulled on the line.

She strolled into the café and sat at the counter. A woman in her mid-forties stood at the cash register with a pencil stuck behind her striking red hair. "I'll be with you in one moment," she said, her Irish accent unmistakable.

Kira looked around the wonderful place. Glass windows surrounded three sides of the building, and the tables were full of locals and fishermen enjoying breakfast and coffee.

"Now, missy, what would you like?"

Kira turned to meet kind eyes and a pleasant face. "I would love a cup of coffee."

"Oh, now, you can't just have coffee, not a skinny thing like you. You need some breakfast. How about some eggs, ham and potatoes?"

"I couldn't. That's way too much food for me. Maybe just some toast."

"Are you sure? The potatoes are a specialty."

She shook her head. "I can't. I'll get in trouble."

The woman looked at her, puzzled. "Why? Are we being watched?"

She laughed. "No, but I can barely fit in my costume now. If I fatten up on wonderful potatoes, they'll probably fire me from the picture."

Recognition registered on the woman's face. "You're Kira Drake. I knew I'd seen you before. I'm Mo McFadden. I own the OB Café."

"It's wonderful to meet you, Mo. I love your place."

Her eyes danced at the compliment. "Thank you. And I love your beautiful accent, even if it is British. Now, let me get you some breakfast."

Just as she turned away, the door to the café opened and a large policeman lumbered inside. "Mo, I'm telling you for the last time that if Flynn doesn't stop jumping off the pier I'm going to write you up. I have laws to uphold. No one else gets to jump off the pier. Why should Flynn?"

Mo put her hands on her hips. "Charlie Vernon, you know as well as anyone that Flynn's been jumping off that pier since she was twelve years old, and she isn't going to stop now. Hell, it's my pier. You will not write me a ticket or give me a fine. Now, sit down and let me get you your breakfast."

Kira noticed that as she got angrier, the Irish brogue grew richer and difficult to understand. Mo finished her speech with a few words in Gaelic that Kira suspected were not appropriate. The police officer did as he was told and took a stool at the other end of the counter. She glanced at the clock and realized that in thirty minutes she had met four interesting characters, including Mo, the café owner. She liked Ocean Beach immensely, and the coffee was extraordinary.

The bell above the door jingled again and the woman named Flynn strolled in—and stopped when she saw Officer Vernon sitting at the counter. He was turned away, talking and guffawing with a table nearby. She slipped onto the stool next to Kira and pulled a menu in front of her face.

"What are you doing?"

"Hiding."

Kira watched as Officer Vernon scanned the patrons while he made small talk and waited for his breakfast. She studied him, as she did everyone, for every person was a potential character, man or woman. His demeanor was overly friendly, and his laughter was an attempt to proclaim his importance. His eyes flickered toward the wet suit and he frowned.

"Flynn, I need to talk to you," Vernon said, already moving toward the other end of the counter.

Flynn swiveled and greeted his scowling face with a toothy smile. "Hi, Charlie. What's up?"

"When are you going to quit jumping off the pier?"

Flynn cocked her head in thought. "Maybe when I'm about sixty-five."

Kira turned away and started to laugh uncontrollably, and several other patrons nearby joined her.

When she glanced back, his face had reddened. He folded his arms across his chest and turned his stare on her. "Do you think that's funny, ma'am?" Suddenly his eyes widened to the size of half dollars. "You're Kira Drake. What are you doing here?"

She stood and faced him. "Um, well, we're going to film a movie here in a few days. You know about that, don't you?" He nodded mutely. "Will you be assisting with crowd control, Officer Vernon?" Another nod. "Good. I can tell you are dedicated to your job." She glanced at Flynn, whose beautiful green eyes seemed to stare at her with total admiration. "Maybe to show my appreciation I could get you two tickets to the premier." He swallowed hard and nodded fiercely. "Fine. Thank you for all you do for the community." She touched his arm and his gaze followed her hand. She sat down while he remained rooted to the floor for another thirty seconds before shuffling out of the café, his breakfast apparently forgotten.

"That's quite the effect you have on men," Flynn said. Kira shrugged and took a sip of coffee before meeting Flynn's continual stare. "Thanks for the diversion," Flynn added. Almost as an afterthought, she stuck out her hand. "Flynn McFadden."

"Kira Drake."

"So I've heard. You must get a lot of that."

She took a deep breath. "Yes, it's one of the consequences of fame."

"So is fame as great as everyone who isn't famous says it is?"

She chuckled at the description. "I suppose I'm lucky, and I try not to forget that." Flynn seemed to appreciate that answer and nodded. Kira looked into the deep green eyes and realized she didn't want her to slip off the stool and disappear. "Flynn, could I ask you a favor?"

Her lips curled up at the corners. "What would that be?"

"I want to learn to surf."

It had not been easy to convince Rona that surfing was a good idea. She swore the woman to secrecy, for if Jonah or her mother knew she was going out in the ocean on what Rona described as a toothpick, they would appear in Ocean Beach as fast as a Lear jet could carry them.

She agreed to meet Flynn later that day at the Ocean Beach Surf Shop. When she arrived, Flynn was still out at another lesson and she was greeted by Phil. He had to be at least seventy, but she could tell he was in better shape than any man of comparable age that she knew. His wet suit peeled halfway down his body, revealing snow-white hair on his chest and rippling muscles free of fat. He definitely was an advertisement on the benefits of surfing.

"Howdy." He grinned, and she was sure he had no problem finding dates with younger women. "Is this your first time?"

"Yes," she said nervously. "I've always wanted to try it, but I've never had the chance."

He smiled with a full respect and admiration for the sport. "You're gonna love it. I promise. And you've got a great teacher in Flynn. Why don't I get you set up with a wet suit while you wait? She should be back in a few minutes."

She nodded and they found one with royal blue trim. She headed off to a dressing room, noticing that Flynn was almost twenty minutes late. She jumped when a door slammed shut, followed by Flynn bellowing at the top of her lungs.

"I can't believe that asshole! He shows up drunk and expects me to teach him to surf, and then he threatens me with a lawsuit for breach of promise. What the hell is that?"

Kira stepped out from the dressing room while Flynn continued to rant—clearly unaware that she was behind her. Phil held up a finger several times to silence her, but she ignored him and continued to purge her anger.

"I can't stand stuck-up rich people. They are the absolute worst. The asshole shows up in a Speedo! A Speedo!"

"Does this asshole have a name?" he managed to ask when she took a breath.

"Sanford something. What kind of a bullshit name is that?"

"An invented one," Kira said. Flynn whirled around and her face turned crimson. "His real name is Horace Corville. He's my costar, and you're absolutely right. He is a total asshole. Frankly, though, I think you made the wrong decision." Flynn raised an eyebrow in question. "I think that a much better choice would have been to let his ass drown out in the water."

They laughed with her, and Flynn's anger seemed to dissipate quickly. They loaded Kira's surfboard onto Flynn's VW bus and hopped in the front. The smell of wet dog assaulted Kira's senses, and she perched her feet upon a stack of surfing magazines that littered the passenger floor. Flynn threw a few empty food containers into the back before she put the bus in gear.

"I'm sorry the place is such a mess," she said.

Kira shrugged, her attention focused on Flynn's lean body. The woman possessed a natural ease in her demeanor, and she could see the shadow of laugh lines around the corners of her mouth. She gazed at her while Flynn watched the traffic on Newport Boulevard. When Flynn applied some lip balm, Kira fantasized about kissing her. She took a deep breath and turned her head away, just in time to catch a glimpse of the ocean. "You're sure this is safe?"

Flynn laughed. "Surfing? Surfing is amazing. I've done it almost my entire life."

"I hear you're studying to be a veterinarian."

"Yeah. I've got a year left. Speaking of animals, are you okay with dogs?"

"Yes, I love dogs. I haven't ever owned one, because my mother doesn't like them, but I've enjoyed everybody else's very much."

"Good," Flynn said, turning down a side street. "I need to make a few stops, if that's okay. I mean, if you're not in a hurry or anything."

She immediately warmed to the idea of spending more time

with her than the allotted hour for a surfing lesson. "Sure."

Flynn maneuvered onto the residential streets of Ocean Beach and Kira admired the historic bungalows of the area. They pulled in front of a brick building, the words *Ocean Beach Veterinary Clinic* painted on the window in gold.

"Is this where you work?"

Flynn nodded. "I want to pick up some hitchhikers. C'mon."

A young woman with stringy blond hair sat at the desk of the clinic, and Kira noticed her striking brown eyes were hidden behind some oversized glasses. When the woman saw Flynn, her entire face smiled. *Someone has a case of puppy love*, Kira thought.

"Hi, Flynn."

"Hi, Amber. This is Kira."

In the few seconds it took for Amber's head to swivel three inches and acknowledge Kira, her expression froze like ice and she glared at her. Flynn didn't notice, her attention directed at the charts piled on the counter.

"Did Mrs. Ormsby bring Radar in today?"

"Yes," Amber said, her sub-zero stare still focused on Kira.

Kira turned away and busied herself at the magazine rack, hoping they would leave soon.

"I'll be back in a sec," Flynn said and headed into the back.

"You'll just break her heart."

Realizing that Amber was addressing her, Kira turned to the reception desk. "Sorry?"

"I've read about you in the magazines. I know what they say."

"I doubt if fifty percent of it is true."

"That still leaves half. You stay away from Flynn. I know you're a heartbreaker. You stomped all over poor Jason Anthony's heart."

She rolled her eyes, remembering the scandal surrounding her reported love affair with Jason, another gay actor. Jonah had staged the whole romance and breakup to lift their careers. "He was just a friend. And I don't date women, so you don't have to worry."

"Sure," Amber said, her mouth forming a knowing smile. "I can tell by the way you look at her."

She tried to hide her surprise, but Amber's grin widened. Perhaps Flynn was attractive, but Kira needed to put her emotions in check. Much to her relief, Flynn emerged from the backroom, three leashes in her hands. Preceding her were an Irish setter, a golden retriever and a German shepherd. She reflexively took a step back at the size of the pack. Flynn must have noticed her hesitancy and ordered the dogs to sit. They willingly obliged and stared at Flynn. She stepped in front of the trio and clapped her hands. Each dog immediately raised his right paw for her to shake, which she did.

"Kira Drake, I would like you to meet Quincy, Lady and Tramp." At the mention of their names, all three tails wagged in unison.

"Are they coming with us?"

"If it's okay with you."

"Absolutely."

Flynn grabbed the leashes again and headed for the door. "See you later, Amber."

" 'Bye, Flynn," she answered with great affection.

When Kira turned to say good-bye, the woman narrowed her eyes, and Kira hustled out to the bus, quickly returning to her seat before Amber could give chase and bite her ankle. The dogs piled in the back, and Flynn cruised down Newport Avenue, stopping in front of the local market. The small store bustled with shoppers and a few tourists buying goodies for the beach. They strolled past a magazine rack on their way to the counter. Kira found her face on three covers, one of which depicted her in a slinky top and shorts outfit. Her lips puckered, offering the readers a sexy kiss. She'd hated that shoot, but Jonah had insisted.

"Now this is sexy." Flynn grabbed the magazine and held it

out.

Kira's face burned, and she pulled it from Flynn's hands, placing it back in the rack. "Stop," she said, although she was secretly pleased that Flynn had noticed. At the counter Flynn greeted a portly gray-haired lady perched on a stool. She was at least eighty, and Kira was rather sure the woman was blind. Next to her was a sign that read, "Shoplifters will be beaten."

"Hi, Gmum," Flynn said.

"Flynn. It's a beautiful day isn't it?" Like Mo, her Irish brogue was rich. "Now, who's your friend, me lass?"

Kira looked at Flynn, surprised.

"Gmum, this is Kira Drake—she's in the movie. Kira, this is my grandmother, Eileen McFadden."

"Kira Drake. It's a pleasure." Gmum stuck out her hand precisely toward Kira, and she shook it over the counter. "I owe you a debt of thanks. Every time you're on the cover of one of these magazines, I make a lot of money. You're very popular."

"That's nice of you to say." Kira noticed that Gmum gazed upward and her head continually moved to the left and right as she assessed her surroundings.

"Now, my darlings, I do need you to step to the side."

Flynn grabbed Kira and pulled her against the wall. In the next second, Eileen McFadden whipped a long wooden bat out from under the counter and slammed it against the chips display. The sound was deafening as the metal rack clattered to the floor and everyone in the store froze.

"Damn filthy thief, you get the hell out of my store before I whack ya!"

Kira's jaw dropped in horror, but she noticed a teenager remove a bag of sunflower seeds from his pocket and place them carefully back in the appropriate box before running out the front door.

Gmum sighed and replaced the bat. "Flynn, be a love and give me a hand."

Flynn righted the chips display and Kira asked, fascinated, "How did you know?"

Gmum chuckled heartily. "Oh, Kira, me darling. The senses are a wonderful thing. You lose one and the others know. They help each other. That young bugger crinkled the bag before he put it in his pocket, and I heard the change jangling. He had the money, but he just didn't want to pay for it. No good little runt. And I know you're standing just to Flynn's right, because your perfume is mixing together with her natural sea smell. And by the way, whatever it is, it's a lovely scent on you, darling."

"That's amazing, Mrs. McFadden."

"Gmum, I thought I'd take Zipper out with us today," Flynn said.

"He'd love it. The poor thing's been cooped up all week."

Flynn squeezed behind the counter and began slapping her thighs. "C'mon, Zip. Let's go. C'mon." Flynn waited until a slow-moving Bassett hound crawled out. The dog's belly scraped the ground as he waddled around the counter and headed for the door, no leash necessary.

Kira repressed a laugh, unsure whether Gmum would find it funny. They said their good-byes, and only when the bus was a block down the road did she burst out laughing. "I'm not sure if Zipper is the best name for that dog."

"He moved a lot faster when he was younger, but it is rather ironic."

Kira glanced into the back. All four dogs lounged about the floor, Zipper lying on top of Tramp.

Flynn pulled up in front of a large two-story Spanish bungalow. "Last stop. This is my house."

She gazed up at the beautiful home. "You live here?"

"Uh-huh. I'll be right back." She ran inside and within seconds returned with a white terrier puppy trailing behind her. He willingly hopped inside and stared at Kira.

"Who is this?"

33

"This is Rufus. He was left on the doorstep of the clinic a few weeks ago. I just couldn't take him to the pound."

"Certainly not. He's absolutely adorable. You're a great dog, Rufus." Hearing his name, Rufus assumed Kira was his new best friend and climbed into her lap. His eyes focused on the road ahead, as though he were Flynn's navigator.

They drove toward the shore, and she asked Flynn questions about Ocean Beach and noticed the passion with which Flynn described her town. She found herself lost in Flynn's life, happy to be the listener for once, rather than the subject of the conversation. She didn't even realize they had arrived at the beach until Flynn parked the bus and turned to stare at her.

"Are you ready?" Flynn gave her arm a squeeze.

The touch penetrated the wet suit and sent a tingle through her body. "I think so."

They unloaded the gear and trudged up the sand and over a dune. Kira had not visited the ocean since her childhood when her parents took her to the Devon seaside each year for holidays. Those trips were pleasant memories, and she had always sworn she would return for a vacation, but she had never found the time—even during her trips to L.A. for various movie shoots. This was her first up-close view of the Pacific, and she was overwhelmed, the sound and sight of the waves spilling onto the shore, the immensity of the place a reminder that she was standing on the edge of the North American continent. Enjoying the water were surfers and, to her surprise, dogs.

Flynn removed the leashes and all of the dogs immediately bounded down the dune and ran right into the ocean, Zipper trailing behind. At one point his short body sank into the sand, and Flynn had to rescue him, but once he made his way to the shore, he seemed to enjoy letting the water roll over his paws. Kira laughed as the dogs frolicked in the waves, chased their tails and fetched toys thrown by several owners. She noticed a group of dogs huddled around a woman with a tennis ball. When she threw it back into the water, the dogs bolted after it, including Rufus, who couldn't keep up with dogs that were four times his size. A whippet seized the ball from the surf and charged up the shore. The other dogs chased after him, clearly not caring that they had no chance to catch the canine bullet.

Curious, she turned to Flynn quizzically. "What is this place?"

"Dog Beach, of course."

She smiled. "Of course."

"I picked this spot because there aren't a lot of tourists. Most of the people here are locals and they won't bother you."

"What? Ocean Beach citizens don't go to movies?"

"Oh, they go to movies, and they know who you are, but they just don't care."

"I see." Kira's ego deflated at the comment.

Flynn touched her shoulder. "Look, it's not that they don't care about your work, they just don't get caught up in all the celebrity stuff. Besides nobody wants to swim with dogs, so we usually just get a handful of surfers and the waves are easy here."

Her gaze lingered on Flynn's hand until she pulled away and started toward the shore. They found a spot and sat down in front of the ocean. Flynn clapped her hands and said, "Okay, so the first part of our lesson today is to study the water and the other surfers. Watch where the water breaks. After a while, you start to get a feeling about where to be. See, right now everyone is out pretty far and that means that there are some great sets coming."

As if Flynn were a prophet, an enormous wave formed—a tube, as Flynn called it—much to the delight of the surfers who rode it until it disintegrated. Flynn gave several pointers, and she tried to pay attention to the techniques Flynn was describing, but her interest in surfing was competing against her attraction to Flynn, which was growing at breakneck speed.

After they studied the surfers, Flynn dropped their boards on the sand. "You need to practice standing on the shore before you try it in the water. Go ahead and lie down like you're ready to catch a wave."

She hesitantly stretched out on the board and waited for her directions.

"Now, you're going to jump up, but you need to make sure that your feet land in the right place. You want your back foot by the tail, and your other foot near the middle of the board."

"Does it matter whether it's my left or right in the back?"

"No, it's up to you. Whatever feels comfortable. Go ahead and give it a try. Jump up and work for a position. Ready?"

"Uh-huh."

"One, two, three."

She jumped up, her feet in a twisted knot. Flynn stifled a laugh as Kira worked to keep her balance. "Stop it or I will push you in the ocean."

Flynn held up her hands in surrender. "Okay. Let's try it again."

They practiced several times, and once Kira could easily pull her body up into a standing position, Flynn suggested they paddle out so she could attempt to surf. She looked at the few surfers already in the water, wondering how many she would jeopardize with her novice surfboarding. She pictured the end of a board protruding from a skull, or worse, drowning someone when she ran into him. That would not make for good press and Jonah really would kill her. Before she could protest, Flynn handed her the board.

They paddled out together and faced several sets of waves. While she only managed to stand once, she calculated she was upright for almost a tenth of a second. Just as her body recognized exhaustion from the constant battle with the water, Flynn motioned them in.

"You looked like you were fading," Flynn said.

She nodded, realizing she must appear absolutely hideous—

not the impression she wanted to leave with Flynn. They sat on the shore for a few minutes while she caught her breath. "I haven't had this much fun in, well, forever."

"It's the best thing in the world and you did great."

Kira blushed. "You're being kind. I could barely get up."

"That will come in time. Don't worry about it."

"So you don't think I'm hopeless as a surfer?" She fished for a compliment, praying that Flynn saw some promise in her surfing ability.

"No way. You've got great potential."

They packed up and Flynn drove her to the hotel. Rufus, dirty, smelly and wet, insisted on sitting in Kira's lap again, which was just fine with her.

"He really likes you," Flynn said. "He's selective about who he covers in seawater and sand."

She held his face between her hands. "I'm honored, Rufus." He responded by licking her on the lips. Surprised, she laughed and hugged him tighter. "Rufus, darling, that was the best kiss I've had in a long time." She looked over at Flynn, who was watching with a mysterious grin on her face. "What?"

"Nothing."

She opened the door to leave and thought of what she could say. "I had a lovely time. Thanks for the lesson."

Flynn shrugged. "No problem."

"I'm really sorry about Sanford and the way he spoke to you."

She looked puzzled and scratched her head. "Why would you be sorry? You didn't pour the booze down his throat, did you?"

"Of course not."

Flynn leaned across the seat until their lips were only inches apart. "Don't apologize for him. Every person is responsible for his or her own actions. He was an ass today, and you, Miss Drake, were excellent company. And a pretty good surfer, too."

Kira's throat went dry and she was unsure if the cause was the compliment or Flynn's nearness. "Please call me Kira. Can I have another lesson tomorrow?"

"I think I can squeeze you in, Kira."

Her desire for another surfing lesson was extinguished when she learned the shooting schedule was pushed up and her freedom was over. The next three days were a blur, full of work from dawn until deep into the night. She thought of Flynn often, but there didn't seem to be a discreet way of contacting her. She didn't have the time, and the shoot wasn't going well, her distaste for Sanford elevated to new levels after his behavior with Flynn. Several time the director had to coax the two of them through romantic scenes, all the while bemoaning the loss of chemistry that had been so evident during the auditions.

On the third day, when shooting finally broke at nine, Rona suggested they hit a local bar for a drink. Kira agreed, desperate for a good pint of ale and a break from movie people. They trekked down Newport Boulevard to the Bullfrog, where pulsating music and gregarious laughter seeped out into the street.

Rona grabbed her arm. "Maybe coming here was a mistake. This place is awfully crowded. Are you sure you want to go in?"

"Why not? No one cares that we're here. This is a great town, and I really want a pint."

She led a hesitant Rona into the Bullfrog through the throngs of people. It was a typical bar, with no attempt at interior design—dark booths and pub tables filled the space and the walls were covered with movie posters. Over the bar sat a cartoon caricature of a bullfrog. Most of the decorations were haphazard, an afterthought. From what Kira had seen so far, the Bullfrog carried the same message as other Ocean Beach establishments— simplicity and quality. In Ocean Beach it was not about the frills.

Most of the bar patrons were gathered in a circle, watching a dart competition. A few of the locals glanced at her, and one raised his glass in salute, but no one accosted her or asked her for an autograph. As she and Rona stepped into the crowd, she noted the competitors—a huge man and Flynn, who was dressed in board shorts and a short crop top. He wore a T-shirt advertising the bar, but it barely covered his enormous belly. She watched the game while Rona retrieved some drinks.

"What are they playing?" Rona asked when she returned.

"Round the Clock."

"What's that?"

Kira explained, "The first person who hits every number on the board in order wins." But Rona was no longer paying attention to her and had instead turned to an attractive man.

"So how's the movie coming?" a voice asked.

She glanced at a woman with many tattoos. "It's going well, thank you. I really like your art." She pointed to an elaborate heart and sword that decorated the woman's bicep.

Their eyes met, and she found something oddly familiar about her. "Thanks for the compliment. I'm Megan. I work at the tattoo place next door."

"I'm Kira, and I guess you already know what I do."

They both laughed and their attention returned to the game when the crowd burst into a cheer.

"Aw, gimme a break!" the large man shouted. "Flynn, if you hit this I'll give you this bar."

The crowd responded with thunderous applause. It was obvious to her that the guy was drunk. "Who is that?" she asked Megan, pointing at Flynn's opponent.

"That's Bear. He owns this place."

"And he has a well-chosen nickname. So will he really give the Bullfrog to Flynn if he loses?"

Megan laughed and shook her head. "No. It's kind of a running joke, but Bear doesn't know it. Every few weeks he gets totally snockered and throws darts with Flynn. He bets the bar and loses. She's probably won the bar at least thirty times. In the end, he'll owe her another few weeks of free beer. That's all she really wants anyway. I don't think she's paid for a beer in three years."

Kira's jealousy radar prickled at Megan's admiration for Flynn. "Do you know Flynn well?"

"She's my sister."

"Oh," Kira said, surprised and pleased. Before she could ask Megan more questions, the bar hushed as Flynn prepared to launch her dart.

Her brow furrowed and her eyes narrowed. Flynn leaned her body forward, making sure that she remained behind the throw line. She eyed her target and chucked the dart in a swift movement. It hit the bull's eye, and the crowd went crazy. Bear looked utterly shocked, but he shook her hand.

"C'mon, Flynn," he said. "Let's go back to my office and I'll give you the bar." He lumbered away, tears in his eyes.

"Aw, Bear, I don't want the Bullfrog. What would this place be without you?"

"You won fair and square, Flynn." Bear's heaving sobs silenced everyone. "It's yours." He pulled out a handkerchief from his pants pocket and buried his eyes in it.

"No way, buddy. You are the Bullfrog. Right, everybody?"

The crowd roared and chanted, "Bear! Bear!"

Bear turned around, drunk and in tears. He went to her and hugged her while the crowd applauded. "I love you guys."

She held up her hand in silence. "Now, Bear, I do think I should get *something* for beating you."

"Anything but the bar."

"Drinks on the house!" Flynn cried, causing another eruption of joy from the bar patrons.

It was a surreal scene, Kira thought. The single beer she had consumed was going straight to her head, lowering her inhibitions. She turned to Megan and asked abruptly, "So, does your sister date women or men? Or both?"

The question seemed to surprise Megan only for a moment,

until a knowing smile crept on her face. "She dates women. Women only. Do you?"

Kira blushed at Megan's bluntness. She certainly couldn't respond. She'd spent her entire career denying everything about her personal life, and she'd developed one of the most believable fronts whenever questions arose about her sexuality, which was rare since she knew she did not look the part of a lesbian.

"I see," Megan said. "Flynn," she called. Her sister turned around and waved at Megan, a huge grin plastered on her face. When she saw Kira, her expression faded into neutrality. Kira couldn't tell if Flynn was happy to see her or not. Perhaps she was upset that she had never called.

Flynn sauntered up to the two of them, her eyes locked on Kira, but her words directed at her sister. "Hey, Meg."

"Flynn, do you know Kira Drake?"

"Yeah, I do. I gave her a surfing lesson the other day."

Megan grinned. "I see. Well, then, I suppose there's no introductions needed. I'll be going now." As she walked past Flynn, she whispered in a voice loud enough for Kira to hear, "She likes girls."

Her cheeks reddening slightly, Flynn laughed, still gazing at Kira. "I thought you wanted to surf again."

"I do," Kira said sincerely. "But they changed my work schedule. I can't fit it in right now."

"That's really too bad." Flynn glanced at the darts she still held in her hands and showed them to Kira. "Do you throw?"

"Yes."

Flynn seemed surprised. "Really?"

"Darts originated in Britain during the Middle Ages, Miss Flynn." She took the darts from Flynn and inspected them. "Hmm. Well, they don't have the steel tips like the ones back home, and your board is a little too close, but I'll give it a go. What are we playing?"

"Shanghai."

She smiled. "I love that game, and I should warn you that I'm good."

"Oh, so we should probably have a wager. Got any ideas?"

She thought of a dozen things she would love to have Flynn do if she won, but she couldn't verbalize any of them. Instead she just shrugged.

"Twenty bucks?" Flynn proposed.

"Okay."

Flynn gathered the darts and found a willing bar patron who was sober enough to keep score. Kira noticed that Rona was nowhere to be found.

"I don't know about your rules, but here we go twenty rounds, and you can only hit the number that goes with the round for your points to count. Whoever gets the highest score for all of the rounds together wins the match."

"And you can also win if you get a Shanghai," Kira added. "If you hit a single, double and triple for that number on that round, you Shanghai and you win. Is that the way you Americans play?"

"Yup. Do you want to go first?"

"No, you go ahead."

Flynn stepped up, took aim and landed a one right away. She hit two more double ones before it was Kira's turn. She missed the board completely and realized how rusty she was. She assumed it was home turf advantage, for Flynn pulled ahead of her quickly. By round five, a small crowd had gathered, clearly divided between the hometown girl and the popular movie star. Not wanting to make a poor showing, she stopped drinking immediately, but Flynn continued to down tequila shots. It seemed to her that Flynn was feeling the effects by round thirteen. She hit the wire on two throws, and both darts fell to the floor. Kira was in the lead, and she felt rather confident that she could hang on, but she misread Flynn's degree of inebriation, and by the last round Flynn was back in the lead.

"This could be it," Flynn said, holding up her final three

darts. "If I hit a few twenties, I don't think you can catch me."

She stared into Flynn's deep green eyes, deciding she could care less about winning. Flynn would never understand that the last hour of standing in a bar and throwing darts with an interesting woman was the highlight of her month.

Flynn scored forty more points and would indeed win the game unless Kira could get a Shanghai. She stepped up and assessed the board. The entire crowd quietly chanted, "Shanghai, Shanghai," and she released her first dart. She hit a double twenty and was one third of the way there. The next dart landed in the single twenty. She glanced over at Flynn, who was licking salt off her hand, running her tongue over the top of her thumb as she prepared to down a shot of tequila. Kira watched in fascination and Flynn grinned. Kira narrowed her eyes. Flynn was cheating. She was trying to distract her from her throw, but it wouldn't work. She quickly turned to the board and chucked the dart. It landed in the triple twenty. Flynn had been shanghaied.

Everyone in the crowd burst into a cheer except Flynn. She downed the shot, set the glass on the bar and slowly pulled her thumb across her lower lip, wiping away the excess salt. Kira eyed her intently, oblivious to all the locals patting her on the back and shouting her name. All she saw was Flynn.

Flynn came over and handed her the twenty dollars. "Good darts."

She quickly returned it to her. "I'm not taking your money."

Flynn pushed it back toward her. "You most certainly are. You won."

She whispered in her ear, "I am being paid two million dollars to make this movie."

Flynn's eyes widened and she nodded. "Fine, I'll keep it." She turned away, but Kira grabbed her arm. "Where are you going?"

"Out."

"Take me with you."

"Where do you want to go?"

"I don't care." Flynn's hard stare caused her to lose her breath momentarily. "Please."

Flynn took her arm and led her down Newport Boulevard toward the pier. As she suspected, Flynn's intended destination was the shore. They followed the ribbon of sand, passing only a few silhouetted figures out for a run or a walk. She noticed some homeless people, camped for the night along the sea wall, huddled in their blankets, ready to brave the chill.

Flynn quickened her pace and took her hand. "I'm not sure we should be holding hands," Kira said automatically, although she made no effort to separate their entwined fingers.

"I already told you," Flynn said. "Nobody in OB cares. People mind their own business. You'll never visit another place in the world with less gossip."

"How can that be?"

Flynn shrugged. "I suppose it's because everyone knows all there is to know about everybody else." Kira offered a thin smile, unable to fully believe her. "Do you want me to let go?"

"No," Kira said immediately, stepping closer to Flynn.

They headed down to the massive rocks that cut deep into the shore and blocked their path, chatting about their lives and families. When they turned around and started back, Kira was disappointed as they reached the pier, filled with equipment and trailers from the movie.

She knew it could be days before she saw Flynn again, and Jonah or her mother could show up unannounced at any time. They reached the steps and she backed Flynn against the railing. "You need to know that at some point in time, I want to kiss you."

A slow smile crept across Flynn's face. "When?"

She thought for a moment and looked around at the people wandering up and down the boardwalk. "I don't know yet. When we're alone." Her hand drifted against the small of Flynn's bare back. "This will have to do for now. It's a promising, intimate gesture, wouldn't you say?"

Flynn's eyes bulged slightly at the touch. Kira sighed, every nerve in her body excited by the feel of Flynn's skin. She took a deep breath and looked at the ground. It was all she could do to resist the temptation of pulling Flynn into the dark shadows under the pier. They stood together for several minutes, listening to the ocean, her hand surreptitiously caressing Flynn's lower back.

"I imagine you're a good kisser," Flynn said. "You have absolutely perfect lips."

She smiled seductively and let her nails gently scratch Flynn's back. "I am a good kisser, particularly with first kisses."

"Why? What is it about first kisses that are special?"

"Oh," she said seriously, "first kisses have a huge responsibility. They should be tender and sweet, assertive enough to show future interest, but soft enough to show lingering affection. They should last long after they're over."

"That's quite the criteria. And you're certain that your first kisses live up to those standards?"

"I guess you'll have to judge for yourself."

"So what if I want a kiss right now?"

"That's impossible. You'll need to wait. Right now anyone looking at us assumes we're just having a lovely conversation, albeit slightly intimate. We could be talking about world affairs or America's expanding federal deficit. No one suspects we're here gazing into each other's eyes thinking about kissing."

Flynn glanced toward the people on the boardwalk before her gaze returned to Kira. "I'm not waiting."

Kira's whole body tingled when Flynn's warm lips met her own. Her knees buckled as Flynn took control of the kiss, and all she could do, all she wanted to do, was respond. When Flynn stepped away, she was grinning, and Kira quickly looked around to gauge the reaction of the people around them. All of the locals were engaged in their own conversations. No one seemed to notice that she and Flynn had just broken one of the time-honored codes of public affection.

"See, I told you. This is OB. No one cares," Flynn said.

Kira shook her head, unable to believe that at least one person wasn't gawking at the sight of two women locking lips. She dropped her hand into Flynn's waistband and stroked her abdomen. "I can't wait to see you again."

"I think we need to be clear about something," Flynn said.

"What?"

"The next time we get together, Miss Drake, you'd better be prepared to do more than kiss."

The sun baked the pier and everyone on it. The morning news had reported that Southern California was enduring a terrible heat wave, and unfortunately, Kira had to stand outside for the day. They were filming a pivotal scene in the movie between her character and the character's best friend. It was one of her favorites because it was well-written, and she enjoyed working with the other actress, Carla Tartaglio. She also savored Sanford's absence, since it was one of the few scenes where they did not work together.

As she and Carla waited for the cameramen to prepare the shot, a splash of yellow caught her attention, and she noticed Flynn entering the café wearing her wet suit. Although it was technically closed to the public, she knew Mo was inside, cheerily offering coffee to all of the production crew. They loved Mo and were shunning the craft services cart in favor of her coffee and pastries. She was sure Mo was making a mint in tips.

Flynn exited the café, a large coffee in her hand, and hustled between the movie people. When she saw Kira, she winked. Kira watched her walk away, the dark red hair nearly glowing in the harsh sunlight.

"Hey," Carla said. "Are you even listening to me?"

Her eyes immediately shot back to her costar. "Of course I am."

Carla smiled. "Who is she?"

"What are you talking about?"

"C'mon, Kira. We've worked on three films together. You don't think I never noticed the trail of women coming in and out of your hotel rooms?"

She couldn't hide her shock, but she couldn't lie to Carla either. "Is it that obvious?"

"Only to me, honey. I know you and I'm observant." Carla touched her hand. "And I don't care. You need to know that. Whoever you sleep with is your business."

Her heart stopped pounding, and a wave of relief swept over her. "Thank you, Carla. And to answer your question, her name is Flynn. She's a local."

"Good, she's safe. Another few weeks and you'll be out of here. You can frolic in between the sheets all you want and not have to worry. No strings attached."

She bit her lip. "Well, we haven't done anything except kissed."

Carla let out a deep sigh. "Oh, God. This is bad. You're falling for her."

"I am not," Kira snapped. Carla snorted and both of them laughed. "What am I going to do?"

"Enjoy it. If she's important to you, figure something out."

The director called for places and they went through the scene several times. Kira's focus intensified and she immersed herself in the work. She was completely in character, bringing a story to life. This was what she loved about acting. Three hours later when the director finally yelled, "Good job," she knew she'd hit it. She stepped aside and saw Flynn, leaning against the pier, out of the way, and talking to one of the minor players, an incredibly beautiful starlet who had a wonderful body but no talent. Kira knew that she had slept with the producer to get the part and wasn't above prostituting herself for any reason.

Kira stormed over to them, forgetting her good manners. "I hope I'm not interrupting."

Flynn cocked her head to the side, a perplexed look on her face. "No, we were just talking about Ocean Beach. I was telling Mindy that OB has a long and interesting history."

Seething, she glared at her subservient costar. "I'm sure Mindy could learn just as much from a book. You do have a library in Ocean Beach, don't you, Flynn?"

Flynn, whose evident shock quickly faded to amusement said, "I'm sure we do. Mindy, if you want to learn more about my quaint little town, you should probably ask for Mrs. Drysdale at the library."

"Okay, Flynn. Nice meeting you." Mindy hastily departed, not bothering to say good-bye to Kira.

"You know, I can see the smoke coming out of your ears." Flynn chuckled.

"What?"

"You're jealous."

"Why would I be jealous?"

Flynn shrugged. "I don't know. You have no reason to be."

She so wanted to take Flynn in her arms, but she looked around and noticed Manny approaching, his bucket full of fish and a wide grin on his face.

"Howdy, Kira, the actress. Afternoon, Flynn. My new friend Kira found a way to get me on the pier so I wouldn't miss my earnings. Thank you, Miss Kira."

"You're quite welcome, Manny."

"Hey, Flynn, your mother said that the clinic called. They're looking for you." Manny tipped his baseball cap to both of them and strolled down the pier.

"I've got to go," Flynn said. "When will I see you again?"

She whispered in her ear, "I have to work tonight, but I want to see you tomorrow. Where can we meet?"

"What's your hotel number?"

"Thirty. I'm on the top floor facing the ocean. Have you got a plan?"

"I will by then." Flynn winked. "Oh, and by the way, three of your costars gave me their hotel numbers, too."

This time Kira laughed.

By the seventh day of her stay at Ocean Beach, Kira realized she had not ever been this happy or felt as much freedom. As the hair and makeup artist twisted her braid and dabbed at her face, it occurred to her that she was in charge of her decisions, at least when she wasn't following the specific instructions of the director. That really was her professional existence, adhering to the authority of a single person, usually a man. Jonah assured her that her success hinged on how people perceived her, and every decision she made could enhance her career or ensure that she plummeted to the bottom of every producer's list. That thought made her shudder, since the trappings of fame were so incredible. It was certainly easier to listen to Jonah, and his wisdom had earned her star power and a lucrative paycheck that increased with each film. With each day that passed in Ocean Beach, however, she rediscovered emotions she thought only existed in the movies—attraction, anticipation and passion.

She knew he would not approve of Flynn, and more importantly, he would tell her that she just needed to stop being gay. He abhorred gay actors on principle. They were their own worst enemies, he said, destroying their careers for love, choosing their personal lives over the opportunity of a lifetime. Yet he was not in OB, and she intended to live her life for herself, shifting the lens away from her own public persona and toward the woman she adored. Should he appear suddenly, there would inevitably be a confrontation, and she refused to think of the outcome.

The entire day's shoot was a mental battle for her, and much to the dismay of Garrison, the director, her mind continually drifted to the upcoming evening with Flynn and the possibilities. Her imagination went wild with visions of Flynn's incredible green eyes and the taut body under her trademark wet suit. Garrison was probably wondering why he had hired her. She would need to be careful or Jonah would be called. That possibility propelled her through the rest of the day, without Garrison yelling at her more than twice.

By the time she returned to the hotel, she was nearly giddy. She stopped by the front desk for messages and found London Bridges once again asleep on his chair, a book titled *What to Name Your Baby* tucked between his arms. She smiled sympathetically and went around the counter and found three messages—one from Jonah and two from her mother. He had also left a message for Rona, which meant that she was expected to keep Kira under the microscope and report back. Kira hoped Rona's loyalty was to her and not to him.

A quick shower and change was all she managed before Flynn arrived at eight. She glanced in the mirror before she opened the door and quickly pulled Flynn inside. Flynn held a pizza box and a sweating six-pack of beer, which she dropped onto the small brown desk in the corner. When she turned around, they both stared at each other. Flynn wore a tank top and rumpled cargo shorts, truly the outfit of a surfer, as Kira had gleaned during her stay. She nearly blushed as Flynn's gaze traveled over her short white shorts and tiny pink spaghetti-strap top. The little top only covered part of her tanned belly, and she would never have worn such an outfit in public. Flynn leaned back against the desk, and Kira suddenly felt horribly exposed. She stuffed her hands into her back pockets and looked down, embarrassed. When she glanced up, it was into Flynn's blazing green eyes.

"What do you want to do?" Kira asked, her voice breaking.

"I'm already doing it."

Her heart raced. She had no control. She stood there quivering, her lips trembling. Flynn's calm tone and easy stance exuded power, which settled over her, exciting her more. "Please, Flynn."

Flynn moved next to her but didn't touch her. She felt the caress of her breath on her face. They continued to stare at each other, fully connected without touching.

"Close your eyes," Flynn whispered, and she obliged. Every nerve tingled in anticipation. She was completely vulnerable and it thrilled her.

She felt Flynn's finger trace her bottom lip. "Let me see if I remember. First kisses should last long after they're over, but what about the kiss before you make love?"

Kira's eyes fluttered open and Flynn's mouth covered hers. Lips and tongues merged, each exploring the taste of the other. Kira shuddered, electricity surging through her body.

"I want you," Kira said. She grabbed the snap on Flynn's shorts, but Flynn batted her hand away.

"We're not starting there, baby. That's where we end." Flynn slipped out of the embrace and went to the overstuffed chair in the corner, then pushed it to the middle of the room, facing the vanity. Satisfied with the positioning, she dropped into the chair and motioned for Kira to join her.

Her lips still burning from the kiss, she slid into Flynn's arms, realizing that she was once again in a place of submission. She sighed deeply and relaxed. Flynn's lips found her neck. "Watch us," she whispered, turning her toward the vanity.

Her gaze drifted to the mirror. It was like watching a movie, and she gasped when Flynn gently rolled the spaghetti straps from her shoulders and bathed each one in kisses. Flynn glanced up, and the sight must have fueled her desire, for she let her hands roam across Kira's exposed cleavage. She arched her back and Flynn's fingers swept across her nipples, but only for a moment.

Kira shifted in the chair, amazed at the wetness between her thighs. Flynn's hands were everywhere now, stroking her arms, her belly, lingering above the waistband of her shorts. Flynn's face rested against her cheek, both of them gazing into the mirror, watching her hands unsnap the shorts and drag the zipper down, exposing her red bikini underwear.

She gasped. "Flynn, touch me."

Flynn groaned, clearly unable to bear the foreplay any longer. Her hand slipped under the satin and Kira moaned softly. She raised her hips, her pleasure increasing with each thrust.

"Keep watching," Flynn reminded her. She saw Flynn's body undulating with her own, one hand moving rhythmically between her legs while the other stroked her breasts, her neck and her cheek. She lolled her head back and imagined she could hear the sea. She was the sea now, ebbing and flowing until she finally crashed against the shore. Eventually they moved to the bed, exploring and touching for hours.

Finally exhausted, she kissed Flynn softly. "I'm so glad you asked to come over."

Flynn raised an eyebrow. "Me? You're the one who set this all up. You flirted with me, came on to me and now you've seduced me."

Kira feigned shock. "I can't be that forward. I'm British."

"Well, I'm Irish, and we're naturally forward and pushy." Flynn kissed her deeply and their bodies collided again. In the morning Flynn was gone, but in her place was a piece of hotel stationery, a rose sketched on it with a sentence: *Next time it will be a real one.*

Kira closed her eyes and went back to sleep, dreaming of roses and surfing.

Chapter Four

Megan McFadden

Usually September in Ocean Beach meant the end of tourist season and the return to normalcy. People who lived in the beach town loved the dual personality that coastal living afforded. During most of the year, the few thousand residents enjoyed the slow pace of life. Yet the community depended on the exorbitant spending of the tourists who flocked there for the summer, over-taking all of the best restaurants, filling the motels and providing an excessive amount of financial opportunities for people like Flynn and Megan, who offered specialized services for a price. The presence of the movie people meant the lucrative summer fling would continue as grips and propmen wandered into Megan's studio, bored with the barely audible pulse of OB and desiring to find a quick source of entertainment, the kind getting a tattoo ensured.

As a tattoo artist working at High Art Tattoo, Megan found a home and comfort zone. She would never be her sister—the good, responsible oldest child going to school and living a respectable life. Flynn was a woman driven by her goals and determination, always rushing forward toward something, the fulfillment of a plan, whereas Megan hovered and often stepped back. When they were children, adults would inquire about their aspirations. Flynn was the one ready with an answer, and Megan frequently shrugged in response. The few times when she blurted that she wanted to be an actress or an artist, people smiled sympathetically and patted her shoulder. During their teenage years, she and Flynn frequently debated their futures, and Flynn often chastised her for not reaching for her dreams and taking risks.

Megan smiled at the irony. The greatest risk Flynn took each day was surfing, riding the tubes and heading for the shore, but Megan's life was nothing but risks. Only Flynn knew of her hard-core life, and her endless nights of clubbing, where she snorted cocaine in the bathrooms and often left with strange men. She felt lucky to have lived past her twenty-first birthday, and as she approached twenty-three with a steady job and a semi-steady boyfriend, she vowed to occasionally dip into the pool of normalcy to find balance. She would never be Flynn, but her desire to achieve yin and yang was strong, and she'd recently etched the symbol in black and white ink on her left shoulder to show her commitment to herself. Flynn had nagged her to follow her dreams, but what Megan told no one, including Flynn, was that she didn't have any aspirations. She couldn't chase a dream that didn't exist.

She gazed out of her second-story window onto Newport Boulevard. It was a Friday night and the street was crowded. She pressed her face against the glass and focused on a small man wearing a loud print shirt and plaid shorts, standing on the corner under the streetlamp. His hands were in his pockets, and he reacted to the sounds of the nightlife. He craned his neck

toward the bellowing laughter of the Bullfrog, jumped when a car backfired as it passed and locked his gaze on a scantily clad woman who strutted before him. Yet he remained planted at the corner, unmoving and unwilling to participate. He was a voyeur, and Megan felt a sudden kinship toward him, and a deep sense of self-loathing. She knew what she was doing. She knew how she lived her life—like a pinball in the machine, smacking against the bumpers unwillingly and haphazardly. She didn't stand on a street corner wearing clothes that announced her difference, watching everyone else walk through their life. No, she hid in the security of High Art, perched above the action, waiting—for what she wasn't sure.

The tattoo shop was quiet, but it would only be a matter of time before a gaggle of women bustled into the place, laughing and pushing one of their friends into an act of sheer rebellion. She laughed when she thought of the hundreds of women she'd inked in secret places. Just a few days before, a promising San Diego lawyer had dropped by, wanting the scales of justice imprinted on her left bicep. When Megan pointed out that the tat would be visible when she wore short sleeves, the woman replied, "I never wear short sleeves. It's against company policy." In most cases, only their lovers knew of their body art, or the people who saw them on weekends in their casual attire.

Two figures ascended the stairs and she smiled when Flynn and Kira burst through the door, clawing at each other, their tongues buried in each other's mouths. They laughed over a private joke, and she laughed with them for no reason other than that their expressions were entirely goofy, the look of two people in love.

"Hello, Megan," Kira thought to say while Flynn greedily sucked on her neck. "How are you this evening?"

She shook her head at Kira's upstanding British manners. "Not as good as you guys, apparently. Hey, Flynn, get a room." She playfully smacked her sister on the back with a magazine.

Flynn raised her head. "What? You can't be embarrassed, Meg. I remember the afternoon when you and Calvin Marcus went at it for eight hours."

Kira's jaw dropped. "Eight hours? My God, Megan, you're a goddess."

"I was younger then. So are you two getting matching tattoos?"

"No," Flynn shot back.

Megan smiled. Her sister had a terrible fear of needles, which was surprising, since she gave shots to animals every day. She had tried to coax Flynn into adorning her body with art, but Flynn wouldn't hear of it.

"I'd like one," Kira said softly.

Megan was shocked. "Are you sure? Won't you get in trouble?"

Kira shrugged and the lovers wandered toward the displays. "It would need to be something small. Something I could hide from wardrobe—"

"And your agent," Flynn said.

"Exactly. What should I get, darling?"

"Whatever you want, baby. Meg, can you recommend anything?"

"Well, how about something to celebrate your newfound love of surfing? Flynn tells me you really enjoy it."

Kira's eyes sparkled and she flashed a dazzling smile. Megan suddenly realized what it meant to stand in front of a celebrity. At that moment Kira Drake was the most beautiful woman she had ever seen.

"What do you have?"

Fifteen minutes later, Kira decided on a yellow surfboard surrounded by exotic flowers. "It reminds me of Hawaii. I've always wanted to go there."

She suggested they position the tat inside Kira's bikini line. "That way the only people who are going to see this are your gynecologist, your dresser and Flynn, or another actor if you ever decide to do a full-frontal nude scene."

"Not going to happen. I have a nudity clause," Kira said primly.

Megan went to work, occasionally glancing up at Kira's brave face during the process. Her beautiful eyes watered occasionally, and Flynn remained at her side the entire time. They had shut the blinds and locked the door, given the location of the tattoo. She knew Kira didn't need Ocean Beach's finest wandering into the shop while her pants were around her ankles. When it was over, Kira gave her a two-hundred-dollar tip, and the two lovers glided back out the door, Kira walking gingerly from her sore hip.

She watched them from the doorway, their hands tucked into each other's back pockets, unaware of the quick looks they got from others, particularly the handful of late-season tourists unaccustomed to seeing affectionate gay couples. One or two did double-takes as Kira sauntered by, certain they recognized her face. A sliver of concern crept into Megan's heart. Flynn and Kira had cocooned themselves from the outside world, but she doubted they could keep everyone out for long.

"C'mon, Meg, don't you want to go?"

She scowled at her whiny boyfriend, Tony. It was a Tuesday afternoon and he stood before her, wearing only his board shorts. Without his shirt, she could see all of his tattoos across his torso and arms. It was like looking at her own gallery show and he was the frame hanging all of the masterpieces she had created.

"Not everyone gets a day off in the middle of the week. I have to be here."

He shook his head. As the concierge at the San Diego Sheraton his workweek was unpredictable. He spent his free time surfing, and he expected her to come with him on a whim. "Ah, Meg. Nobody's gonna care. The tourists are all gone. Who's going to come in for a tat on a Tuesday afternoon?"

"Doesn't matter," she said with a shrug. She turned her back to him and busied herself with a display of nose rings. He sighed in exasperation and slammed the door on his way out.

She knew she would need to lose him soon, but she wasn't good at relationship confrontation. She could speak her mind in an angry fury or during a debate with Flynn, but breaking up was different. It always took some event to open her eyes and force her to shift her life. Every time she finally worked up the nerve to break up with a guy, months had passed, and when it was over, she went through a period of great self-pity, where she cursed herself for being so weak and wasting so much of her life. Yet she couldn't seem to break the cycle.

Flynn had tried to help because she didn't have these problems. When a relationship didn't work, she broke it off and began looking for another opportunity. She was so cool. Maybe it was a gay thing. Megan had wondered if she could ever want a woman, and she'd actually kissed one of Flynn's friends after a drunken binge at a party, but neither of them had ever pursued anything once they sobered up. She idolized Flynn, who seemed to enjoy playing the field, although this relationship with Kira was definitely different, and Megan was seeing a side to Flynn that she didn't know existed.

Voices drew her attention to the door as three strangers entered the shop, including a woman with an '80s punk hairstyle about ten years too late. She wore a black leather jacket and faded jeans that completed her bad-girl image. Megan found herself drawn to the brown eyes that met her own. She barely noticed the other two women who accompanied the punker, a blonde with ratty hair and a tall brunette who looked vaguely familiar. Neither woman said hello, both content to stay in the background.

"Hey," the punker said with a nod. "How's it going?" She leaned across the glass counter, her arms draped over the display case. "I'm looking for something unique to add to my collection."

"And what do you have so far?"

She removed her leather jacket and pulled up her T-shirt, revealing a muscular back with three tattoos. Megan stared at the unique works of art. A leopard's face in a swirl of stripes sat across from an angular design of color that was inviting and interesting but did not depict any recognizable scene or form. It was the third tattoo, however, that grabbed her—a waterfall tattoo that covered much of the woman's middle back. The detail was unbelievable.

"These are amazing."

The hairstyle nodded. "They're my own creations."

"Really? I love them."

"A friend does the needlework, but I do the designs." The woman pulled her T-shirt back down. "I'm Rocco, and I would love to know your name."

Accustomed to the tattoo parlor come-ons from guys and women getting inked, she smiled pleasantly and glanced at the two women who were chatting over by the tattoo wall. "I'm Megan."

Rocco smiled. "It's great to meet you, Megan. I'm working on the movie as a set designer, but today's my day off. I saw your shop and thought I'd check out your bird collection. I'm looking for something to fit on my lower back." She pushed down her jeans far enough to expose a broad patch of virgin skin.

Megan directed Rocco to the other counter. "You might like this one. It's my own personal design, and it would go well with what you've already got. It's a phoenix. You know, risen out of the ashes, symbol of renewed life."

Rocco stared at the tattoo intently, Megan growing more uncomfortable in the silence. She felt her work was being judged by someone whose opinion mattered, and she swallowed hard when Rocco looked up at her.

"You're right. It's perfect for me."

She prepared the works and the two other women sat across from Rocco, giggling and whispering. Megan knew the behavior, which usually meant the observers were embarrassed and nervous. When the needle actually touched Rocco's back, they squealed in fright, another response she expected. She rolled her eyes and ignored them. Only when the brunette spoke distinctly to Rocco, her British accent crisp and clear, did Megan realize why the woman was familiar. She was Kira's personal assistant, Rona. Megan wondered if Rona realized Kira was busy outing herself all over Ocean Beach, her mouth permanently attached to Flynn's lips.

"Doesn't it hurt, Rocco?" the blonde asked.

"Not if you're used to it, Sissy."

Megan noticed she sat like a pro—still, as though she was enjoying the burning needle. *She probably is*, Megan thought.

"I could never get a tattoo," Rona said. "I have no desire. However, apparently her highness wants one. I've already told her I'll kill her if she actually does it."

Megan suppressed a smile, envisioning the small blue flowers surrounding the little yellow surfboard, permanently inked into Kira's hip. She also wondered if Kira knew that Rona referred to her as "her highness."

"She's totally in love with that local girl," Sissy said. "I had no idea Kira was a muffdiver. I'm shocked. Rona, shouldn't you be doing something about this?"

"There isn't anything I can do. I've tried talking to her, but she won't listen."

Rocco laughed. "You haven't tried that hard, Rona. You've been too busy shopping."

"That is true. There are so many great shops here. If Jonah finds out, I'm going to be in big trouble. I'm supposed to keep my eye on Miss Kira at all times. It's all about her."

Megan could hear the disdain in Rona's voice, and she was certain Rona was jealous of Kira's fame.

"You just better hope Garrison doesn't call Jonah," Sissy said.

Rona slapped her hands on her knees. "Don't you think I know that? She's totally infatuated with her. And I don't get it. Flynn is so butch, and Kira could have anyone, and she picks an obvious bull dyke."

"I wonder if her pussy is the same color," Sissy joked.

"God, that would be horrible." Rona moaned. "All that red hair. How awful."

It was all Megan could do to bite her tongue and focus on her job. At one point Rocco shot her a quick glance, and she imagined that she'd pressed the needle a little too hard as her emotions took over.

"Rocco, have you ever been with a redhead?" Rona asked. "Maybe you could provide some explanation as to what her highness sees in the carrot-top surfer? Are redheads more fun?"

"All women are wonderful lovers," Rocco said.

"And a few men, too?" Sissy added wickedly.

Rocco smiled and lifted her head slightly. "Once in a while."

"So, Rona, what are you going to do about Kira?" Sissy asked.

"If history repeats itself, I won't have to do anything. This happens a lot. Kira meets a local, has a fling, and when Jonah shows up, the love affair magically ends. He writes her new toy a check and the toy disappears. I'm not that worried."

Megan realized if she continued to listen to the horrible woman, Rocco would pay the price. She set down her needle and grabbed her earphones. When heavy metal music flooded her brain, she returned to her work, noticing that Rocco had turned her head to smile. Two hours later she completed the design and was surprised to see that Sissy and Rona had already left.

"Where'd your friends go?"

"They're not my friends. They finally bored themselves with

all of their sniping."

Megan laughed and handed Rocco a mirror. She twisted her body for a first look at the new addition. Megan wrung her hands, anticipating her reaction. It was always difficult for her the first time customers saw their new art. Almost all of them were thrilled, and only a few clients had refused to pay. In those cases she obliged, unwilling to fight over money. It was all about the balance between art and economics.

Rocco smiled in complete pleasure. She sat up and faced her. "You do exceptional work."

"Thanks." Megan quickly bandaged Rocco's back and stepped to the cash register, sensing that Rocco's eyes were still on her. When she looked up, Rocco was indeed staring.

Out of the blue, Rocco was at the counter, caressing her shoulder. "Do you know the most erotic place where a woman can get a tattoo?"

"Where?" Megan had her own opinion, but she'd actually heard this line before. What was new was the incredible feeling of Rocco's touch.

"The slope of her breast." Rocco's fingers lazily wandered to the tender skin of her cleavage. Megan inhaled deeply but said nothing. "There are so many perfect designs."

"Do you have any?" she asked, her legs turning to jelly with every stroke.

"Several. I noticed your tajitu." Rocco's gaze settled on the yin and yang emblem.

"I never knew that's what it was called."

Much to Megan's dismay, Rocco stepped away and slipped her hands into the back pockets of her jeans. "I learned that when I was in China."

"You've been to China? Wow. I'll bet that was a great trip."

Rocco nodded. "It's an amazing place. I take it you've never been there?"

Megan snorted and came around the counter, closing the

cash register. "I've never been anywhere, except here and Tijuana."

She wasn't sure what was happening, but she wanted Rocco to stay. She wanted to talk with her, she wanted to know her, and Megan *definitely* wanted to feel her touch again. She sat down on the customer chair, and Rocco joined her. Their shoulders and thighs collided, and Rocco clearly took the connection as an invitation. She unbuttoned Megan's shirt and slipped it off. Megan wore no bra and suddenly felt very vulnerable—and terribly excited. Tuesday afternoons were usually boring.

"Can you please close the blinds and lock the door?"

Rocco obliged and rejoined her on the chair, staring into her eyes. "How about instead of a cash arrangement, you and I work a trade? I'm an artist and I've inked a lot of people. I'll give you the Chinese symbol for strength to go with your tajitu. It's beautiful and would fit perfectly right here." Again Rocco stroked the flesh of Megan's breast, and Megan gasped slightly. "Then we'll be even. What do you say?"

"Um, okay." Rocco went to the bench and prepared the works while Megan leaned back in the chair and closed her eyes, imagining herself in a different place—China. She had no idea what it would look like, but she had seen pictures of the Forbidden City and the Great Wall.

"You look so relaxed," Rocco said as she smoothed Megan's hair.

Megan's eyelids fluttered and she gazed into Rocco's deep chocolate brown eyes. Rocco caressed her cheek, outlined her neck and circled her nipples. Megan sighed, amazed that another woman's touch could affect her so quickly. She'd always thought she was straight, but all she could think about was Rocco's hand. *Skip the tattoo*, she thought. *Just fuck me.*

"You're like me," Rocco said. "You don't cover your body with just any tattoo. You're picky."

Megan smiled at the compliment. "Yeah. If it's permanent, I

63

want it to be meaningful."

"Exactly."

As if she could read Megan's mind, Rocco's fingertips dropped down to her stomach, below her belly button. "What are you doing?"

"Truly taking advantage of this situation." Rocco kissed her gently, while the palm of her hand stroked Megan's exposed belly.

During the next twenty minutes she found her reason to dump Tony.

Chapter Five

Rona Miller

A twinge of guilt nagged at Rona as she entered the Antique Emporium on Newport Boulevard. Instead of tending to Kira's needs and, more importantly, Jonah's edicts, she wandered up and down the dozen aisles searching for antique thimbles to add to her grandmother's collection. So far she'd found two in the Ocean Beach shops, and like Kira, she loved the little town, and she was grateful that the location filming had been extended for another two weeks. The buildings on Newport Boulevard were old and fashionable and their façades preserved despite a change to the interior. Just prior to entering the emporium, she had visited the converted movie theater, its marquee still in place, now the home of an eclectic boutique. She had investigated every shop on the block during her time in OB, since Kira had made it clear that she wanted to be alone with Flynn. Both she and Kira were savoring their time away from Jonah's watchful eye. He was the puppet master and they were the puppets, except Kira was exceptionally paid for her job while Rona languished in the shadows.

She had learned early that life was about understanding your station. It was the British way, and although Britain embraced the American concept of success, it could only throw one arm around its former rebellious child, considering Britain still operated as a monarchy and the royal colors separated the upper echelon from everyone else. She knew that the only way to escape her dreary youth in north Liverpool was to climb out on the back of someone else—someone who would give her a ride. That someone was her best friend Priscilla. She owed everything to Pris, who made sure that she didn't spend her adult life working as a seamstress beside her mother and three sisters.

Pris managed to get them both airline tickets to Los Angeles where they could pursue their dream of show business. She never asked how Pris got the money. Priscilla was wild and willing to do anything for the right price, and Rona certainly enjoyed the fruits of Priscilla's labor, but she never wanted to know the details. After ten auditions in Los Angeles for various commercials and TV pilots, none of which even resulted in a second callback, she grew impatient, convincing herself that an acting career was beyond her grasp and above her station. True or not, what she learned was that she didn't have the wherewithal to suffer an actor's life, nor the stomach to survive on instant soup or peanut butter. She was a restaurant girl who readily accepted the charity of others. If it wasn't Pris coming to her rescue, it was someone else, and eventually that person was Jonah Israel.

She met him on a movie set where she served as the personal assistant to one of the most demanding and well-known divas in Hollywood. Whereas most people were afraid to confront the temperamental bitch, she frequently criticized her boss for intolerable behavior and reprimanded her for stupid decisions. Such candor would normally have resulted in immediate dismissal, but the diva found Rona endearing, since the night they had met at a Hollywood party. Rona was schlepping drinks on a tray, working for a friend's catering business, and the diva was a guest. She turned and asked Rona what she thought of her couture. Rona told her that she'd seen better dresses on the salesladies at Harrods. The diva hired her immediately.

Jonah had been amazed that the actress endured her abuse, but what he didn't understand was that Rona lacked a basic characteristic found in Hollywood—fear of losing her job. She would not stomach the temper tantrums of pampered stars, and she regularly told them what she thought, even when she knew they would disagree. She had been summarily fired several times and never cared. Part of the beauty of accepting one's station was to recognize that life did not move forward, only sideways. One job was as good as another, and if she was canned, there would always be another famous starlet in need of someone to pick up the dry cleaning or pay the bills. Employment apathy was standard for her, until she met Jonah.

She knew almost instantly that working for him would be different. He lived his life a cut above everyone else, resplendent with the small touches and unexpected thoughtfulness that most others ignored. Clients were courted, birthdays were remembered and expensive gifts purchased for any occasion. The day after her first interview with him, a deliveryman appeared at her door with an elaborate floral arrangement and a note urging her to accept the job. Jonah oozed class, and she was impressed. He paid better than anyone, and he treated her like a valuable member of the team. His elaborate, tangible gifts offset his cruel nature and the tongue-lashings she often endured.

The more she thought of him and her job responsibilities, the faster she combed through the antique store. She glanced at her watch and decided to get back to the hotel. She'd check in with Kira. Maybe the three of them could go to dinner. Despite what she told her friend Sissy, she secretly liked Flynn, but she knew Kira would never be able to sustain a relationship with another woman. This fact saddened her somewhat, simply because she knew that Kira would never be happy with a man, which was her inevitable future if she wanted to continue her rise to fame. Rona was counting on Kira's success because she had every intention of doing what she did best—riding on the coattails of someone else's astounding luck. She would do whatever Jonah asked, for although he was exceedingly self-serving, she knew that as his interests were achieved, both she and Kira would benefit.

When she arrived back at the hotel, the worthless desk clerk slept while the phone rang incessantly and people wandered through the lobby. She watched as one couple hustled through the exit with their luggage and zipped into a waiting cab without paying their hotel bill. She just shook her head. She would never understand Americans. She ascended the stairs and was not surprised to see the Do Not Disturb sign swinging from Kira's doorknob. She leaned against the door, and when she didn't hear sounds of erotic pleasure, she knocked. An eyeball appeared at the peephole, and Kira opened the door dressed only in a sheer robe.

"Hey," Kira said.

Rona recognized complete and total satisfaction radiating from her face. She had never seen her so far into the clouds. "You two want to get some dinner?"

Kira looked over her shoulder, to where Rona imagined Flynn lay on the bed. Kira nodded. "That would be great. We need to get out of this room for a while. Why don't we meet you down at the Bullfrog in half an hour?"

The door quickly shut, followed by laughter, and she imagined how Flynn and Kira would spend the next thirty minutes.

In the lobby the stoner boy had awakened and was taking a message. When he saw her, he pulled the phone from his ear and held it out. "It's for you, Miss Miller."

She didn't bother to return the toothy smile as she took the receiver. "Hello?"

"Rona, what the hell is going on?" Jonah barked. "I've got Garrison calling me in the middle of the night telling me that Kira's ruining the film. Says she's lost her chemistry with Sanford. What's her problem? Aren't you doing your job?"

She bristled at his accusation, aware that he was right to question her vigilance. She wasn't keeping a close eye on Kira, but she quickly denied this to him. "It's under control."

"It doesn't sound like it. This is totally unlike Kira. She has a reputation as the most accommodating actress in Hollywood and it gets her the parts. You cannot allow her to lose focus. I don't care who she's met or what's going on, but I expect you to fix this."

The line went dead, catapulting her out of the haze she had enjoyed since coming to Ocean Beach. Like a train suddenly righted on the track, she immediately vowed to scrutinize Kira's every decision, and she would need to have a long talk with her later that night, even if it meant she had to climb into bed between Kira and Flynn.

The Bullfrog was packed wall-to-wall with locals clutching their drinks and one another, enjoying various states of inebriation. It appeared few people drove cars in OB since everything was close, so the bartenders kept the alcohol flowing. Several glances came in her direction, and a few people smiled. She had to admit this was one of the friendliest towns she'd visited in the States, and it reminded her of the local pubs she frequented in London.

"What'll it be, ma'am?" the owner named Bear asked from behind the bar.

"Gin and tonic."

Bear's massive hands reached for the bottles automatically

while his eyes studied her. "You're Kira's friend."

"Yes."

"But are you really a *friend*?"

The question ruffled her. "Of course. I've been Kira's personal assistant for five years. Why would you say something like that?"

Bear handed her the drink and leaned over the bar. "I'm only thinking of Flynn. I'd hate to see her get hurt. I don't know Kira well, but Flynn's the best." He pointed a large, stubby finger at her. "Remember that. By the way, they all went into the bathroom."

She found the ladies' room and heard raucous laughter inside. She tried to open the door, but it was locked. "C'mon, Kira. Open up."

The door opened an inch and she was surprised to see Rocco's face on the other side. Rocco opened the door wide enough for her to gain admittance, but what she saw almost caused her to drop her drink all over the cement floor. Kira stood by the sink, her pants down and her underwear low enough to reveal a tattoo on her hip. Flynn and the tattoo artist—Megan—admired the artwork while Kira gushed about how much she loved it. Furious, Rona stood there mute, watching as Rocco rejoined the trio, pulling Megan against her and kissing her passionately. Flynn followed suit with Kira, her hands working their way underneath the sheer fabric of Kira's underwear. No one seemed to notice or care that she was standing just a few feet away.

She could feel the situation sliding out of her control. She'd assured Jonah that she would handle Kira, but it was apparent she could not compete with Flynn, or rather Kira and Flynn. The hard fact was that in a span of a few short days, Flynn and Kira had become a couple. Rona refused to accept it. The thought of Kira's career exploding was enough to make her physically ill, since their livelihoods were clearly tied together.

It was Flynn who finally raised her eyes and saw Rona. She pulled her hands out of Kira's panties, despite Kira's protests.

"Hey, Rona," Flynn said.

"Hello, Flynn."

When Kira's eyes met Rona's, she laughed like a teenager caught by her parents. She offered no greeting but pointed to her new tattoo. "Isn't it marvelous?"

A wave of nausea overtook her and she thought she might need to duck into a nearby stall. All three of the women now stared at her, Megan's glare particularly unfriendly. "Kira, I need to speak to you now." Her tone was urgent and Kira immediately pulled up her pants and followed her out of the bar and into the street.

"Is Jonah here?"

"Let's just walk," she said. They strolled to the pier, away from the tourists and locals. She whirled around and faced her. "I'm afraid for you."

"Why? Because I got a tattoo?"

"That's horrible enough and you know it, but that's not the point. You've let down all your defenses. Not just with this woman, but with the public. Kira, these are your fans, and some of them will hurt you—it's inevitable. It's like you've decided they're all your best friends."

Kira shook her head. "This is a wonderful town. It's not like everywhere else. They don't care."

"You're kidding yourself. These locals are no different. Look at the way everyone notices you when you and Flynn walk into the Bullfrog." When Kira didn't respond, she knew she'd struck a nerve. She grasped her shoulders and looked her in the eye. "I agree that these people have a special quality, but in the end, at least one of them will hurt you. No one is immune from money and power, and you and Flynn are parading around like a straight couple."

"It shouldn't matter that Flynn's a woman."

She nodded. "You're right. It shouldn't, but it does, especially for you. If your affair with Flynn gets out, it could ruin you. And it will get out."

"Don't call it an affair. I'm in love with her."

Rona closed her eyes. In the five years she'd known Kira, she had never proclaimed her love for anyone and had mocked Rona for the two times she'd fallen in love. Kira was not the lovelorn type, and Rona had assumed Flynn was just another fling. "Please don't say that. More importantly, please don't *believe* that. You don't have time for a relationship, especially with a woman."

Kira sighed in exasperation. "I can't control the timing. It's happened. We love each other, and it's incredible."

Rona's heart ached for Kira. She shook her head. "What about your mother? What about Jonah?"

At the mention of his name, the resolve in Kira's face washed away like sand during low tide. She looked toward the water, evidently unwilling to debate the issue further. They stood together, gazing at the sea until Kira headed back to the Bullfrog. Rona debated whether she should call Jonah. Loyalty to Kira pulled at her heart, for so often it had been them united against him, but it was always concerning small issues, funny things. In the end they knew he was right when it came to her career, and they always followed his instructions.

She decided to wait a little longer. Perhaps now that they had spoken, Kira would see the inevitable ending to this little drama. She shuddered when she thought of what would happen if Jonah found out. He believed celebrities chose between true happiness and fame, since attempting to attain both was a guaranteed car wreck. And his attitude about car wrecks was always the same. If you're going to crash, take control to minimize the damage. She knew Kira was about to crash, and if necessary, she would take the wheel in order to survive.

Chapter Six

Flynn McFadden

Flynn McFadden loved the ocean and Ocean Beach. It was home. It was comfort and stability. She felt it needed her, and she needed it. To try to explain her relationship with the water would be difficult. She was never a religious person, and her Irish mother and Italian father had totally soured on the Catholic faith before she was born. Yet she believed there was a God, because only God could create something as majestic as the sea. She guessed the sea was her religion, and she revered and respected it. As an Ocean Beach native the sea was her backyard, and she never tired of playing in it. Her earliest memories were of the water. According to her mother, she took her first steps across the Ocean Beach pier. Once she was upright, her mostly no-good father took her down to the shore and led her into the Pacific Ocean, where she returned almost every day for her entire life.

Until she met Kira, she believed her life was complete. There were only so many hours in the day, and her internship, combined with surfing lessons, left her little time to date—or so she had thought. Meeting Kira changed her priorities, and although it was hard to admit, she preferred spending time with Kira to surfing. Fortunately, Kira's work schedule rarely forced her to choose since her free time usually began late in the evening. By then all Kira wanted to do was have a quiet dinner with Flynn, throw darts at the Bullfrog and make love. This consistent routine pleased Flynn immensely, but she suggested they move to her house rather than stay at the hotel. Kira jumped at the opportunity to distance herself from Rona, whose wariness of Flynn grew day by day. Flynn didn't trust Rona, but she kept her thoughts to herself, unwilling to say anything against a woman who had been loyal to Kira for years.

They were truly harbored in their own world, and although she knew it couldn't last, she hoped they were constructing a future that could weather the inevitable changes that would come when Kira wrapped the location shoot and Flynn returned to school in two weeks. Their love was immense and somewhat terrifying. If Kira did ask her to give up everything, she was certain she would—even life in Ocean Beach. She prayed that dilemma would never arise.

As she lay in the dark with Kira nestled in her arms, the chestnut hair tickled her naked flesh. She relaxed, certain that it would all work out, her eternal optimism overriding the twinges of doubt that surfaced when they were apart.

She tipped Kira's chin up and kissed her. "I love you."

"I love you, too." Kira wrapped her arms around her and buried her face in Flynn's chest. "Give me a pet name, darling."

She laughed. "What do you want it to be? Sweetie? Honey? Sugarlumpkin?"

"Anything but the last one."

"What about *muirnîn*?"

"That's beautiful, darling. What does it mean?"

"It's 'my love' in Gaelic."

Kira sighed and kissed her again. "Say it again. Say it to me over and over."

Flynn whispered in her ear until their bodies could no longer bear to be apart. She loved Kira's body and explored every part of it with her mouth. As her lips wandered between Kira's legs, Kira sighed, encouraging Flynn further until she satisfied her fully into complete ecstasy. Kira readily reciprocated, and Flynn had taught her how to work a much more forceful stroke. She needed Kira inside her immediately.

"Deeper," Flynn said. She closed her eyes and moaned softly with each thrust of Kira's wonderful fingers until her body exploded—three times. Her heart pounded, and the room spun. No one had ever made love to her like Kira.

They drifted into the afterglow, staring into each other's eyes and smiling. Kira took her hand and admired her ring. "This is exquisite. I love it."

She gazed at the silver band. The unique design had caught her eye several years before at the Farmers' Market. It was crafted by a local artist who loved surfing as much as she did. The silver swirled to one side, representing a wave growing into a barrel. She watched Kira's delicate fingers trace the outline of the design, Kira's touch soft against her skin.

She sat up and removed the ring, holding it up to her. "Give me your hand."

Kira obliged and she slipped the silver band over her middle finger, the only one large enough to provide a snug fit.

"Flynn, I can't."

Yet even as she objected, Flynn could see the pleasure she took in wearing the ring. She held it up to the moonlight seeping into Flynn's room. "It's beautiful." She turned to her. "Are you sure? This is the only jewelry you wear."

Flynn caressed her cheek and brought their lips together.

"And when you wear it, I hope you'll think of me."

"Always."

Normally Flynn viewed heavy rains as a bummer and a lost surfing opportunity, but the downpour caused a delay in the shooting schedule and they found themselves holed up in the house on Narragansett Street, Rufus and Flynn's six other mutts faithfully at their feet. Even Mo had closed the café and refused to brave the weather. Only Gmum kept her store open. She tended to make more profit when people spent time at home eating junk food and watching the stupid box, her nickname for television.

Flynn and Kira spent the afternoon lying in each other's arms on the couch while Mo sat in her chair knitting a sweater. Flynn popped a huge bowl of popcorn, and they enjoyed an old Humphrey Bogart movie followed by a Katharine Hepburn classic.

"Can I just stay here forever?" Kira said.

"Of course, dear," Mo replied.

"Is she serious?" Kira whispered to Flynn.

"Yeah."

An hour later, just as the opening credits rolled for *Gone with the Wind*, the doorbell rang.

"Who could that be?" Mo rose from her chair and answered the door while Flynn took the opportunity to roll on top of Kira and kiss her passionately.

A few moments later, a cough brought their attention to the doorway.

"Dad!" Kira exclaimed. She climbed off the couch and threw her arms around a tall man with silver hair. His smile was warm and friendly, and he spoke softly to her, his British accent evident.

Flynn adjusted her shirt and joined the introductions. It was evident that Kira was the most important part of his life and she cared equally for her father. Flynn felt a pang of jealousy at her own lack of a father, but it was gone in an instant.

Kira wrapped her arms around Flynn's waist. "Dad, this is Flynn. Flynn, this is my father, Stephen Drake."

"It's a true pleasure, Flynn." Stephen shook her hand, a broad smile on his face, and Flynn reciprocated.

"Where's Mum?" Kira asked with a total lack of enthusiasm.

Stephen sighed and his expression shifted, becoming serious. "She's coming, my darling. In fact, I'm here to give you a little notice. She and Jonah are on their way."

Kira sighed and flopped down on the loveseat. "Is there a particular reason?"

Stephen bit his lip and looked at her. "I think you know why. The reports are not good."

Meaning the reports from Rona, Flynn thought. Why couldn't Rona keep her mouth shut?

Kira simply shook her head and glanced at Flynn with pleading eyes. "Well, we need to enjoy it while we can. When he gets here, he'll make my life miserable."

"Why?" Flynn asked. "How can he make your life miserable? You just don't let him."

"It's not that simple, Flynn," Mo interrupted. "Don't be judgmental about things you don't understand."

Her mother's words silenced her, and she took Kira's hand in her own and kissed it.

"Come, girls, it's time to make dinner." Mo turned to Stephen. "Where are you staying, Stephen?"

"Over by the airport somewhere."

"Well, I insist that you join us for dinner."

"Oh, please let me assist as well," he said. "I've been told that I'm a rather good cook."

"A great cook," Kira added.

The four of them prepared dinner—or rather, Mo and

Stephen prepared most of dinner while Flynn and Kira went out to feed the McFadden menagerie, a task that should have taken very little time but instead consumed most of an hour. Granted, they took a detour into the back of Flynn's bus. When they returned, just as Stephen placed the serving bowls on the table, both Stephen and Mo chuckled at their appearance. They looked at each other and started laughing. Kira had buttoned her shirt incorrectly and Flynn's T-shirt was inside out.

"I guess there's no hiding what we were doing," Kira admitted.

Stephen kissed his daughter on the cheek. "I'm just glad you're finally happy, sweetheart."

Dinner was a pleasant affair, and Flynn couldn't remember laughing so hard in a long time. Megan joined them midway through the meal and only added to the funny stories Stephen and Mo were sharing. Flynn noticed that as the wine disappeared, the stories grew in length and color. Mo burst out laughing at something Stephen had said, and he squeezed her arm affectionately.

Kira leaned over and whispered in her ear. "If my father wasn't the most faithful person in the world, I think he'd have a go with your mum."

"What?"

"Look at them, darling. They're flirting with each other."

Mo and Stephen sat close together and were engaged in their own conversation. Megan had already abandoned the table for her own evening plans, and Flynn realized she and Kira may as well have been invisible to their parents.

"Mom, do you want some help cleaning up?"

Mo glanced at her. "No, honey, don't worry about it."

"We'll take care of it," Stephen said. "You girls go have some fun."

Before the parents could change their minds, Kira pulled Flynn out the front door.

"What's the rush?" Flynn asked. "Where are we going?"

Kira turned and faced her. "We now have approximately twenty-four hours before my life turns into a living hell. We're going to the Bullfrog for our nightly visit. I'd like to throw some darts, get bloody drunk, and then we're going back to the hotel where we can be alone. You're in charge of the evening from that point on."

By late Wednesday afternoon, Flynn was exhausted, having risen at dawn to surf followed by a grueling ten-hour shift at the animal clinic where back-to-back appointments kept her busy for the entire day. Normally she would gladly head home and straight for the refrigerator and a cold beer, but she found an extra burst of energy while strolling down Newport Boulevard at the Farmers' Market. She had not seen Kira for three days, since the morning after the rainstorm. She knew her schedule, combined with Jonah's visit, meant they would be apart. Kira had told her to come by that night. By then she would have explained their relationship to him and proven that the film was on track.

Flynn bypassed all of the wonderful crafts and vegetables, heading straight for Myrtle and Tim's booth. They were known as the romantic twosome, selling the necessary props for couples in love.

"The actress?" Myrtle asked, as she handed Flynn a carton of chocolate-covered strawberries.

"Could be. She's special."

"You deserve it, Flynn. Here, take her these." Myrtle reached behind a crate and withdrew six incredible sunflowers.

"Well, thanks, Myrtle. These are perfect."

"Trust me. Roses are overrated. With these you'll be original, and you'll get some great sex. I guarantee it."

Flynn laughed and waved good-bye, heading straight for Kira's hotel room. The courtyard seemed unusually quiet. There were always movie people smoking and drinking at all hours. She had no idea when some of them slept. Yet no one crowded around the patio tables and only the rippling of the waterfall filled her ears as she headed upstairs and gently knocked on Kira's door. When no one appeared, she knocked again, but she sensed something was wrong. Kira never took long to answer.

She raced to the front desk where London Bridges dozed lightly, a book of baby names resting on his chest. Why was he reading that? she wondered. "London, where is everybody?"

"I'm awake." He jumped off the stool.

"London, where's Kira? Where are the movie people?"

He stood stiffly in front of her, his eyes wide. "They're gone, Flynn. They finished today and packed up."

She couldn't believe it. They weren't supposed to go for another three days. She glanced at him, and he looked at the floor. "Is there something you want to tell me?"

He shook his head slowly, but after a few emphatic horizontal twitches, he changed directions and started nodding. He looked like a spastic dog.

"London, what's going on?"

He reached under the counter and withdrew an envelope. Her name was written on it, and she detected a trace of Kira's perfume. Inside was a folded piece of newsprint. She sucked in her breath at the picture that was splashed over most of the page, a front page from a national gossip rag. It was obviously taken at the Bullfrog, judging by the tables and the décor, and she and Kira were dressed as they had been the night of the rainstorm. They sat together intimately, and it was clear that they were about to kiss, but their faces were still far enough apart to recognize Kira Drake and her paramour—a woman. The headline declared a similar message, and she could only imagine how Kira had reacted, and more importantly her mother and Jonah.

She searched the envelope for a note, an explanation, but there was nothing else inside. Kira probably thought the picture really was worth a thousand words. It was probably worth thousands of dollars as well, and Flynn wondered who had taken it. She would certainly find out.

"Where did they go? Did they tell you?"

"I don't know." He stared at the counter and wouldn't look at her.

She frowned. He was perhaps the worst liar in the world. His actions betrayed him the moment he opened his mouth. "I need you to tell me where Kira went. I have to find her."

He straightened the glasses on his twitching face. Flynn suspected he was struggling with his conscience. "I can't, Flynn. That scary man told me that if I told anyone, especially you, he would send someone after me."

"London, I've got to know. You have to tell me."

"I'm sorry." His face disintegrated into pain and he retreated into the back room. At the click of the door lock, she raced around the counter and pounded on the door, but he wouldn't answer.

She had known him for years, ever since he and Megan were in high school together, which meant she knew all of his fears, and while Jonah Israel could conjure up images of faceless scary men, there was a much more realistic and horrifying face nearby. She stormed out of the OB hotel and hustled down Newport Boulevard to High Art Tattoo. She went to find the person he was most afraid of—Megan.

She had just finished covering a woman's entire torso with a jungle scene, she told Flynn, but Flynn didn't care, pulling her down the street, explaining what had happened. When they entered the hotel, she ran behind the counter and grabbed him while Megan calmly took off his glasses. Flynn could feel him shaking in her arms.

"London," Megan whispered. "What's the deal?"

"I . . . I . . ." His jaw moved in circles, but no sound came out. Eventually his mouth just fell open. Megan cradled his chin with her fingers.

Although Flynn held him, Megan's slight touch seemed to send a charge through his body, and he went limp. He was deathly afraid of her, Flynn knew, because he was completely in love with her.

Megan smiled. "London, if you tell Flynn where the movie people went, I will kiss you right now."

"San Diego Sheraton," he whispered.

With those three words, Flynn got what she wanted.

Flynn drove Megan into downtown San Diego to the Sheraton, where her now ex-boyfriend Tony worked. If anyone knew which room was Kira's, it would be him. At the sight of Megan, the young man grimaced. He was definitely a hardcore surfer posing as a respectable hotel employee, but Flynn could see the multiple holes in his ears that went unadorned during the workday, and the edges of an elaborate tattoo protruded from the collar of his white button-down shirt.

"Hey," he said.

Megan leaned over the counter, exposing her cleavage. "Hi, Tony. I need a favor."

"What?"

"Tell me which room is Kira Drake's."

Tony swallowed hard and looked around. "I can't do that, Meg. I'm paid to keep people's lives private."

She took the newspaper article from Flynn and showed it to him. "Here's the deal. I know you're still pissed that I broke up with you, but it's not like I left you for another guy. I can't help what happened." Word had spread that Megan was now totally in love with Rocco, who had returned to L.A. two days before.

"I just don't understand what that woman's got that I don't."

Growing impatient, and unwilling to spend another second massaging his bruised ego, Flynn faced him. "Tony, you can't know so don't try to understand. What women have going on between them is amazing and we don't need any guys to be involved. So just get over it."

"You see this woman with Kira Drake, that's my sister." Megan pointed to Flynn. "She's in love with Kira. Isn't that cool?"

At first he didn't seem too interested in Flynn's problems, and then his eyes narrowed. "Wait. Is that awful blowhard son-of-a-bitch agent with her?"

Flynn nodded. "Yeah. That's Jonah Israel. He totally controls Kira."

Tony shook his head. "He's made my life hell ever since he got here. His damn picky room service orders. Nothing's been right. Asshole sent his dinner back three times last night. Go on up to sixteen-oh-five. That's where you'll find her."

Flynn took the elevator to 1605 and knocked on the door. When she heard the locks click, she thought about what she would say. At the sight of Rona her face fell.

"I need to see Kira."

"I don't think that's a good idea. She doesn't want to see you. You've done enough."

"What the hell does that mean?"

"Somebody from your little town practically ruined her career."

"I doubt that," she said, although she couldn't be positive. "Everybody knows how I feel about her."

"That's the problem, Flynn. Now you need to go."

"I'm not leaving." She pushed past Rona. "Kira!" She darted between the three rooms in the suite while Rona watched. Kira was not there. "Where is she?"

Rona shook her head. "You need to let it go, Flynn. You guys had some fun, but Kira's going places. She's going to be a big star. What you had was a little on-location fling. Happens all the time. Kira's had several local girls."

She bristled at Rona's comments and stormed out of the hotel room. If that was true, then she really was a loser. She waited at the elevator, and when it opened, she nearly walked into Kira, sandwiched between a woman who no doubt was her mother and a burly man that she assumed was the infamous Jonah Israel. A moment of surprise ensued and no one moved or said anything. Kira glanced up at her, and in that instant Flynn knew Rona had been lying.

It was Jonah who recovered the fastest and broke the silence. "Miss McFadden, I presume. Kira has nothing to say to you. Good day."

He pushed past her, his hand clamped on Kira's arm.

"Kira," Flynn called.

Kira tried to turn around, but her mother and Jonah pushed her along. Flynn watched the distance grow between them and hung her head. The elevator doors had already closed, and she once again pressed the down button and waited. When the second elevator arrived, Stephen Drake strolled out.

"Flynn? What are you doing here?"

She shoved her hands in her pockets and shrugged. "I had to come. It was stupid." She boarded the elevator and pressed the lobby button. Before the doors could close, he stepped back inside and rode down with her.

"Flynn, I can't imagine how you must feel."

Too numb to respond, she just stared at the pattern on the elevator carpet. For some reason it reminded her of a cresting barrel on the Pacific, and then she thought of her ring, the one she had given to Kira.

The elevator descended the sixteen floors, returning them to the lobby. He put his hand on her shoulder. "What if I could give you an interview? I could buy you some time alone. I don't know if it would help, but it's worth a try. Don't you think? You are in love with her, correct?"

She gazed into Stephen's kind eyes, grateful that she had

someone on her side. She reached toward the panel and pressed sixteen.

"Dad, how long is this going to take?" Kira said, her voice full of exasperation as Stephen shut the door to his hotel suite. When Kira turned around, Flynn was sitting on the couch, wringing her hands. Her eyes swept from Flynn to Stephen. "What's going on?"

Stephen caressed his daughter's cheek. "This is for you to decide. You choose your happiness." He opened the door to leave, but he looked back at Flynn. "You'd better hurry. They'll start looking for her rather quickly."

Once they were alone, Flynn said, "Rona says that there really wasn't anything between us. She said you date lots of local girls all the time. I guess I just wanted to know if this was all a joke."

Kira closed her eyes and shook her head. "No, it wasn't a joke. You don't understand. This is out of my control."

Tired of hearing her pitiful excuses, Flynn stood up, her Irish temper rising inside her. "What are you talking about? This is your life. You're in charge of it, not your mother. Not Jonah. You make your decisions."

Kira sighed. "You don't get it. In my work, the *public* is in control. They decide whether I'm worth anything. They go to my movies, or not. They buy my line of hair products, or they don't. And when they don't, when enough of them no longer care if Kira Drake is on the screen or appearing in commercials, I'm done. My career is over. And being a lesbian is a liability." She grabbed the gossip rag from the coffee table and held up the photo. "This picture could destroy my career. It might not, but it will definitely cause damage." Flynn folded her arms across her chest in disbelief, and Kira touched her cheek. "It will. How much and for how long might be the only thing I can control.

Look at it. See it from the eyes of middle-class America in nineteen ninety-two. They can barely say the word *homosexual*."

Flynn tried to interpret the picture the way that she described. The grainy images defined just enough to incriminate Kira, her lips inches away from those of another woman. The picture cheapened their relationship. They were in a bar, hiding in a corner. "I get it. It looks smutty."

"I'm not supposed to look smutty—ever," Kira said haughtily. "My career does not afford me that luxury."

"It sounds like your life is your career."

She looked away, crying again. "It was until I met you. I do love you, Flynn. I'm caught in a bad moment here."

The door flew open and Jonah barged in. Without acknowledging Flynn, he handed Kira his pocket handkerchief. "Fix your face. Your mascara is running." She dabbed at her eyes carefully while he planted himself at the desk. He reached into his suit jacket and withdrew a fountain pen and checkbook. He turned to Flynn and peered at her over his glasses. "How much?"

"What?"

"How much will it cost to make you go away?"

She stood frozen, too stunned to reply.

He rolled his eyes and started writing. "So, it's Flynn with two n's and McFadden with two d's, correct?"

"Jonah, stop." Kira said the right words, but they lacked the conviction to make them believable. Flynn also noticed Kira couldn't make eye contact with her anymore. She sunk into the sofa, her back to Flynn. She was hoping he would save her, and Flynn felt her drifting away like the tide in the morning.

He ripped the check from the register with a flourish and brought it to Flynn. "I understand you're in school. This should cover all of your expenses for the rest of your educational career."

When she refused to take the check from him, he let it drop to the coffee table and strode out of the room without another word, as if he knew he'd won. She read the figure. One hundred thousand dollars. Her mother was paid only fifty grand for the entire pier, and she got double that for sleeping with the star. Kira remained motionless on the couch, unwilling or unable to turn around and face her. She stared at the check, Jonah's illegible handwriting scrawled across the official lines, in haste and without care. In her opinion the check was much more revolting than the photograph. She looked back at Kira, whose eyes were downcast, her hands clasped.

"If this was a movie, you'd say something clever, and we'd rewrite what I think is a predictable ending." When Kira said nothing she added, "I hope you keep on surfing."

Kira's shoulders sank, and although she didn't turn around, Flynn thought she was crying. She glanced around the room, at the expensive furniture and the enormous fireplace. She would never be able to afford such an expensive suite, but this was Kira's life. Not the Ocean Beach Hotel. That was a joke. Ocean Beach was a joke. Suddenly feeling as though she were the biggest fool on earth, she bolted from the room, leaving Jonah's hush money on the coffee table.

"She's gone, isn't she?" Mo asked.

Flynn gave a slight nod and dropped onto a stool at the counter. She buried her head in her hands and felt the soft caress of her mother's hand against her hair. She looked up, crying. "I loved her, Mom."

"I know you did. And she loved you. She really did."

"Do you think she'll call?"

"No, dear. I don't. That girl is like a boiling potato stuck in a covered pot. She's got so many pressures around her, so many people counting on her. She's responsible for their rent, their food, their life. Look at that mother. From everything Kira said, it's obvious she can't stand her. All she wants is for her daughter to be famous, and she doesn't really care about her happiness. And that agent." Her mother scowled. "He sounds like the devil."

"I just don't understand what happened."

Mo handed her a cup of coffee. "Something did, darlin'. I can't figure it out, but that girl was pushed away from you, and I doubt she'll be back."

Mo pulled a flask from beneath the cash register. "You need a little more than coffee, my Irish girl."

When she took a slug of the doctored coffee, she felt the breath leave her lungs. She nodded in pleasure and her mother patted her hand.

"I could say a bunch of kind words, that it's all for the best, how sure I am that you'll find someone else. I could say all of that, but it wouldn't make you feel better. Nothing will help right now, and nothing probably will for a long time. So, since I can't make you feel better, I want you to come over here."

She followed her mother outside to the edge of the pier. The sun had just touched the horizon and would set in a few minutes. It was the time when the light blended with the sea for the perfect moment.

Mo wrapped a protective arm around her daughter, and somehow the touch helped. "Since I can't make it better, at least I can show you one of the best reasons to carry on."

Chapter Seven
Francesca Drake

In total darkness Francesca Drake saw the light—or rather her future. She was ten and her mother, Penelope Astley, had saved two farthings to take her to the cinema. She had never been inside the cavernous theater, and her mouth hung open in amazement. The fresco ceiling, a mural of a garden scene, reached from the sky, its magnificence truly overwhelming. Wall sconces painted the theater in shadows, providing enough dim light for the patrons to find their seats but creating a somber, calming mood. It was the enormous screen, however, that riveted her attention. Framed by long, flowing gold drapes that billowed at the sides and swept across the wide proscenium, the screen was the focus, and once she sat in her plush velvet seat, she never turned around. She was certain that whatever waited behind the gold curtains was worthy of the majestic surroundings. The cinema was sacred, and she felt as though she was at church.

When she and her mother exited the dark theater to the sidewalk of Longfellow Road after their first visit, her life was changed, and all she wanted was to return. She went home and raided her secret box, spending every farthing she had ever saved the next Saturday when she returned alone. She saved up again until she could afford a third visit. And a fourth. The ushers grew fond of the "pretty little girl," as they called her, who went to the movies alone, and they began letting her in for free. She huddled in the shadows watching the films whenever she wasn't in school. Her mother assumed she was out with friends, but the movie house had become her world, and all of her friends were now two-dimensional.

She fantasized about Hollywood, clipping pictures from magazines and reading the discarded newspapers for shreds of information about her idol, Bette Davis. She fancied herself a burgeoning starlet, and when she finally came of age, she began auditioning for local companies and British television. She secured a few bit parts, but she was always certain her big break was around the corner. Her parents supported her dreamy notions, as long as she continued to attend her mother's weekly formal tea, the place where Penelope was certain Francesca would meet her future mother-in-law. She dutifully kept her promise and went to dinner with many men. At first she had been reticent, but it became apparent that they were only placating their mothers as well, and they had no intention of forming a permanent liaison with her. Some were gay, several had secret girlfriends, and the others were just a wonderful romp in the sack. She found she got the best of both worlds—pursuit of her dream and interesting evenings with handsome men.

She had no intention of settling for life in London. She wanted glamour, a huge house in a place called Beverly Hills, a chauffeured limousine and true luxury. Eventually there might be a traditional life but that was not the priority. Each month she took another step toward her goals. It was painstakingly difficult to have the end in sight, to know the path of the dream and be shackled to the present. When she landed the lead role in a rather large London production, she felt the restraints loosen. Perhaps this was her moment. The production was brilliant, and the producers predicted a smash with rave reviews after opening night. Within two weeks, however, the curtain fell on her.

If asked by a reporter, she could pinpoint the moment she lost control of her life. It was March 25, 1968, the day she learned that she was pregnant with Kira. If she wanted to be specifically scientific, she might claim that her life was permanently changed the moment she went to bed with Stephen, a fledgling British literature professor who looked much better in the hazy light of a pub than he did the morning after. When she hurried out of his flat after their night of passion, she only felt slightly guilty about leading him on. She actually skipped away, having enjoyed the sex with no lasting commitment—or so she thought. They had slept together one night and Kira was the result.

At first Kira was the anchor that permanently disabled her and forced her to give up acting and her freedom. She resented the little girl tremendously until it became evident that Kira could obtain what she had wanted since childhood. Francesca would know the life of a celebrity, even if she lived it at an elbow's length away from her daughter. As Kira's star shone brighter in the sky, she guarded her daughter with extraordinary vigilance. At one point Stephen lobbied for more children, but she wouldn't hear of it. Her energy was entirely directed toward Kira, and although her marriage suffered for it, she didn't care. Her dream had been destroyed, and Stephen was, albeit indirectly, the person to blame.

Kira's total lack of appreciation for her efforts appalled and frustrated her, and it nearly broke her heart when she realized Kira's sexual tendencies ran to the abnormal. Yet she had managed to steer her love life, often without her knowledge. Most people readily compromised love for money, and she had grown quite cynical of the parade of women in Kira's life who were easily prostituted for the right dollar amount. One woman even agreed to use cocaine in front of Kira, repulsing her enough to sever the relationship. She knew it was for Kira's own good. There would be no "I told you so" or "If you had only listened to me." Stardom afforded no hindsight, and she wouldn't sacrifice their opportunities for Kira's naïve mistakes.

This woman Flynn was a mistake. Rona's updates greatly concerned her; Kira's heart was exposed and vulnerable. Unfortunately, to excise Flynn from their lives required tremendous measures that brought great pain to Kira momentarily, but like everything else, it was all for her benefit. Rona's plan had gone brilliantly, and while Kira's career was momentarily tarnished, it would recover, and, like a small child learning not to touch the hot stove, she would be much more careful about parading her lovers around in public.

Then Francesca's master plan would reach its zenith, with Kira the darling of Hollywood. She would marry and her wedding would be splashed all over the tabloids. Perhaps a scandal or two during the engagement would draw some more ink on her. She would see the benefits, since a marriage would allow her ample opportunities to have casual flings with any woman she wanted, and no one would suspect.

Francesca smiled, as she did each time she unfolded the pages of Kira's road map. It was all clear. She'd have to share it with Jonah, perhaps some night after they had made love and he was a little drunk on Champagne. She didn't know if Stephen suspected, but if Kira needed any evidence that a marriage was the best cloak for infidelity, she need only look to her mother.

Chapter Eight

Stephen Drake

A cool breeze drifted across the shore, and the palm trees shuffled in response. Sitting on the deck of Kira's new seaside mansion in Oahu, Stephen felt an overwhelming calm as he gazed out at the crystal blue water. Kira caught a wave for a splendid ride and raised her fist in triumph when she washed ashore. Her surfing instructor stood nearby and critiqued her performance with a much more critical eye, but to Stephen, she blended with the ocean effortlessly. Her life in Hawaii was vastly different than in London, and much to his surprise, she seemed happier here in an environment that was nothing like her home. She had changed, and it concerned and pleased him at the same time. While her decisions were unpredictable lately, as he watched his daughter twist through the water, he knew she had finally found a sense of peace since she had lost Flynn eight months before.

When she had announced she was moving across the ocean to another continent, Francesca came unglued, unable to believe her movie star daughter would leave the U.K. for sandy beaches and surfing in the U.S. Lately it was all about surfing. After Kira purchased the thirty-thousand-square-foot home, she first called a surfing instructor, not the phone company or an interior decorator, but Jason, the surfing instructor.

When Stephen eventually dragged his insufferable wife to the island, they were appalled at the sight of her new home. Although she had lived on the property for a month, boxes climbed toward the ceiling of each room, furniture sat haphazardly placed, and the house was in total disarray—except for the kitchen. The kitchen was fully organized and stocked with appliances that a world-famous chef would envy. Apparently she had hired a cooking instructor named Echo. When Echo bounded down the stairs one morning for breakfast, he recognized that Kira and Echo were doing more than making ratatouille.

Yet, two months later, Echo disappeared from Kira's life. Apparently since she had moved to Hawaii, Kira's casual relationships with women had increased significantly, now that Jonah had carefully camouflaged her sexual preference with a boyfriend named Dax. No last name—just Dax, a bronze beefcake who paraded in front of the cameras with her, his arm possessively wrapped around her waist. Jonah decided that the best way to erase a lesbian image from the mind of the American public was to replace it with a strong heterosexual one, ensuring that women would envy her terribly for her good looks and handsome boy toy. That was Dax, and much to Stephen's surprise, she didn't care. She willingly allowed Dax to enter her life and even agreed to be photographed topless from a distance with the stud hovering over her, prepared to make his move. Stephen had been outraged at the sexual exploitation of his daughter, but he was clearly in the minority and nobody ever cared about his opinion. She didn't fight it, so why should he? Dax was the reason for his visit, and he decided it was better to confront the issue sooner rather than later.

He watched her and the instructor stroll across the sand, the lesson concluded. As Jason pointed toward the water, Stephen imagined he was discussing technique, and Kira was listening attentively. She asked questions and the conversation ended as they parted, Kira to the deck and Jason to his car. Originally Jonah had suggested using Jason as her cover, but she would not hear of it. Her newfound love of surfing would not be entangled in the joke that was her personal life.

She lugged her surfboard up the steps and smiled at her father. "Dad, what are you doing here?" She pecked him on the cheek and retreated to a corner of the deck and an elaborate shed. He followed her into the room, which housed all of her surfing equipment. Her collection of surfboards was growing rapidly, and she carefully placed the board in its proper stand.

"Did you see me go into the green room?" she asked excitedly.

"I'm sure I did, but I didn't know that's what it was called. Is the green room a good place?"

She laughed. "Oh, Dad, the green room's a great place. It's the inside of a great wave." She took a breath and narrowed her eyes. "So what's up?"

"Well, I just wanted to visit but we also need to talk."

She nodded and they returned to the deck loungers. "What terrible errand are you running now?"

He sighed in exasperation. "Sweetheart, don't say that, please. It makes me feel horrible."

She scowled and leaned back in her chair. "I know, but why do they always send you to do their dirty work?"

He knew *they* were Jonah and Francesca, and now Dax had been added to that group as well. "They send me, darling, because *they* know that you and I have a strong relationship, and that if you'll listen to anyone, it's me."

"That's true. Because you'll never lie to me." She stared at her father for confirmation, and he nodded slowly. "So what is it?"

"Jonah thinks that you and Dax should get married."

She sat straight up. "What? Is he crazy? There is no way I'm sleeping with that oversized blond ape."

He reached over and touched her arm. "No, darling. Jonah couldn't care less about sex. It's about appearance, and it's the time to take full advantage of your stardom. You've just won your Oscar for *The Autumn Months*, and if your face is plastered all over the covers now, it will be great PR for *Beach Town*."

At the mention of her latest film, she deflated and fell back into the lounger. He knew that when she began the publicity tour for the movie next month and was forced to spend hours in front of reporters and interviewers, she would need to give the greatest acting performance of her life, since she absolutely refused to talk about the picture or Flynn, even with him. In fact, she didn't discuss anything of substance, unless it was surfing, and then he had no idea what she was talking about.

"Do you think I should do it?"

"I don't know what to tell you, darling. Jonah's right. A wedding would certainly help your press, and Dax seems to be upstanding."

She snorted at the comment. "Right. Anyone who'll sell himself for money, Dad, is a prostitute, even if there's no sex involved."

"You're probably right there," he said. Secretly he suspected that Dax was gay and his lack of attraction to Kira the only reason the entire ruse worked. "I can't tell you what to do, and nobody cares about my opinion anyway."

She looked at her father sympathetically and patted his arm. "Tell Jonah I'll do it, but I have conditions. First, we are not having sex, and there will be no titillating pictures of our honeymoon, which will be in Tahiti. The waves are incredible right now, and if I'm going to do this, then I'm getting something out of it." She rose and went to the door. "Are you staying for a few weeks?"

"I'd like to," he said with a smile. "I'll even make dinner tonight. How about shepherd's pie?"

"Wonderful." She kissed him on the cheek and ran inside to shower, leaving him to enjoy the serenity of the view.

He suddenly felt he understood why she loved her retreat on Oahu. Away from Francesca and Jonah, he felt a huge burden lifted from his back and a sense of healing occurring. It was hard being "The Shadow," as he often referred to himself, for he had always been the peripheral parent, the one on the side. Kira knew he was there for her, but Francesca ran the show, and until the filming of *Beach Town*, that hadn't bothered him much.

He had met Francesca Astley accidentally in a pub. He was a grad student awaiting notice of a professorship in British literature at the University of London. He was young, brash and, according to many women, handsome. His life growing up in Chelsea had been happy, and he was known as a level-headed chap who knew how to treat a lady right, having been schooled by his father, a barrister, and his mother, a teacher.

That night he and his friends had already consumed several pints of beer when Francesca and her theater troupe descended on the pub, their uproarious and obnoxious behavior dreaded by the regular patrons. When he first saw her, another bloke was lighting her cigarette. She scanned the room and spotted him. They spent the next several minutes pretending not to notice each other until she brazenly walked across the pub and asked him to dance. He accepted and soon found himself asking her the predictable question about her plans for the rest of the evening.

They went back to his flat and, after a splendid night of enjoyment, realized in the light of day that they were too young, too self-absorbed and too involved in their individual lives to have a relationship. She kissed him wistfully and floated down the steps, her hair glistening in the morning sun. As she waved good-bye, he felt a tinge of regret, assuming he would never see her again, but six weeks later, he found her outside his door one evening, sobbing.

She was pregnant. Yes, she was positive. Yes, it was his. He insisted they get married and assured her that he would be a good provider, and their night of passion was surely a sign of the love they could build. Not wanting to face her parents without a father for her child, she accepted. Kira's birth, however, was troublesome, and she was a difficult baby, crying for days at a time. Francesca sunk into a terrible depression, and he struggled to keep his wife sane, his baby fed and his new fledgling career as an academic afloat.

The first five years were disastrous until providence pulled Francesca from her depression and gave Kira her first break. It was Christmastime and the three of them were standing in front of Harrods, coveting the gifts they couldn't afford. Kira was wearing her red velvet Christmas dress and white tights, a dress Francesca had insisted on buying, even though it meant eating cabbage soup for a month. He only argued until he saw Kira in her new clothes. She looked beautiful. They were all so engrossed in their own Christmas fantasies that they didn't notice a well-dressed man standing next to them.

"Excuse me. Are you the parents of this young lady?"

"Of course," Francesca said. "May I help you?"

"My name is Thomas Whitehead, and I am the manager of Harrods. Might I say your daughter is angelic?"

Francesca beamed at the compliment. "Thank you. We think so."

"And I believe others would say the same. I'd like your daughter to appear in some advertisements for our store. She would be paid, of course."

Stephen started to formulate some questions, but before he could utter a word, Francesca and Whitehead were already headed to his office to sign papers. It was the beginning of Kira's career, which blossomed from a few print ads in *The Times* of London to magazines and commercials. An agent appeared one night at their home, and Francesca found an immediate ally, for now it was two against one. While Stephen supported the opportunity for Kira to model and act, he was an academic and believed her to be a bright girl, one whose schooling should not be interrupted for a photo shoot. As the agent encroached upon their lives, Stephen stepped into the shadows, unable to win the battles he chose to fight. Eventually he fought less and less, until he just retreated into his own world, allowing a growing entourage to plan his daughter's life.

Now as he sat on a Hawaiian beach, thousands of miles from home, his daughter about to marry a man she detested, he wondered if he had failed as a father. It was a thought that slipped in and out of his mind, sometimes as a whisper and at other times, like now, as a speeding freight train. One day he would truly address the question and make a change—just not today.

His reflections were interrupted by the sound of feet ascending the deck. A buxom Polynesian woman appeared wearing tight jeans and a small bikini top that struggled to confine her large breasts. She smiled beautifully, and he reminded himself not to stare at her chest.

"Hello," she said pleasantly. "My name is Aikane."

"I'm Stephen, Kira's father. You have a lovely name."

"Thank you. My grandfather named me. It means friend. It is a pleasure to meet you, Stephen. I am a friend of Kira's. Her masseuse."

He nodded, although he noticed Aikane brought nothing with her that might be necessary to give a professional massage. "She's upstairs taking a shower."

"Perfect. She'll be ready for me afterward. It is a pleasure to make your acquaintance."

"Aikane, will you be staying for dinner?"

"At least."

Stephen reached the immense steps of the School of Veterinary Medicine and leaned against a towering pillar. Watching the hundreds of students linger on the mall and professors engaged in academic conversation as they strolled from building to building, he felt a wave of regret. He had given up that life several years ago, Francesca demanding that she needed his help as Kira's career soared to the sky. He checked his watch just as the double doors of the building swung open and several groups of students emerged. Flynn was one of the last to exit, alone.

Her eyes remained downcast and she passed by without noticing him. He paused, suddenly unsure of why he was there. Doubt of his plan lasted only a second before he called her name.

"Flynn!"

She spun around, and it only took a moment before recognition filled her face. "Stephen, what are you doing here?"

He motioned to a nearby bench and they sat down. "I guess I'm the self-appointed messenger. I thought you deserved some sort of . . . response. I can't provide an explanation, but I can say I'm sorry about the way things turned out for you, Flynn. I really am."

Her eyes were dark with pain. "I appreciate the thought, Stephen. Is it true that she's getting married?"

"I'm afraid so. It's a marriage of convenience. She doesn't love him. She loves surfing." When Flynn didn't reply, he reached into his pocket and withdrew a shiny object. At the sight of the silver ring she had given to Kira, her face fell. "She thought you should have this back," he said, holding the ring out.

She stood up, her eyes moist, and shifted her backpack from one arm to another. "No, that was gift." He suspected her refusal was borne from a sense of decorum as much as her eclipsed emotions. "If she doesn't want it, then she can throw it away, but I'm not taking it back."

He stood and pocketed the ring. They glanced about the campus, and he knew there was nothing to say. Only Kira possessed the answers to the questions he knew they both wanted to ask.

"Well, it was nice seeing you. I don't know why you felt you needed to come here—"

"Because you didn't take the money."

"Of course not."

"That's why I'm here. You're different. You really loved her. Kira's previous girlfriends may have cared for her, but they readily sold her out to turn a profit."

She stared into the quad. "For what it's worth, I don't know who took those pictures, but I'm positive it wasn't anyone in OB."

"I know you're correct," he said, avoiding the sordid details of Rona's scheme. "You and your friends did nothing wrong, Flynn. I'll tell you that the time Kira spent in Ocean Beach was probably the happiest in her life."

Flynn stared across the mall, unwilling to look at him. "I want you to know," she said, her voice crumbling, "that I would never do anything that could hurt Kira or her career. Not now, not ever."

He watched as she quickly walked away toward the rest of her life.

Fifteen Years Later

Chapter Nine
Stephen Drake

After the director yelled cut, he stormed toward Kira, his temperamental star, and at that moment, the most untalented soul on the face of the planet. Stephen hated to admit it, but her performance was flat and uninteresting, which was quite surprising, given the fact that the script was good, written by a first-rate novelist and Oscar winner. She even had the benefit of an inside track to understanding the character's motivations and feelings because she and the writer were engaged in a torrid affair. Yet her performance was sub-par, and the director's frustrations were legitimate. Kira was costing the producers a fortune.

Stephen remained on the periphery, watching Kira and the director discuss their differences and her inability to carry the scene. Soon their voices silenced the rest of the crew, and the director, a famed Italian with numerous movie credits, was gesturing in her face. She crossed her arms and turned on her heel, heading off to her trailer. The director threw up his hands and sunk into his chair. The writer quickly followed and disappeared into the trailer. If Kira was true to form, she would emerge again in thirty minutes. Stephen imagined that the writer had some sexual and persuasive ways to calm his daughter, but he didn't wish to dwell on it.

The next three weeks dragged by with little change. Stephen remained a silent observer, watching the movie evolve into a picture that would gain nothing but mediocre reviews and yet again affirm that Kira's best performances were behind her and she was washed up.

Since the deaths of Jonah and Francesca two years before, her life had changed dramatically, almost shifting in a one-hundred-and-eighty-degree turn. Without Jonah and Francesca to choreograph every decision, she was left to her own devices and was clearly making up for lost time. Over the past few years she made a few bombs and took her lumps. While he doubted any producers would describe her as a diva, she certainly had become opinionated and strong-willed—or, as he believed, her true personality, the one he remembered from childhood, finally resurfaced. She was in charge of her own career now, and her agent, a wonderful woman named Austin Prentice, was truly a partner, working *with* her. Of course, if her career did not rebound soon, if a hit did not emerge, he wondered if there would be much of a career left and she would lose the only thing that mattered to her.

She was in a slump and she needed a boost, but neither he nor Austin knew what to do. At those moments he almost wished that Francesca had survived the car crash that killed her and Jonah, her lover—*almost*. Her deception had floored him and provided Kira with the tangible proof necessary to truly hate her mother, a reason she searched for most of her life.

Now it was just Stephen and Kira, and she had found no one to share her life, not that she ever looked. The sham marriage lasted only a year, just long enough to convince the public of her heterosexuality. Dax met a man, and for the right price he and his new partner agreed to remain silent and allow the public divorce to sail under the radar.

Now, her personal life remained secretive, an easy accomplishment. Flynn was the only person who ever won her heart. She devoted her life to acting, leaving everything else behind. He learned that her self-confidence was rooted in her career, and professional failure weakened her personality. Each time a poor review appeared in a magazine or newspaper, she was devastated, and at forty, there was nothing else to enjoy except surfing. For Kira, surfing was a religion, and when she wasn't filming, she stayed at home in Oahu on the water.

After the film wrapped, he followed her back to Hawaii, hoping to find a way to help her. After a week he noticed a consistent routine—surfing, work and the occasional female visitor who shared her bed. He found himself studying his daughter for the first time in her life, rather than simply enjoying her company. He noticed how she prepared dinner, when she answered her e-mail, how she reacted to her lovers, even her surfing technique, which he was totally unqualified to judge. Yet, while watching her surf, a realization struck him. He couldn't explain why, and he didn't know the technical surfing terms, but it was only when she rode the waves and shifted back and forth on the water that she showed any true passion. When she emerged from the sea, her smile was genuine and her body language carefree. He realized that as much as she enjoyed filmmaking, there was no passion in her work. The smiles and energy she showered on the camera and the public were just a different type of acting. His epiphany helped him see that his daughter, a multimillionaire, whose face had graced hundreds of magazine covers, was coasting through life and would have little to enjoy at the end.

And then the truth hit him. Every analysis he proposed for Kira also applied to himself. He was as miserable as his daughter, and the most pathetic part was that he was twenty-five years older. He decided it was time to act. He had wondered over the years if he was a good father. He saw an opportunity to improve his own life and give her a chance to choose a different path. Sitting on the balcony watching his daughter, he pulled out his cell phone and called his housekeeper in London. They spent ten minutes talking, and when Stephen pocketed the phone, he was a changed man.

Two days later, as he and Kira enjoyed their eggs Benedict, the doorbell rang. When he returned holding a FedEx box, Kira looked up from the newspaper.

"What's that?"

He slit the flaps open and pulled out two shoeboxes. "Sweetheart, there's something I need to tell you."

Fear clouded Kira's face. "Dad, is something wrong?"

Realizing his error, he immediately covered her hand with his own. "Oh, no. At least, I don't think so. And I hope you won't either." He removed the lids from the shoeboxes and showed her the contents—packets of letters wrapped with rubber bands.

She dragged her hand across the top of the first box and pulled a stack from the back. "These are from a woman." She scanned the envelopes and frowned. "The return address says San Diego." She looked up at him. "Who sent these to you?"

He smiled slightly. "Mo. Mo McFadden." He watched her accept his answer with a slight smile of her own. He studied her response, teetering between his own joy and respect for the pain she still carried from the past.

"So, what's been going on? How is Mo?"

"She's wonderful. Her life is good. We've been writing letters to each other for many years."

"I see. Is it just correspondence or have you been seeing her?"

"Only once. I thought that arranging a trip to the States would be betraying your mother, but one time, when I was flying out to see you in Los Angeles, I thought that stopping by to see Mo would be justifiable because I was so close. We had dinner and walked around the harbor."

She examined the letters, her fingers tracing the edges of the envelopes. "Did you see Flynn?"

"No. Mo and I have always kept our connection private. I doubt Flynn even knows her mother has been writing to me." Suddenly serious, he looked her in the eye. "I want you to know that I never cheated on your mother. I just needed a friend and Mo was always a good listener."

"It's too bad Mum couldn't show you the same consideration," Kira said. Regaining her composure, she managed a genuine smile and squeezed her father's hand. "I understand, Dad. Mum wasn't much for anyone else's world. I certainly can relate to your feelings. I stopped telling her anything of significance when I was ten. You're the one I've always turned to."

Her revelation pleased him, and he kissed her on the cheek. "We've always had each other."

They sat in silence, the clock on the mantle ticking away the moments of their lives. "How is Flynn?"

He heard the hesitancy in her voice. She had not asked about Flynn in more than fifteen years. He held up a special stack of letters. "Flynn's well. These letters are about her and Megan." He opened five envelopes and unfolded a newspaper clipping from each one. "This one is the announcement when she graduated from vet school and joined the clinic. The next one shows her with her staff at the clinic, when the practice was turned over to her. Standing next to her is her partner, Luz."

Kira strained her neck toward the granular image of a dark-haired woman, her arm wrapped proudly around Flynn's waist. "She met someone. I'm glad."

"And this is a wedding announcement for Megan. She and her girlfriend, Rocco, had a commitment ceremony about eight years ago. They opened a tattoo salon in West Hollywood. They're doing well, the tattoo artists to the stars."

Kira laughed slightly and shook her head.

"This is a birth announcement for Flynn's son, Kellen."

She read every word, tears welling in her eyes. She wiped her cheeks and set the clipping down slowly. "I can't believe she has a child. I'll bet she's an amazing parent."

He nodded. "Mo says Kellen is a great young man." He searched through the most recent letters and withdrew a small wallet-size photo. "This is his school picture from last year. He's thirteen now."

She stared at the handsome young man. Like every early teen, Kellen was caught between the looks of his youth and the adult he would become. She said nothing and gave the photo back to her father.

He handed her the final newspaper clipping, an obituary. "I think for a while it seemed like Flynn had the perfect life. Luz was a wonderful partner, but unfortunately, there was a terrible car accident, and Luz died five years ago."

"Oh, no," she said, her voice full of anguish.

"Apparently she was visiting a relative in central California and went over a ravine on Highway One on her way home."

"My God, how awful." Her troubled eyes met his. "Has Flynn recovered? Is she all right?"

He chose his words carefully. "I think Kellen forces her to live in the present and keep moving forward, but from what Mo has told me, Luz was everything to her."

"I'm sure it was devastating," Kira said. She stood and moved away from the table, putting distance between her and the life of her former lover. "Why are you showing me all of this now? I probably could have gone the rest of my life without discussing Flynn ever again."

He avoided her gaze, slowly folding the clippings and placing them back in the envelopes. He struggled with the words, because he had no answers and no real understanding of his feelings. There was no way to explain it all to her. When he finally turned to her he said, "I'm sharing this with you, darling, because I want my life back."

Chapter Ten

Mo McFadden

Filled with nervous energy, Mo expended it by polishing the counter endlessly and bustling through the Ocean Beach Café among the customers. Even the morning rush couldn't occupy her mind, which continually drifted to her worries. She glanced at the clock incessantly, sensing the hands were not moving at all. Everyone eventually filtered out the door and she was left alone. She flipped the door sign to Closed and waited.

"Hey, Grandma," a voice called.

She beamed at the sight of her handsome grandson. "Hello, Kellen."

He kissed her on the cheek before grabbing his breakfast from the doughnut plate and plopping down on a stool. "So what's up?"

"I can't tell you until your mother and aunt arrive."

Kellen had finished his second doughnut when the door jingled and Megan and Flynn entered, drawing an automatic smile from Mo. It was a rare treat, having her whole family together, especially now that Megan lived in L.A. Although it was only ninety minutes away, it might as well be a three-day drive for as often as they traversed I-5 to see each other.

Flynn looked at her watch. "Okay, Mom. We're here, and I've only got a little time before Mrs. Ramirez brings Flopsy in for her checkup."

She bit her lip and took a deep breath. "You three know that you are dearest in my heart, and no one could ever mean more to me than you do—"

"Oh, God, you're dying," Megan cried.

She momentarily closed her eyes. "No, Megan, I'm not dying, and please don't interrupt. I'm not good at explaining these kinds of things." She looked at all three of them before continuing. "As I said, you are all important to me, but I've come to realize that there is room for someone else."

Kellen's eyes went wide. "Grandma, are you trying to tell us that you have a boyfriend?"

She blushed and they voiced their surprise. Flynn asked, "How can you have a boyfriend we've never seen? Kellen and I live in the same house with you. I'm sure I'd notice if some man were standing in the kitchen wearing your robe and making French toast."

"Flynn," she said, her cheeks warm. "I am of a different generation, and we are much more discreet."

"Sounds boring," Megan added. "So, Mom, how long have you been seeing this guy?"

She debated her answer. "In what sense?"

Megan held out her hands. "How many senses are there?"

"We've known each other a long time as friends, and we've only recently discovered that we have other feelings."

Kellen jumped up. "It's Manny, isn't it."

"No!" Flynn and Mo said in unison.

"Do we know this person?"

Although Megan asked the question, Mo's gaze settled on Flynn. "You do. You met him once a long time ago, and I've been writing to him for many years. I've been writing to Stephen, Stephen Drake."

Megan shook her head. "I can't believe it, Mom. After everything that woman did to Flynn."

"What are we talking about?" a puzzled Kellen asked.

"Grandma's new boyfriend helped break your mother's heart," Megan said. "Sounds like a really great guy."

"Megan, that is incorrect. Stephen wanted them to be together."

Megan snorted in disbelief. "Yeah, sure."

"It's true, Meg," Flynn agreed. "Stephen actually tried to help." Flynn turned to her mother with kind eyes. "I guess I still don't understand what's happened."

Mo sat down next to her daughters and folded her hands on the table. "Well, I imagine it all started that night he visited the house during the rainstorm. Do you remember that night, Flynn?" When Flynn nodded, she squeezed her hand. "We hit it off immediately, and before he left, he asked if he could write. I told him I very much enjoyed receiving letters. I think he was lonely."

"How long did you write to him?" Kellen asked.

"For the last fifteen years."

"Wow, Grandma. That's a lot of letters. Did you ever see him?"

"I've seen him twice, once about eight years ago when he stopped by for a short visit on his way to Los Angeles, and then I just saw him recently. You see, Kellen, Stephen was married for a long time to a woman he didn't love, but he had made a commitment, and he would never dishonor it, not that she didn't."

"His wife had an affair?" Flynn asked in astonishment.

Mo scowled. "Yes. I never liked that woman." She took a deep breath and gazed at her oldest daughter, whose thoughts were unreadable. "Flynn, Stephen and I are close, but I care about your feelings. I'd like to know what you think."

Flynn smiled at her mother's concern. "Mom, I'm happy for you. If you're worried about my feelings for Kira, you shouldn't be. Those wounds healed a long time ago. Luz saw to that."

"So it doesn't bother you when you see all those pictures of her on magazine covers or in the movies?"

Kellen's eyes widened. "Mom knows a movie star?"

"Your mother was in *love* with a movie star. A big movie star," Megan said. "Then she broke your mother's heart."

"That was long before you were born, Kellen," Flynn said quickly. "A *lot* of women broke my heart before I met Luz. And in answer to your question, Mom, no, it doesn't bother me."

Mo realized the conversation had wandered too far into the serious realm for the teenage boy. Kellen grabbed another doughnut and stared at his family. "So what's the big deal?" he asked between bites. "Good for you, Grandma. I don't even have a girlfriend. So when do I get to meet this guy? Is he here in OB now?"

"No, he had to leave immediately. He was only in town for an evening. Just long enough to do what he needed to do."

Megan raised an eyebrow. "And what was that?"

"He asked me to marry him."

Chapter Eleven
Flynn McFadden

Twenty-four hours after her mother's announcement, Flynn still didn't allow herself to think about the upcoming wedding, Kira's arrival in two days or that summer fifteen years before. She was too busy with her own life, a convenient list of to-do items that kept her in constant motion and afforded little time for reflection or remembrance. Yet a few glimpses of the past had edged their way into her mind—Kira's laugh, the first time they kissed, her incredible body standing in the shower—and the hair. She clearly remembered the beautiful chestnut hair.

She had pushed the ugliness of their breakup to the back of her mind, and she refused to think of that awful day in the hotel with Jonah. She knew she would eventually need to confront the memory, for it was inextricably tied to Stephen Drake. For now she could ignore it, since she still had several patients waiting in the lobby and an evening of fun with Megan, who had decided to stay in OB for the rest of the week, until after the wedding on Saturday.

At least her journey through the past would be fast, she mused as she grabbed the file for her last patient of the day. Stephen and Mo had decided they had no time to waste, her mother thought a June wedding would be lovely and, fortunately, Kira was between films and could attend—if they could throw it together in the next four days. There would be no great fanfare. They would hold an engagement party at the Bullfrog and the wedding on the pier. It also helped that everyone in town owed Mo favors. Whatever she wanted, she would get.

Flynn glanced at her wall clock and headed toward the treatment room to greet her final patient of the day, Dewey, and his owner, Mrs. Tillowix. Dorothy Tillowix was a rich matron whose husband built the Ocean Beach Hotel decades ago. When he died of a heart attack at forty, a scandal ensued and gossip spread through the town, accusing his young bride of foul play. No one could prove Mrs. Tillowix had poisoned her husband, and Flynn suspected that Mrs. Tillowix's greatest crime was feeding her husband incredibly fatty foods, which she now continued to give her dog, Dewey. Every month Mrs. Tillowix brought the extremely overweight bulldog to see Flynn, whether he needed it or not.

"Hello, Mrs. Tillowix," Flynn said warmly. "Hey, Dewey." Flynn patted Dewey's head and his snorting ceased momentarily. She enjoyed her visits with the elderly dowager, who once won a contest named I Look Like My Pet. Indeed Mrs. Tillowix's round body and wrinkly face was a near match for Dewey. She glanced from owner to animal and her smile widened. "So how's our boy doing today?"

Mrs. Tillowix pursed her orange lips and took a deep breath. "I'm a bit concerned, Dr. McFadden. Dewey hasn't been eating much from his bowl lately. I set his bowl on a little stool so he doesn't have to bend his neck too far, and yesterday he knocked it clean off."

Mrs. Tillowix's British accent momentarily reminded Flynn of Kira, talking and laughing as they trudged up the beach after surfing. She focused on Dewey's chart, erasing the image. She checked Dewey's weight and furrowed her brow. "Mrs. Tillowix, it says that today Dewey weighs sixty pounds. That's two more pounds than last month. If he's not eating his food, how is he gaining the weight?"

Mrs. Tillowix shifted in her chair, her black bag moving from knee to knee. She avoided Flynn's gaze and looked down. "Well, I can't be sure," she mumbled.

Flynn took a deep breath and set the chart down on the counter. She folded her arms across her chest. "Mrs. Tillowix, I thought we had an agreement. Dewey was not to have any more table scraps. It causes him to gain weight and it's unhealthy. And, as you have seen, it increases his dislike of his own food."

Mrs. Tillowix's head shot up and she looked sincerely at Flynn. "Oh, Dr. McFadden, I didn't feed him any table scraps. No, I listened to you after last time."

"Then do you have any idea why Dewey is gaining weight?"

Mrs. Tillowix cocked her head to the side just like Dewey and Flynn almost laughed. Mrs. Tillowix was deep in thought, and she couldn't wait to hear her response. "Maybe it has something to do with his birthday cake."

"His birthday cake?"

"Well, of course. Dewey's birthday was on the third. So he got to have a cake."

She closed her eyes for a moment, reminding herself that to Mrs. Tillowix, Dewey was a person, a companion. "What kind of cake did Dewey have?"

"Oh, his *second* favorite. White with butterscotch frosting." She pointed her finger at Flynn and sat up straight. "I was careful this year, Dr. McFadden. I remembered what you told me about feeding dogs chocolate. No more chocolate fudge for my

Dewey Doo Doo, no siree." She puckered her lips and kissed the dog's snout. "Not after last year's scare."

"I'm glad you remembered that, Mrs. Tillowix. How much cake did Dewey have?"

"One piece a day."

Her eyes widened and her jaw dropped. "A *day*? How many days did Dewey have cake?"

Mrs. Tillowix's expression soured. "Well, eight of course. It's always proper to cut a cake into eight slices."

She scratched her head and debated what to say. "Mrs. Tillowix, if I understand you correctly, you have fed your bulldog birthday cake for eight days straight, and yesterday, when he didn't get any cake, he knocked over his food bowl. Right?"

"Yes, Dr. McFadden."

"Well, I think I know what happened."

Mrs. Tillowix simply gazed at her, as if Flynn was about to reveal the meaning of life.

"Mrs. Tillowix, Dewey had a temper tantrum. You stopped giving him something that tasted wonderful, and instead, you fed him his regular meal. He got upset, and he refused to eat it." She scratched Dewey behind the ears, and his heavy breathing increased, as if to agree.

Mrs. Tillowix's eyes twinkled and she clapped her hands. "Oh, of course, Dr. McFadden. That makes perfect sense."

"So, do you understand what the problem is and what you need to do?"

"Yes! I need to make another cake!" Mrs. Tillowix jumped from her chair and threw her arms around Dewey. "Come to Mommy, my love dumpling. Mommy's going to make you a wonderful cake."

Flynn waited until she had finished lavishing affection on the frothing bulldog. "Um, Mrs. Tillowix, unfortunately, that's not the answer."

"What?"

"You cannot make Dewey any more cakes. You cannot give Dewey any more human food of any kind at any time, not even for special occasions." She paused for effect and adopted a serious expression. She knew she was hurting her immensely, but she knew Mrs. Tillowix must understand. "Mrs. Tillowix, if you continue to feed Dewey human food, you will kill him."

Mrs. Tillowix nodded her head slowly, the meaning of Flynn's words bringing tears to her eyes. She looked at her dog and caressed his face. "I'm so sorry, Dewey. I just wanted you to have a nice birthday."

Flynn's heart melted as she watched the two of them. An idea came to her. "Mrs. Tillowix, come with me." Flynn lifted Dewey off the table and guided the dog and Mrs. Tillowix to her office. She sat at her desk and found the Web site she was looking for—Doggie Goodies. Several pictures of dog biscuits, cookies and cakes appeared on the screen. "Mrs. Tillowix, look at these. If you want to give Dewey a treat, you could buy him these over the Internet."

Dewey jumped up and Flynn pulled him into her lap. Mrs. Tillowix studied the pictures and read the description of the doggie cake. She sighed and walked away, shaking her head. "Those look wonderful, Dr. McFadden, but I don't know how to use all of these electronic gizmos. I wouldn't know what to do. Can I buy these items at the pet store down on Newport Boulevard?"

"I'm afraid not. There isn't a place nearby that sells them. You'd have to go downtown. They might have them."

Mrs. Tillowix frowned. "That's unfortunate. I don't drive anymore, you know."

Flynn nodded and thought of a solution. "Mrs. Tillowix, what if I order them for you, and then you can pay me? Could we do that?"

The smile returned to the old lady and she clapped her hands. "That's wonderful, Dr. McFadden. Thank you. I won't take any more of your time. Say good-bye, Dewey."

Dewey gave a final snort, and Mrs. Tillowix and Dewey waddled out the door together. Flynn looked back at the screen, realizing that she was missing a business opportunity with her clients. She scrolled through the pictures, an idea swirling in her brain. She clicked through several Web sites and began taking notes on a pad of paper.

"What are you looking at, Doc?"

She jumped at the question, surprised to see Megan so early. She turned the monitor so Megan could view the dog treats. "Look at this stuff. I'll bet it's really cheap to make, and look how much it goes for."

Megan chuckled. "Great. Why don't you build a doggie bakery next to your new dog shelter?"

She stared at Megan. "That's not a bad idea."

Megan sighed. "C'mon, Flynn. You've got enough to deal with right now."

"You're right." She shut off the computer and stood up. "Have you seen the shelter?"

"Nope. That's why I'm here." Megan pulled a digital camera from her purse. "Rocco wants some more pictures for your Web site." Rocco had become the official Webmistress for the Ocean Beach Veterinary Clinic, and she constantly updated the progress on the animal shelter.

"Great, let's go."

She hung up her white coat and led Megan out the back, noticing that the clinic was dark and the staff had departed for the evening. She glanced at her watch, realizing it was after seven. She had once again lost track of time, which happened frequently. Often she would collapse into her office chair at the end of the day and stare at Luz's photograph that sat next to her computer, or she'd surf on the Web or stroll through the skeletal frame of the animal shelter, imagining what it would look like when it finally opened—anything to avoid her room at home, which had seemed so lonely for the past five years. More than a few times she'd thought of moving, but now that Luz was gone, she needed help with Kellen, and Mo understood children far better than she ever would. It was almost a blessing that she and Luz never scraped enough money together to buy their own place. Luz loved Mo and never cared that they all lived together, using all of their extra money to support the clinic—and now the shelter.

Flynn knew that the animal shelter would serve the community, but it was also a huge distraction that occupied her empty days. Progress was slow as she and her board of directors sought contributions and grants. She spent most of her free time begging San Diego corporations for money and learning the steps for achieving nonprofit status. The cash flow had increased, and she was proud that the bulk of the funds were coming from Ocean Beach folks. She smiled when she realized Mrs. Tillowix had made the most generous donation of one hundred thousand dollars.

Flynn didn't bother to narrate their tour, as Megan knew the floor plan by heart and had heard all of her interior design ideas. The entire foundation and framework were upright, and the roof was ready to install. Megan snapped several photos before they wandered to a stone wall that outlined the perimeter of the entire property. Flynn admired the modest parcel of land that she acquired through her inheritance from Gmum, three sprawling acres that overlooked the Pacific. Gmum also left some cash, and Flynn was able to relocate the OB clinic to the wonderful land. Gmum only asked that a plaque be placed in the lobby, a tribute to her beloved Zipper, who lived to be fourteen. That was years ago, and it was all Luz's idea. Flynn had asked Luz several times if she was sure that was what they should do. Wouldn't she rather buy a house? But Luz was insistent. The clinic needed to expand. Flynn's eyes misted at the thought of her dead partner, and she took a deep breath, forcing down the emotion.

She straddled the wall, affording herself a view of the shelter if she looked over her right shoulder and the Pacific Ocean if she looked to her left. She did not wish to turn her back to either. Megan joined her and withdrew two longnecks from her purse. She popped the lids with her bottle opener and handed her sister a beer.

"To Mom and Stephen," Megan said. Flynn raised her beer and they clinked bottles before downing hefty swigs. "So, have you thought about her much? Do you know what you'll say?"

Flynn didn't answer right away. "I guess I'll say hello," she decided. "I don't know." She glanced at Megan, a skeptical expression on her face. "I really don't remember much about that summer. It was a long time ago, and our affair, if you could call it that, only lasted a few weeks."

"They were pretty memorable, though," Megan said. "She's a movie star, for Christ's sake. Don't you remember all of the phone calls from our relatives after they saw the picture on the cover of that magazine? You had your fifteen minutes of fame."

"Twelve minutes too long." She had hated the fact that her name got out as the other woman in the "kissing picture" with Kira Drake. She did the smart thing and took her mother's advice by not saying anything, not granting any interviews and not accepting any money for the real story. She meant what she had said to Stephen Drake that day at the university—she would never hurt Kira.

She glanced at her new building, fortifying her resolve to talk about the second most difficult time in her life. "It's been weird. I'll see these little memories in my mind, and they trigger a feeling. The only time I'm avoiding is that afternoon in the hotel." She stared down at her beer. "I don't want to remember that."

"That's the most important one. That's when Miss Kira Drake showed you her true colors."

She said nothing. There was no point in arguing with Megan. The few times they ever discussed that summer always ended in a disagreement. Flynn realized after the last fight that Megan was only trying to be her sister's ally.

"Meg, just let it be. We know nothing about her or her life." Flynn swallowed hard. "If Luz were here, she would be the first one to throw her arms around Kira and give her a big hug."

Megan sipped her beer, and she knew she had made a point. "Luz was an amazing person, but she's gone."

Their eyes met for a second before Flynn looked away. "I know she's dead," Flynn said, although uttering the words made her lips quiver.

Megan furrowed her brow. "You know in your head but you don't in your heart. And I worry for you." She squeezed her sister's hand. "I just want you to be happy. You need to date—but not Kira Drake."

Flynn didn't protest, for it would be a pathetic lie. Megan was her confidante, the one person who knew her emotions and all of her anxieties. "I want to be happy, too."

"Okay, then let's get this evening moving. I thought we'd hit some clubs over in Old Town."

She scowled at the thought. "Clubs? Why don't we just go throw some darts at the Bullfrog?"

Megan hopped off the wall and shook her head. "We can do that anytime. Tonight we're going out on the town. Even someone who's over forty can handle a little excitement once in a while."

Chapter Twelve
Kira Drake

Traffic through La Jolla moved quickly for a busy Tuesday morning, and Kira was tired of listening to the voice on the GPS feature of her rented Land Cruiser. She glanced at the dashboard and found the appropriate switch to deactivate the system. It was annoying and she didn't need it anyway. She knew La Jolla well, having stayed in the area before during a previous movie shoot. She had arrived a day early to prepare herself mentally for the reunion that was to come, and only her assistant, Robert, knew she was in California.

He had found a magnificent bungalow for her, and after a few hours of surfing in the incredible La Jolla waves, she drove into San Diego to run errands for her father and look for a wedding present. She had narrowed her choices to a Swarovski decanter or candlesticks. Familiar exit signs appeared and she spotted the exit for Rosecrans Boulevard, the road to Ocean Beach. On a whim, she took the turnoff and headed west toward the water. She was looking for a street that she was sure she would remember when she saw it. Curiosity overrode anxiety, and she was waiting for the emotions to come, whatever they might be. If she was going to be surprised by her reactions to Ocean Beach, at least it would be in private. Robert's ring tone, "I Walk the Line," filled the Land Cruiser's interior and she smiled slightly.

"Hello, Robert."

"Hey, Kira. How's California?"

She looked through the windshield at the blooming summer flowers and the swaying palm trees. "Beautiful."

Robert Duncan hailed from El Mira, Texas, and she fell in love with his accent and easygoing manner at their interview three years ago. The fact that her mother and Jonah hated Robert was an added bonus. They called him simple-minded, but in fact, he graduated at the top of his business class at the University of Texas at El Paso and was accepted to law school—an opportunity he declined in order to work for her.

"What are ya doin' now?" he drawled. "Surfin'?"

"No, I surfed this morning." She caught a glimpse of the ocean and knew she was close to the street. "I'm going downtown to pick up the wedding rings for my father and continue my search for a proper wedding gift. But first I thought I'd stop by Ocean Beach. You know, check it out before I have to see everyone tomorrow."

"Huh. You sure about this?"

She smiled at his concern. He never lectured and only gave her advice when she asked. It made her value his opinion more, and in the last six months, she had found herself turning to him often as a friend. He was the greatest straight man she knew, and his girlfriend was adorable. "I'm okay," she said. "I just want to brace myself for what's coming."

"Well, how's the house? Does it have all the right fixin's?"

"It's wonderful, Robert. And the company did an excellent

job of stocking the cupboards and the icebox. I feel quite comfortable."

"So you doin' okay?"

"I'm fine. I miss you."

"I miss you, too. Did you get the scripts? Those Fox folks are expectin' an answer next week, you know. Austin wanted me to make sure I reminded you of that."

"Yes, you tell her that you did remind me. I promise I'll read them between surfing sets while I'm here." Ahead she saw the sign for Narragansett Avenue. "I need to sign off, Robert."

"Are you goin' to that Bull Terrier bar?"

She laughed. "You mean the Bullfrog? How do you know about that place?"

Now it was his turn to laugh. "Well, darlin', you don't have any idea how tequila affects you, that's all I'm gonna say. The other night when you got hammered, after you found out about your daddy, you babbled for hours. I know more about that Irishwoman and the Bullfrog and surfing then I ever thought I could know."

"Oh, God. Did I really say that much?"

"You said enough to fill up most of Houston. I'll let you go. I gotta head out anyway. Becky and I are goin' to a barbeque tonight at her folks."

Kira smiled at the memory of her last barbeque with Robert and his fiancée, Becky. Her family owned a huge ranch in eastern Texas, and they were known for their pig roasts. She dreaded attending it, but she had a blast and met a wonderful woman who shared her bed for the rest of the trip, showing her true Southern hospitality.

"I'll talk to you tomorrow," she said before flipping her phone shut and tossing it in her purse. She studied the houses on the west side of the hilly street and with each passing block, she remembered a little more about the large, white structure that sat on a corner with many windows—on the top of a hill. Kira peered two blocks ahead and saw a house that looked familiar. When she pulled up beside it, she recognized it as the McFadden house instantly because of the old blue back door that she and Flynn used many times. And there was Flynn's old VW bus, sitting in a corner by the guesthouse. She gazed at the faded yellow paint and the rusty roof rack that held all of Flynn's surfboards. It was clearly not used anymore, but Kira imagined Flynn couldn't part with it, or perhaps she was saving it for her teenage son.

Her mouth was dry and her hands were shaking. Seeing Flynn would be much harder than she imagined, and she suddenly wished she had asked Robert to come with her. She felt alone, and the only other person she would call, her father, was at the center of this visit and about to join the McFadden family. She leaned against the steering wheel and gazed out at the ocean in the distance. It calmed her, and she decided to drive down Newport Avenue for one more stop.

Chapter Thirteen
Kellen McFadden

People turned and stared whenever Kellen McFadden walked his pack toward Dog Beach. Regardless of how many dogs he handled, however large or small, the canines all behaved well for him, despite the fact that he was only thirteen. The dogs started to tug on their leashes as he reached the crest of the dune, all of them knowing what waited on the other side. Their manners diminished as they headed for the shore, and he required all of them to sit at attention while he removed each leash. The six wagging tails swished back and forth at full speed, their eyes glued to the surf, their daily playground. With a whistle and a motion, the freed animals bounded away in different directions, looking for fun. Rusty and Smoky frolicked in the water, while Scrunchy, Izzie and Joe joined a game of fetch with another dog owner. Only Rufus, his own ancient mutt, stayed close to him, his little furry face glancing about, unable to play in the water like a puppy but just happy to be outdoors.

"You miss those days, don't you, Rufus?" he said, and Rufus looked up as if to acknowledge his master.

As the proprietor and sole employee of Big Woof Pampering, he assumed responsibility for at least six dogs on a daily basis. He provided every service imaginable to dog owners, including walking, grooming and sitting. The business had started by chance one day when he was at his mother's vet clinic and a patient mentioned she needed someone to feed her poodles while she was away in Maui. He readily volunteered, and word of mouth plus his mother's recommendations ensured that his business thrived, particularly now, during the summer months with many of the locals heading for other places, avoiding the influx of tourists.

Always eager to earn money, he'd made his mother and Luz proud with his entrepreneurial skills, beginning with the lemonade stand at the end of the pier. It took Grandma almost a week to realize that the reason the lemonade at the café wasn't selling was because he was competing against her just one hundred yards away. Flynn and Mo encouraged him, though, particularly because of his generosity. After he spent a day at the lemonade stand, he gave away most of the profits to the homeless people that lined the boardwalk next to Ocean Beach.

He glanced out at one of the female surfers and a fleeting memory of Luz floated by him with the sea wind. The woman looked slightly like his second mother and a knot formed in his throat. Five years had passed since her death, but sometimes it felt near, a memory that sat in the corner of his heart. He walked farther down the shore with Rufus, enjoying the pleasant June weather. Glancing back and forth at his frolicking pack, Rufus looked up at the dune and bounded away. He was headed straight for an attractive woman sitting on a blanket. Kellen's mouth dropped open when Rufus invaded her personal space and plopped down at her side.

He rushed toward her, stunned by his dog's behavior. "Rufus, what are you doing?" He turned to the woman, who fortunately was smiling. She was about his mother's age, and he figured she was a surfer, judging by the Ron Jon T-shirt she wore. He suddenly felt much more comfortable around her and wondered if she was a local he had missed. "I'm really sorry. I've never seen him do that." He patted his leg and Rufus ran to him.

"His name is Rufus?"

"Yeah."

"I knew a Rufus a long time ago. This couldn't be him, could it?"

"Well, maybe. Rufus is pretty old. He's almost sixteen."

The woman's eyes moved from him to the little white dog. A look of recognition crossed her face and she smiled pleasantly. She threw her arms open and Rufus jumped into her lap. "It's good to see you again, Rufus."

"How do you know my dog?"

The woman stumbled for an explanation while she scratched Rufus behind the ears. "I knew your mom a long time ago. I'm Kira. My father is Stephen Drake."

"Oh, hi. I'm Kellen. Your dad's marrying my grandma on Saturday."

He was about to ask her if she had seen his mother when a shrieking growl clashed with the roaring surf. He automatically rushed to the shore and the source—two fighting dogs. He quickly withdrew a can of dog mace from his pocket and sprayed both of them in the face. They immediately yipped and separated. The larger mutt ran off and joined a man and a woman sitting in foldable chairs reading books, their ears plugged with MP3 players. He scowled, knowing that they were tourists and totally unaware of the incident that just occurred.

He dropped to Scrunchy, the little spaniel mix, who whined in pain. "Oh, God," he said, noticing a gouge at the base of Scrunchy's neck. "Mrs. Mullen is going to be pissed. Hang on,

Scrunchy." He scooped up the dog in his arms and headed up the dune. He turned around, suddenly remembering that he had five other dogs with him.

Kira gathered her blanket and ran to his side. "Let me help you. My SUV is over there. I'll hold him while you get the others."

He nodded and followed her instructions. They piled into the Land Cruiser, and he smirked when he realized Joe the Doberman was licking Kira's ear. "Jeez, Joe," he scolded, pushing the dog back in the seat.

"It's fine," Kira said with a giggle. "I just hope your little friend is okay."

He looked down at Scrunchy, who was panting heavily, a bloody gash on his neck. He directed her through the side streets of Ocean Beach. At times it seemed as though she already knew when to turn and his directions were unnecessary. Whatever existed between her and his mother must have left an impression, if she still remembered Ocean Beach. They pulled up to the front of the clinic, which was partially blocked by a large delivery of two-by-four beams.

"Is the clinic being remodeled?" Kira asked as she stepped out of the car.

"Yeah, we're adding a shelter for unwanted animals," he said, already heading toward the door with Scrunchy. "Can you handle these guys?"

He noticed that she hesitated a second before she nodded, grabbed the other leashes and led the animals into the lobby. Before he realized what was happening, the other five exuberant dogs tangled their leashes and tumbled through the entrance, dragging Kira behind them and disturbing the many waiting dogs and cats that were already anxious about visiting the vet. The sudden movements upset the other patients, who started tugging on their leashes and barking in unison with the new arrivals. The din was excruciating, and Kira could do nothing to silence her five charges. He tried to calm the dogs while cradling Scrunchy, but he couldn't be heard over the barking.

Other human voices added to the noise, shouting orders to the dogs and one another. Two vet techs hurried around the counter to assist them, but the Doberman jerked the leash, sending Kira sprawling onto the floor. She lost control of all the dogs, and the vet techs chased them around the lobby.

"Kira!" he cried. He rushed to her and looked over her. "Are you okay?"

"What's going on out here?" a commanding voice boomed, silencing everyone, including the animals.

He closed his eyes, recognizing the angry tone of his mother. Kira scrambled to right herself from the linoleum floor as his mother rushed to her.

"My God, I'm so sorry," she said to her backside. "Let me help you."

She extended her hand, and Kira turned around to face her. When their eyes met, his mother's expression conveyed utter shock. He watched in amazement as they studied each other. His mother blinked and pulled Kira from the floor.

"Hello, Flynn."

She shook her head and looked around. "How—" she began, but quickly changed her question to, "What are you doing here?"

"She helped me, Mom," he quickly said. "Scrunchy got hurt at Dog Beach and Kira gave us all a ride." He looked from his mother to Kira, whose eyes darted from Flynn to the ground.

When Scrunchy let out a low moan, her attention returned to the animal. Without another word, she took Scrunchy from him and disappeared into the back of the clinic. He watched Kira, frozen in the same spot, her hands at her sides.

"Kira, are you okay?"

She blinked and turned to him, a soft smile on her face. "I should probably go. Can you handle everyone else?" she asked, motioning to the five panting heads at his feet.

"They're fine now that they're really tired out. Thanks for your help."

Kira nodded and opened the door for his pack. "Can I give you a ride?"

"No, that's okay," he said, but he stopped at the edge of the sidewalk. He opened his mouth to speak just as Jeanette, one of his mother's vet techs, appeared. "Excuse me, Ms. Drake?"

"Yes."

"Dr. McFadden asked if you would please step into her office."

"All right." She squared her shoulders and sighed. "Well, I guess your mom wants to see me."

"Can I ask you another question?"

"Certainly."

She smiled and he felt a lump form in his throat. For her age, Kira Drake was amazingly beautiful. He could easily imagine why his mother would fall in love with her. "My Aunt Megan said you broke my mother's heart. Is that true?"

Her face crumbled. "Yes, Kellen, it is. We were both much younger. This was before you were born, and I didn't treat your mother well. I think you should know because we're all going to be together for the next several days, and I'm sure certain unpleasant things will be mentioned." He nodded in understanding. "I also think you should know that my relationship with Flynn has nothing to do with your grandmother and my father. I know your mother would agree with me about that."

"Okay," he said. He turned away from Kira with his dogs, somewhat saddened and wishing he had never asked the question, since the answer made him like Kira a little less than he did a few minutes before.

Chapter Fourteen

Kira Drake

Kira looked down the sidewalk at the young man who was Flynn's son. She should have recognized him immediately, for his eyes were exactly like hers. She touched the door handle and debated whether to go back inside or retreat to La Jolla, grab her surfboard and let the ocean wash away the tension that had taken hold of her shoulders. The idea was so appealing that she released the handgrip just as a harried mom barreled outside, her Chihuahua and little girl in tow.

"I'm sorry," she said absently, continuing along without noticing Kira.

Holding the open door, she decided that she couldn't avoid the inevitable. She went back inside, scanning the clinic lobby for the vet tech, who had disappeared. Her eyes met the stare of a middle-aged African-American woman sitting at the center of the reception desk. Kira didn't remember seeing her before, and the woman showed no sign of recognizing her. A pencil rested behind her ear, and she had a look of authority that wilted Kira's confidence.

"May I help you?"

"Yes, I need to see Dr. McFadden."

The woman whose nameplate identified her as Mrs. Jenkins looked over the top of her glasses with searing eyes. "Do you have an appointment?"

"Um, no."

Mrs. Jenkins added a condescending smile to her expression. "Dr. McFadden is extremely busy. She doesn't have time today for people without appointments."

Kira smiled pleasantly, hoping she could charm Mrs. Jenkins. "I'm sorry, I don't think you understand. Dr. McFadden asked to see me."

Mrs. Jenkins frowned, clearly disapproving of her explanation. She leaned over the counter and said slowly, "We don't have time for anyone without an appointment."

Kira bit her lip and tried a different route. "Okay, I'd like to make an appointment."

Mrs. Jenkins nodded, clearly thinking they were finally getting somewhere. She turned to her computer and tapped a few keys. "Name of pet."

"I don't have a pet."

"You're not stupid, are you? You do know that the sign outside says Flynn McFadden, D.V.M., and that means she's an *animal* doctor?"

She bobbed her head up and down in agreement, deathly afraid of the large woman. "I understand. I'm an old friend . . . well, I guess you wouldn't say I'm a friend anymore, because we haven't kept in touch, but I knew Flynn a long time ago, before Kellen was born. I was just in here with him, and we had somewhat of a row. Flynn asked—"

"Are you the lady that caused all that commotion and kissed

the floor?"

Her face burned and she offered a slight nod.

Mrs. Jenkins shook her head and scowled. She reached for a pad of paper. "Name?"

"Kira Drake."

She began to write and her hand stopped. She looked up at Kira and recognized the face she had certainly seen a hundred times. "Kira Drake? The actress?"

"Yes."

"Oh, my Lord. I've heard all the rumors about you. Is it true you left Flynn for a man?"

"No, that's not true."

Mrs. Jenkins narrowed her eyes. "But you dumped Dr. McFadden. And you married that man in order to hide your sexuality. Hmm. I see."

Kira's jaw dropped, but before she could protest, Mrs. Jenkins disappeared into the back. When she returned, it was with pursed lips. "Dr. McFadden would like you to wait in her office. Come with me please."

Mrs. Jenkins opened the swinging gate and she followed her into the back, down the hall and past several animal prints that lined the wall. Mrs. Jenkins motioned to an open door and she stepped into Flynn's small office. She sat in one of the cushioned chairs that faced Flynn's desk.

"I don't suppose you ever met Flynn's *wife*?" Mrs. Jenkins asked from the doorway.

She steeled herself from making a rude comment and turned to her. "No, I never met Luz. I hear she was a wonderful person."

"The best," Mrs. Jenkins said with great emphasis before disappearing back down the hall.

She closed her eyes momentarily and reminded herself that she only had until Sunday morning in Ocean Beach, and then she would be on her way to Vancouver for her next shoot. She slumped down in the chair, not caring that her posture was extraordinarily unladylike and unbecoming to an Academy Award-winning actress. Ever since her father told her of his relationship with Mo, she fretted over one inevitable moment, a conversation with Flynn. She had spent the better part of the last fifteen years editing the memories to suit her, but the past twenty-four hours had brought everything from the *Beach Town* shoot to the surface, jagged pieces floating against each other, the edges blurred and none of them distinct. With each passing minute, those memories grew more acute, and the pictures, the sounds, even the smells and tastes of those few weeks she spent here long ago sharpened and cut at her heart.

She gazed around Flynn's office and noticed some colorful renderings covering the wall space behind Flynn's desk. She realized they were of the animal shelter Kellen mentioned. Without her glasses she couldn't read the small print at the bottom of the picture, and she was certainly not going to put them on when Flynn could walk in and see her wearing them.

She was impressed by the degrees on the wall, the stacks of file folders on Flynn's credenza awaiting her important decisions and the thick books with impressive titles like *General Guide to Veterinary Medicine*. Kira always knew Flynn was smart, but the proof stared at her from around the room, and she felt even more insignificant. She couldn't help but notice the framed photos that lined one shelf of her bookcase. They were pictures of Flynn with Kellen, Mo, Megan, Rocco and Luz. The most prominent photo sat at the corner of Flynn's desk, next to her computer—a framed headshot of Luz, an open and welcoming smile covering her face. Jonah would approve of Luz's smile, she thought. He believed in the power of the smile. She wanted to rise and study the pictures closely, but she didn't wish to have Flynn enter her own office and find Kira perusing her personal life. Instead she sat patiently, staring at the computer screen.

Her eyes focused on the displayed Web page, a catalogue of

dog treats. Kira was fascinated by the pictures, unaware that such products even existed. She leaned over the desk and started to read, careful not to disturb Flynn's files or work. She didn't hear the click of the knob, and it was only when Flynn stepped into her peripheral vision that she stood straight up and met her bewildered expression.

"I'm sorry. I just noticed these dog treats on your computer."

Flynn motioned for her to sit, and she retreated to her own chair, avoiding an awkward hug, for which Kira was grateful. "I've been doing some research. I have several patients who'd like them. At least I think they would." Flynn turned the monitor toward her and scrolled down to show her the many offerings.

"It's incredible," Kira said. "How are they made?"

Flynn seemed relieved—Kira certainly was—to have begun a conversation in the middle and skipped the difficult beginnings. "Um, let's see." Flynn pulled her reading glasses from her pocket and clicked on a few more links. She pointed to a Web page and Kira leaned closer.

"Do you need these?" Flynn joked.

Kira sighed and rummaged through her purse, retrieving her glasses. "No, I have my own."

Flynn said, "It stinks to be over forty sometimes, doesn't it?" and they both laughed.

Kira scanned the ingredients and shrugged. "Oh, well, this doesn't seem so difficult. You could make these."

"Well, I couldn't, but I imagine someone who bakes could do it. I still don't cook."

Flynn turned the monitor back and faced Kira, who quickly removed her glasses and flashed her best smile. It was the smile that Kira had perfected after twenty years in the film industry, one that had helped her sail through most of the unpleasant situations she endured with fans, the press and studio presidents.

They sat in silence as the last fifteen years dissipated between them. It only took her a few seconds to realize that little had changed about Flynn. Her curly hair remained a beautiful dark red, and her eyes were still the warm green that enflamed Kira during their lovemaking. A few lines bisected her face, but that was the price a surfer paid for worshipping the sun every day of her life. The long white coat and stethoscope that hung around her neck announced her importance, and Kira couldn't help but feel a surge of pride. "Flynn, look at you. You're a doctor."

"Yeah."

When she said nothing else, Kira realized it was her responsibility to guide the conversation. Flynn was the recipient of the surprise attack, and she was the one who showed up unannounced at the clinic. Unfortunately, there was no script. The winner of several major awards, including an Oscar, Kira struggled for words. "I'm sorry for what happened in your lobby."

Flynn chuckled and waved it off. "Don't worry about it." They stared at each other, and Kira realized the silence was easy, almost comforting. Flynn cleared her throat and folded her hands in her lap. "Where are you staying?"

"Up in La Jolla."

Flynn nodded and Kira was relieved there was no explanation required. She realized there was a question she was dying to ask. "Did you know about our parents?"

Flynn shook her head and gazed at her desk, appearing to assess the amount of work she had left to do. "No, I had no idea. I was shocked."

Flynn's tone disappointed her, since it seemed to convey a slight disapproval of Stephen and Mo as a couple. "I see. Um, you seem to be doing incredibly well. Kellen says you're building an animal shelter. That's wonderful."

Flynn beamed at the compliment. "It's a labor of love. We've spent a lot of time raising money. I think in a year we'll have enough to make it all happen."

"I'm sure you will. I also want to tell you that Kellen is truly smashing."

At the mention of her son, Flynn's smile widened. "Yes. He's amazing. What about you?" she asked courteously. "I read somewhere you weren't married anymore. Do you have any children?"

Kira squirmed at the thought of her sham marriage. "No, I don't have kids. The marriage lasted for about twenty minutes. The best thing that came out of it was some wonderful surfing in Tahiti during the honeymoon."

Flynn arched her eyebrows at the mention of one of the world's greatest surfing locations. "You seem to be doing well."

Kira looked away. "I've been fortunate to be so successful." She took a deep breath and returned her gaze to Flynn, who stared at her intently. "Well, I can see from your waiting room that you're busy. I should be going."

"Are you coming to dinner tonight?" Flynn asked quickly.

Kira swallowed hard, unprepared for the invitation and not ready to face the McFaddens without her father, who wouldn't arrive until the next day. "That's kind of you to offer, but I have some errands to run in San Diego. I was thinking I might stop by the café later and see your mum."

"She'd like that."

"I was planning on inviting you all up to La Jolla tomorrow night for dinner, if you wanted to come."

Flynn tapped her pencil on her desk, and her eyes drifted to the picture of Luz. Kira couldn't tell if the glance was intentional, but when Flynn spoke to her, she was still focused on the beautiful headshot of her dead wife. "Can I think about it?"

"Of course." Kira pointed to the photo. "That's a beautiful picture."

"Did your dad tell you about Luz?"

"Only a little." The mention of Luz disintegrated the conversation, and Kira stood abruptly. "Why don't you call me if you decide you want to come?" She reached into her bag for a piece of paper and scribbled a few numbers. "This is my cell phone, the landline for the house in La Jolla where I'm staying, and I've included the number of my personal assistant, Robert, just in case you can't find me. I'm sorry I've taken so much of your time, and I am sorry about what happened earlier. I'll always remember it as truly one of the most awkward moments of my life."

She made a beeline for the door and struggled with the handle. She twisted it left and right, but it refused open. She looked back at Flynn, who sat with her hands laced behind her head, an amused grin on her face.

"A little help here," Kira called. "I'd at least like to make a graceful exit and preserve a kernel of my dignity."

Flynn slowly pulled herself out of the chair and ambled to the door. Kira jiggled the knob with intensity, her frustration and anger growing. Flynn waited until she finally dropped her hands in defeat and stepped in front of her, slowly twisting the knob while she pushed the door in with her shoulder. "Sometimes you just need to finesse a situation to make it work. Brute force isn't always helpful."

"I'll remember that."

Chapter Fifteen
Mo McFadden

The last of the customers finally left, protesting Mo's close-at-sundown rule, although the merciful June sunsets meant people could stay until nearly eight o'clock. She prodded the tourist for twenty minutes prior, but he just couldn't understand. She flipped the sign on the door and began her nightly routine. The bell tinkled again, and she turned to face the intruder. "We're closed," she said, assuming that the customer had returned for something. At the sight of Kira, she threw her arms out and rushed to her. "It's wonderful to see you. Flynn said you might stop by."

"It's so good to see you, Mo."

She stepped back and looked at Kira directly. "My darlin', you still look as amazing and gorgeous as you did that first day you walked in here all those years ago. I remember it clearly. I wanted you to eat potatoes and you only wanted toast."

Kira laughed in embarrassment. "I'm sure it had something to do with my agent. Thank you for the compliment. I should have you call some of my producers. It seems I'm past my prime, and the only parts I can play now are mothers and best friends."

"How could anyone think that? You still look so young." Kira's blush reached her shoes and Mo understood exactly why Flynn had fallen so fast for the actress. "Sit down, sweetheart. Let me get you some coffee." Kira perched on one of the counter stools and she poured them both a cup. "Now, I want to hear all about your life."

Kira sighed and took a sip. "Honestly, it's really mundane. I make movies and I spend time at my house in Hawaii. It's hardly a life, but I know I have no cause to complain."

She raised an eyebrow. "So there's no one special in your life?"

Kira looked down. "I'm sure my father has shared with you his concern about my love life and lack of commitment."

She smiled sympathetically. Stephen had indeed often mentioned that Kira had chosen random affairs over love, and he suspected it was because she could never expose her heart again after losing Flynn. "Darlin', I'm not going to judge you."

She returned the smile, relieved. "It's just now that I'm older I feel like I missed out on something, something important."

"What?"

"I'm not sure, really. A relationship. Maybe a family. I know my father worries about me and he shouldn't." She shook her head, and Mo couldn't blame her for feeling frustrated. "I'm sorry. I never should have mentioned it. How horrible I must sound. Poor little rich girl isn't happy. No one wants to listen to that."

"Well, you're right to some extent," she admitted. "You've had some extraordinary opportunities and lived a life millions of people wish were in their grasp, but, my dear, you're missing the point."

"Which is?"

"This is the life you have, the plot of land that you got. What you do with it is your choice."

"You sound like Flynn. That was essentially the last thing she said to me fifteen years ago, that I had a choice."

She squeezed her hand. "No one knows, honey, why anything happens. Why some people are given golden moments and others toil for a day's wages. You can spend your life trying to make it something else, or you can live with it and make it your own—the best it can be."

"That's an incredible way of thinking. I wish I could adopt it."

"I can't take credit for it. Flynn and I learned it from Luz." She gestured to a small photo hanging on the wall over the cash register. It was her favorite photo, taken one day while Luz was working in the café, leaning over the counter, with a smile that radiated positive energy. "Luz lived for three things—Flynn, Kellen and surfing, in that order. Her life was beautiful in its simplicity."

Kira studied the picture, and Mo imagined Kira saw someone who was an exact opposite of herself. "I heard she died in a car accident."

She let out a long sigh. "On the interstate. It was late. She was coming back from visiting a cousin in Long Beach. She had a blowout at the wrong time and the car went over a cliff. She died on impact. I thought it would be the end of Flynn. Her grief was as deep as the ocean, and for two years she wandered through life without much purpose. Kellen was only eight, and while she tried to be a good mother, Luz was the primary parent while Flynn was the breadwinner. It was a huge shift for Flynn, and she had to really get to know Kellen, to test herself as a parent. I think she's done a wonderful job, but she's still lonely. I think if it weren't for Kellen . . . well, I don't know. He's a marvelous young man." She grinned broadly at the thought of her grandson.

"I met him on the beach. He's quite mature."

She nodded.

"I never told you, Mo, but losing you was almost as hard as losing Flynn. I know we didn't know each other for long, but I felt closer to you than I ever felt to my own mother."

Her eyes filled with tears. "You're kind, dear. I was sorry to hear about your mother. Despite your differences, I'm sure it was difficult when she died. I know it was for your father."

Kira changed the subject. "I was surprised to see that you and my father kept in touch. I am so happy for both of you and the life you'll have together. You deserve it."

"I'm glad you approve, my dear. Your father and I share a kinship for many things. His friendship over the years has been irreplaceable. He's a remarkable man, and I'm glad he finally told you the truth about everything, and I'm thrilled that you're here in Ocean Beach."

Kira's smile faded. "I think you're probably the only one. Well, maybe Kellen, too. I think everyone else would rather I disappear. I walked by the Bullfrog earlier and thought I heard Bear growling at me."

They chuckled together. "There, there, honey," Mo said. "Don't worry. The folks at Ocean Beach are a good lot. That was all a long time ago. It's time to let it go, and a wedding is just the thing for mending fences." She patted Kira's hand and stood. "Now, I need to close this place up."

"I could help."

Mo gasped. "I would never ask a movie star to help fill saltshakers." Both of them laughed and Kira reached for the large container of salt that Mo handed to her. Kira struggled to pour more salt into the tiny glass bottles than on her lap.

The doorbell tinkled and they both looked up.

"Flynn," Mo said. "I'm surprised to see you."

Flynn grinned slightly and wandered over to Kira's table and sat down next to her. "Hi. What are you doing?"

"Theoretically I'm adding salt to these shakers; however, it appears that I'm just making a glorious mess."

Both of them laughed at the salt, which covered Kira's clothes, the floor and the table. She had created a miniature salt playfield. "Let me show you how to do that," Flynn offered.

Kira handed her the shaker and the salt container.

"The key," Flynn said, holding both up for Kira's inspection, "is the distance. You want to keep them close together, and your pour angle should be such that the salt doesn't spill out." She brought the two together and effortlessly transferred the salt.

Kira looked on in amazement. "How did you do that?"

"Are you kidding? I spent my entire youth filling salt and pepper shakers."

"Now, that's not all you did," Mo interjected. "You had many jobs—"

"Yeah. Mopping the floors, washing the windows, cleaning the tables—"

"No, that was Megan's job." She stood before them, her hands on her hips. "Well, Miss Kira, I think you've proven that you have a dismal future in the restaurant industry. Thank goodness you can act. Why don't you two go for a walk and leave me to this mess? Have Flynn show you her animal shelter. She loves to give tours." At the suggestion of spending time alone together, both women looked panic-stricken and neither uttered a word. "Now, don't jump at the opportunity too quickly." Kira glanced at Flynn, and Mo knew it was entirely up to her daughter.

When Flynn offered no words of encouragement, Kira rose and wiped off her pants. "Let me get a dustpan, Mo, and get this picked up for you before I go."

"No, no. Don't worry about it, darlin'. I'll spill just as much doing the rest of them."

"Well, I should get back to La Jolla," Kira said, claiming her purse from the counter. "I guess I'll see you and my father tomorrow night."

"I'm looking forward to it."

"How's the surfing in La Jolla?" Flynn asked.

Kira seemed startled by Flynn's question and paused a moment. "The waves have been magnificent."

Flynn nodded and stared at the floor. Mo sensed the distance growing between the two women. There was so much to say but evidently neither knew how to begin. She wished she could do more and thought it best to just give them some space. She shuffled behind the counter and opened the register.

"How come you haven't surfed in OB since you got here?"

Kira shrugged. "I guess I thought this was your turf. I wasn't comfortable."

Flynn didn't respond but simply tapped her foot on the floor. "Sea World is having a fireworks display tonight. You can see it from the animal shelter. Would you like to walk over there with me?"

Kira nodded. "Sure."

Chapter Sixteen
Flynn McFadden

Flynn led Kira down the pier toward the lights of Ocean Beach. She couldn't explain what possessed her to invite Kira to see the shelter, and it was total curiosity that propelled her to the café in the first place, knowing that Kira would most likely be there visiting her mother. The image of Kira sprawled on the clinic floor surrounded by barking mutts had remained in Flynn's mind all day.

"What happened to your grandmother?" Kira asked.

Flynn chuckled and shook her head. "Oh, Gmum lasted for another five years after you left. She had a heart attack lifting a box of potato chips in the storeroom and died on the spot. Best thing that could have happened to her. Mom sold the store to Manny, and he had Gmum's old bat put into a display case, right over the cash register."

"Sounds fitting. How is Manny? I haven't seen him yet."

"Go by the market and say hi. I know he'd love to see you."

"I will."

Flynn felt the mood lighten, pleased to have found an easy topic of conversation—everyone else in Ocean Beach.

"So what's the story on Megan? My father showed me the picture of her and Rocco at their commitment ceremony."

"It's amazing. Rocco changed her life. She's a wonderful woman with a great spirit, and Megan must have seen that. About a month after *Beach Town* finished they moved to L.A. Megan totally cleaned up her act and eventually they saved enough money for their own tattoo shop."

"I think that's wonderful."

"Do you still have your tattoo?"

Kira laughed. "Of course. I love surfing and it's still appropriate."

She cleared her throat and Flynn wondered if she'd embarrassed her.

"So what about Charlie Vernon? Is he still bothering you about jumping off the pier?"

"Oh, yeah. At least once a week. He'll never change." She smiled slyly at Kira. "Why don't you jump off the pier with me and Kellen tomorrow?"

"I couldn't do that. I'd be scared to death."

"It's no big deal, and it's a total rush. You'd love it."

"I don't think so."

"If my thirteen-year-old son can do it, you can."

"Your son is in much better shape than this forty-year-old actress. Besides, if I get hurt, I'm screwed."

"You won't get hurt."

"No," Kira said definitively. "I'll pass."

"Okay, but you're really missing out."

Kira wrapped her arms around herself as the wind blew past them. "Tell me about Luz."

Flynn bit her lip and shrugged. "She was indescribable. She

was an illegal from Mexico. Bear gave her a job as a waitress at the Bullfrog, but she was terrible. I think the only reason he hired her was because he thought he'd be able to get some. He didn't know she was on the other team. She spilled a drink on me the first time we met, apologized several times, and I told her it was okay. We looked at each other, she smiled and I was a goner. Mom gave her a job at the café after we got together, so she could work during the day. She was really happy with everything in her life up until the day she died." She stopped and took a deep breath, suddenly overcome with emotion. Kira reached for her, and Flynn looked at their connected fingers, amazed that she could hold the hand of one woman and speak of another.

"I'm sorry," she said.

"There's nothing to be sorry about." Kira stepped away and started walking again. "So how did you decide you wanted a child?"

"I think I've always wanted kids, and Luz did too. We knew I'd have to be the one to have the baby. Luz could never deal with all the questions from the hospital. She didn't have any papers."

"How did you get pregnant?"

She grinned. "This is Ocean Beach. There are many potential donors."

"Do you know who Kellen's father is?"

"Yes."

"Does Kellen?"

Flynn shook her head. "Not yet. He hasn't asked. Someday I'll tell him, but not now."

They reached the clinic and Flynn led Kira around to the animal shelter. She jumped up onto the concrete foundation. "Okay, so this is a hallway." She walked in a straight line, holding out her hands. "Over here will be a treatment room, and over there will be a grooming area. Then there will be rows of dog pens. The cats will be off this way, but they won't need as much space. There's going to be a play area, and a dog run and a meet-and-greet space for potential owners. The best part will be the training facility, where we can hopefully rehabilitate some of the animals so they're adoptable again."

When she finished her speech, she looked at Kira, leaning against the stone wall, the chestnut hair curling around her face. She was beautiful in the moonlight. Flynn's mouth went dry and she stuck her hands inside her back pockets.

"I'm sorry. I really get going when I talk about this place."

"Well, you should be proud of it." Kira came toward her and Flynn felt a tingle shoot through her body. "You're going to save lives and that's entirely admirable. You're incredible, Flynn."

Suddenly the black night was illuminated in fireworks. They gazed skyward at the shooting rockets and sparkling lights. Kira's dark brown eyes reflected the bursting explosions, and Flynn was once again absorbed in her beauty. Their shoulders were almost touching and she could smell the scent of lilacs from her shampoo. Kira turned to her and they stared at each other, no longer fascinated by the pyrotechnic display. She reached for Flynn, touching her cheek with her palm.

The touch stunned her. "We should probably get back," she said. "I have a surgery in the morning."

Kira immediately withdrew her hand. "Of course."

They headed back up the street toward the café, Flynn noticing Kira's quick pace, as if she longed to be alone. She could still feel the cool touch of Kira's palm on her cheek, and she chastised herself for her reaction. She tried to think of something to say amid the thunderous pounding of each rocket as it exploded, but her mind lingered on the unexpected moment of tenderness.

While she would never admit it to Megan, she had kept watch over Kira's career for the last fifteen years. Before Luz, she regularly scanned the magazines in Gmum's store, searching for articles and pictures. Even after she and Luz became a couple, she would stop at the magazine rack when she was sure Luz wasn't around. She felt guilty, but she couldn't help it. Gmum understood. "It's all right, Flynn," she said. "Kira will always be in your heart."

She continued to see Kira's films, although she was usually moody when she and Luz left the theater. Luz understood—until the night she screamed Kira's name while they were making love. Why Luz didn't walk out on her was a mystery, but she never made that mistake again. Once the Internet arrived, Flynn regularly checked Kira's fan Web sites and silently cheered when she was nominated for a Golden Globe or an Academy Award. Although she never won again after *The Autumn Months*, Flynn believed she was the most talented actress she'd ever seen. She was sure Luz was aware of her never-ending obsession, but her lover never worried about their relationship. She knew Flynn was as loyal as the dogs she treated, and there was no competition. Yet it was Kira who stood next to her now and Luz who was gone.

She realized that she had not asked Kira any personal questions or shown any interest in bridging the span of years. "So, how's your life?"

Kira whirled in Flynn's direction. "What?"

"How's everything going? I saw your last picture. It was pretty good."

Kira snickered loudly. "You're being kind. It totally stunk and everyone knew it."

"What about everything else? Are you with anyone?"

Kira avoided her gaze and stared at the sidewalk. "No. I'm devoted to my career, as you probably remember. I don't have time for a real love life."

"So you're celibate?" she teased.

Kira glanced at her, as if judging her tone. "No, I just don't get involved."

"Ever?"

"That's right. What about you? Do you have a girlfriend?"

"Me? No . . . I, uh . . . no."

"I would have thought women would flock to an eligible doctor."

Kira grinned. It was her turn to tease. Flynn's cheeks warmed as she remembered her last date three months ago, a disastrous evening with a flight attendant who talked endlessly about work. "No," she said, avoiding Kira's stare. "Um, I'd like to come to dinner tomorrow if I'm still invited."

Kira smiled and touched her arm. "Of course. That would be wonderful." She hesitated. "You know, I should thank you for what you did all those years ago."

Flynn looked at her quizzically. "What are you talking about?"

"You could have ruined my career with all that talk about the kissing picture, and you didn't."

Flynn felt her gaze, and she shrugged. "I couldn't do that."

They had hit a roadblock and neither made any effort to converse further, both of them eyeing the pier, Flynn hoping they reached it before the lag in conversation seemed obvious. Just as they were about to climb the steps, Stephen and Mo began their descent.

"Dad," Kira said, rushing up the steps to the landing and embracing her father. "When did you get here? I thought you weren't coming until tomorrow."

"I only arrived an hour ago. I finished my business in London early." Stephen pulled Mo against him and planted a kiss on her cheek. "I'm not going to be away from my girl for another second."

Flynn remained at the bottom of the pier steps, watching Kira reunite with her father. She was poised as she talked with Stephen and Mo, but there was something about her face, a sense of falsehood that Flynn couldn't place. When she turned away from the engaged couple, their eyes met, and Kira readjusted her expression, as though Flynn had caught her in a lie.

Chapter Seventeen
Megan McFadden

On Wednesday evening, before they left for La Jolla and dinner with Kira, Megan excused herself to the patio and called Rocco on her cell phone.

"What are you doing?" she asked.

"Hey, baby. I'm painting the bathroom. You're gonna love it."

She grinned at Rocco's enthusiasm. Undoubtedly the bathroom would be a wild design manifested from Rocco's creative mind. "I'm sure I will, honey."

"You sound better than you did yesterday. Everything going okay between Flynn and Kira?"

"Flynn said they took a walk last night and had a nice talk. I guess it only got a little weird in a few places—"

"Like how weird?"

"She didn't give any details. I just want this to be over, for Flynn's sake. I don't want her falling for this woman again."

"What if that's what she wants?"

She smirked. She hated it when Rocco was logical, and she knew Rocco hated it when she tried to control other peoples' lives. "I seriously doubt anything will happen, but I just know Kira. History will repeat itself if Flynn lets it happen."

"Don't mess with history, Meg. Stay out of it."

"But—"

"No buts. Listen, your sister isn't a kid. She can take care of herself. You need to be supportive. Has it occurred to you that Flynn may be the last thing that Kira wants?"

"No. Who wouldn't want my sister? She's unbelievable. She's successful, cute, an incredible surfer."

Rocco laughed into the phone. "Yeah, I know that last part carries a lot of weight with you. I'm just saying that you may be making something out of nothing. Be smart. Be the observer. Be the good sister. Okay?"

She closed her eyes and smiled. This was why she adored Rocco. "You are so wise, my love."

"I know. That's why *I'm* painting the bathroom and you're on vacation. How did this happen?"

"You had to work, remember? But you'll be here tomorrow night, right?"

"That's the plan. I'll start down before the rush hour and be there in time for the engagement party at the Bullfrog."

She noticed her mother beckoning and said good-bye. They all piled into Flynn's FJ Cruiser with Rufus and headed up to La Jolla. Not surprising, Kira had rented a seaside bungalow with a private beach.

It was Kellen who voiced what everyone was thinking when they pulled up into the driveway. "Wow. This place is awesome."

Kira greeted them at the door wearing a tailored blouse and jeans. Megan thought she looked practically the same as she did fifteen years before. Kira smiled and extended her hand. "Hello, Megan. It's nice to see you again."

"Hello, Kira." Their eyes met briefly before Kira looked away, obviously uncomfortable. It should be an interesting evening, she thought.

They passed through the great room, and Kellen headed to the patio door and an extraordinary view of the Pacific.

"Something smells wonderful," Mo said. "What are you making?"

"We're having beef Wellington. I hope that's all right for everyone."

The four adults nodded in agreement and Rufus started to whine. He trotted to the end of the counter and stood on two feet, his nose extended in the air, focused on a paper bag sitting on the edge. "What's with Rufus?" Kellen asked. "He hasn't danced on two paws for years."

"I think I know what he's after." Kira opened the paper bag and pulled out a cookie.

"You shouldn't give dogs chocolate," Megan warned, not caring if she sounded condescending.

Kira looked at Megan and shook her head. "It's not chocolate. It's a dog treat." Kira held it out and Rufus barked insanely. When he finally sat, Kira offered it to him and he devoured it in seconds. "I'd say he likes it."

"Where did you get these?" Flynn asked, opening the bag.

"I made them. It wasn't that hard. I just went to that Web site you showed me and a few others, and I combined some of the suggested ingredients, and that was the result."

Flynn pulled one out and smelled it. "I can see why Rufus's nose went crazy." She handed a treat to everyone for inspection and read the ingredients. She smiled at Kira. "You went to a lot of trouble."

"It was no big deal. I love to cook and I was already working on dinner."

Flynn touched Kira's arm and smiled. "Still, it was a kind thing to do for Rufus."

"I wonder how they taste," Kellen pondered, licking one end.

"Go ahead and try it," Kira said. "I ate one myself, and it wasn't so bad."

Kellen took a small bite of the chewy treat. "I've had worse in the school cafeteria."

They all laughed, and Megan watched Flynn and Kira closely. While Mo and Stephen joked with Kellen about Rufus, Flynn and Kira spoke quietly, as though there was no one else in the room. She pointed to the recipe that she had taped to the side of the bag, and Flynn stared into her eyes. Megan was certain she was only half-listening to the explanation, for she was gazing at Kira with that same goofy expression she wore throughout that summer long ago.

Kellen wandered back to the patio door and gazed out. "Can we surf now, Mom?" he asked excitedly. "You ought to see those breakers."

A wide grin spread across Flynn's face. "Go for it, son. I'll be out in a minute."

Kellen rushed out the front to unload the boards and the gear. Flynn turned to Kira, her grin still evident. "So, are you going to surf with us?"

Kira shook her head fervently. "Oh, no. I need to prepare dinner."

"I could do that," Stephen offered. "I'm quite familiar with beef Wellington, my dear."

"And I could help," Mo chimed in. "You should go and surf."

Kira opened her mouth to disagree, but it was obvious to Megan that she couldn't say no. To object would be rude and leave the impression that she didn't wish to spend time with them. There was only one reply she could make, and Megan gave a slight smile, enjoying Kira's discomfort immensely.

"Very well. For a few sets." She turned to them with her most hospitable face. "There's a bathroom and extra bedroom downstairs for both of you to change," she said, pointing to an open door. "I'll join you in a few minutes." They watched Kira trek up the stairs, as though she was being sent before a firing squad.

A few minutes turned into half an hour before she emerged from the house in her wet suit, the chestnut hair pulled back into a ponytail.

"Let's see what she can do," Megan yelled to Flynn across the water.

Kira paddled out into the sea and joined the routine. Flynn, Megan noticed, was trying to watch Kira and surf at the same time. When Flynn wiped out for the third time, Megan cursed under her breath. Finally Flynn gave up and swam to the shore. She sat on the sand and watched the three of them ride the waves. Megan had to admit that Kira was a decent surfer. She'd never be as good as Flynn, but she'd obviously had extensive lessons and she could hold her own—and she surfed alone. Unlike Megan and Kellen, who talked in the water and applauded after good rides, Kira was in a zone by herself. She didn't acknowledge them or, apparently, wish to be recognized. She physically distanced herself from them, hanging back from the best waves, allowing them, particularly Kellen, to have the prime opportunities.

When Kira finally paddled to the shore, Megan drifted in the water, noticing the interaction between Flynn and Kira. The body language told the whole story. Flynn was impressed and made several gestures praising Kira's surfing technique. She moved closer to Kira and touched her shoulder. Much to Megan's dismay, Flynn was flirting. She knew the stance, the cocking of the head—it was Flynn in hunting mode. Megan was pleased to see Kira's response, though—total disinterest. She nodded to Flynn, but her arms were crossed and she looked back at the house several times. She seemed uncomfortable and probably wanted the conversation to end. Perhaps Rocco was correct and Kira had no interest in her sister.

By the time they had all retreated from the sea and changed

clothes, Stephen and Mo had covered the dining table with bowls and platters full of food. Megan's mouth watered at the smells that rose from the table. She sat down and plucked a warm roll from a basket before passing it to Flynn. The asparagus, beef and a British potato dish she couldn't name all found their way to her plate.

"Excellent," Kellen said. "This looks great."

When they had all been served, Stephen raised his glass of wine and the others followed. "I would like to propose a toast to my wonderful bride-to-be, Maureen. I am grateful for your love and I cannot wait to begin sharing my life with you."

"And I you, Stephen," Mo said.

They saluted and began to eat. Megan had to admit it—Kira was an amazing cook. She glanced at Kira, who was smiling down at the ground toward a begging Rufus.

"So, Kira, why don't you tell us about your latest movie?" she asked pointedly.

The table, which had just moments before buzzed with idle chitchat, went silent. Kira looked up from Rufus and cleared her throat, a sad expression in her eyes. "I wish I could tell you it will be good, Megan. But frankly, don't waste your money. It's crap."

Megan was momentarily taken aback by Kira's honesty and busily speared her asparagus. "Is it better than *A Delicate Affair*? I mean, *that* movie stunk."

"Megan," Mo said. "Stop it."

"I'm just being honest, Mom. Kira's had some bombs in the last few years. I'm just hoping her career picks up." She looked over at Kira and carefully avoided Flynn's razor stare. "How would you assess your career, Kira? Are you really past your prime?"

"Megan," Flynn said sharply. "What the hell are you doing?"

She whipped her head around at Flynn—a traitor. Her anger broke the surface and she fled from the table and out the patio door. She couldn't understand how easily Flynn erased the past.

Certainly the intervening years with Luz buffered all of the drama and pain, but Flynn had to remember the nights she agonized over Kira, while Megan held her while she wept in her arms. Perhaps Flynn had forgiven everything, but she would not.

The patio door slid open and Kira joined her on the deck. Neither one of them started the conversation, so they let the sea fill the silence with its own language.

Finally, Megan eventually said, "She moved on, you know."

Kira's expression remained pleasant. "I know."

"Luz was amazing. She was the perfect match for Flynn. I don't know what God was thinking when he broke them apart."

Megan hoped her words cut deeply into Kira's heart, but Kira showed no reaction. "I know how you feel about me, Megan, and it's justified. I hold no ill will toward you but I doubt we'll ever be friends. I just want to get through the next few days, and then I'll be gone on Sunday. I suppose as *family* our parents will expect us to spend holidays and such together, but I promise that I'll always have a convenient excuse for my absence. You don't have to worry about sitting through Christmas dinner with me, but I hope we can be civil to each other for a little while. My father's been alone most of his life in one way or another, and he's the best man I know. Your mother is such a good person, and I'm sure they'll be happy together." Kira smiled, tears in her eyes, and Megan realized it was the first time she'd seen any real emotion from her since their arrival. "And by the way, it's extraordinarily belated, but congratulations on your nuptials with Rocco. My father showed me the announcement not long ago."

She couldn't help but return Kira's smile since it was *Beach Town* that brought Rocco to OB all those years before. "We're happy."

Kira looked out at the ocean and laughed. "I remember the night we were all gathered in the bathroom at the Bullfrog and Rocco let Rona in. I thought she was going to have a heart attack when she saw my tattoo."

She narrowed her eyes and shook her head. "You must have a much better memory than I do. I can't remember that."

"That's because you've had so many wonderful memories in between. It all floats together. It makes for a happy life."

Megan leaned against the balcony railing and studied her. "So if that's true, then does that mean you haven't had a happy life?"

Kira's face remained frozen in a smile, but she detected a slight wavering in her eyes. "Of course, I'm happy. I'm a star. I have an Academy Award, fame, money and a beautiful home."

"But happiness is more than that."

"Ah," Kira said dramatically. She turned and went across the deck. When she was far enough away so that Megan could no longer see into her eyes, she faced her. "I guess I see happiness as the absence of fear or guilt. If I don't feel either of those things, then I'm happy."

"What about joy, elation or passion?"

Kira shrugged. "I don't have an answer, really. Surfing?"

The patio door opened and Kellen appeared. "Can we eat dessert now?"

Both Megan and Kira chuckled and rejoined the family for another one of Kira's extraordinary recipes—macaroons and nesselrode pudding. After three helpings of pudding and half a dozen cookies, Kellen begged for another round of surfing, and Flynn acquiesced and joined him. Kira shooed the other adults from the house, arming them with coffee and cookies, determined to be a cleanup crew of one.

"We're going for a stroll on the beach," Stephen said. "Megan, would you like to join us?"

Megan shook her head and sat on a deck lounger, cradling her coffee. "No, I'll just stay here."

Mo arched her eyebrows. "Are you all right, Meg?"

Megan smiled and nodded. Her mother stared at her for a long moment before turning away with her fiancé. Megan gazed out at Kellen and Flynn, their shadows rolling across the sea on the crest of the waves. She wasn't really okay. She missed Rocco horribly and felt out of place in OB without her. She'd never tell her mother the truth, which was that, since Luz died, she hated to visit. Although she loved Kellen dearly and despised being an absentee aunt, Flynn was not the same person, and her heart ripped apart for her sister every time she spent time in their childhood surroundings. Maybe if Flynn would move out of that damn house, she thought. Once Rocco arrived, she would be a filter between Megan and Flynn, and Flynn's broken heart wouldn't smother Megan as it did when they were alone.

She glanced through the patio door at Kira, replacing the centerpiece on the table. She thought of what she would say to Kira when Kira joined her on the deck. An apology was definitely in order. Rocco would have kicked her under the table if she'd been there. Instead of coming out to the deck, Kira remained inside once the work was over. She sat down on the couch with a glass of wine and patted her legs for Rufus to jump in her lap. Megan watched as Kira laughed and played with the old dog. Only alone did she seem comfortable. Her entire aura shifted and she was relaxed. She cuddled Rufus and let him lick her face. She was playful and happy, and Megan was suddenly reminded of the day fifteen years before when Kira and Flynn appeared in the tattoo shop. The look on her face then was similar.

Eventually Flynn ordered Kellen out of the water, and once the surfboards had been repacked on the top of Flynn's FJ Cruiser, it was time to leave. Kira walked the family to the SUV. There was an awkward moment until Kellen threw his arms around Kira, unfettered by the memories of the past. Megan retreated to the front passenger's seat with a slight wave, and Mo and Stephen gave Kira a hug before climbing into the back with Kellen. Megan adjusted the side view mirror and watched Kira and Flynn. Kira stood straight as a rail, her arms crossed, her face devoid of expression, while Flynn casually leaned against the

SUV, holding the homemade dog treats. The contrast between them was obvious until Kira laughed, and at last her stone façade was broken. She playfully slapped Flynn's arm, and they moved closer together. Finally they looked away, apparently embarrassed. Flynn squeezed Kira's shoulder and kissed her cheek before jumping into the driver's side of the SUV. Megan noticed the smile plastered on her face, and she laughed.

"What?" Flynn asked weakly, still smiling.

They stared at each other and Megan felt warmth in the exchange that she hadn't experienced in years. What if Kira was the one for Flynn?

She turned and looked out the side window. Kira quickly ascended the flagstone steps and retreated into the house before Flynn could put the car in gear. The scene was disturbing, and it took a moment for Megan to discern why it bothered her. Kira never looked back at them, never waved to Rufus and didn't watch them depart. Such good-byes were much different when Mo, Flynn and Kellen visited Megan in West Hollywood. She waved and yelled at them, sometimes following them down the driveway, throwing kisses while they screamed, "We love you!" until the car disappeared out the drive. It was a good-bye with a longing for the next visit. She understood as Flynn pulled onto the interstate that the family had been dismissed by Kira, who felt no desire to have them return.

Chapter Eighteen

Stephen Drake

Stephen almost felt guilty for manipulating his daughter into spending her Thursday with him. Over the phone he could hear her hesitancy in the breathy sighs and indecisive words she chose. He knew she would much rather stay confined to the beautiful home she had rented in La Jolla, surfing, reading scripts and answering e-mail. Yet he refused to allow her to make La Jolla a California version of her life in Oahu. He insisted that he needed her help with the final wedding details, such as his tux fitting, the seating arrangement for the reception, which he and Mo had cleverly waited until the last minute to plan just so her assistance would be needed, and the menu for the engagement party at the Bullfrog. It was the last agenda item that almost broke the deal, but he was certain that Bear would welcome her cheerfully. Apparently Megan already spoke with Bear and persuaded the burly bar owner that Kira was not an evil lesbian heartbreaker and that Flynn was fine.

It was Megan's behavior in the last twelve hours that surprised him the most. At dinner she was openly needling Kira, but by morning, she was offering to make Kira's existence in OB more pleasant. He didn't understand, and Mo swore she didn't berate Megan into passivity. He chose not to question her motives, but he was glad for her change of heart.

As they strolled down Newport Boulevard, Kira's arm looped through his, he could feel the tension surging through her body. He knew she had made the ultimate sacrifice for him—returning to the place of her greatest heartache and disappointment. He hoped she would somehow reunite with Flynn, a woman he knew was perfect for her, but he realized such a thought was merely wishful thinking and the stuff of movies. He almost chuckled. He had lived in her world for too long.

"Are you counting the hours until you can leave?"

"Of course not, Dad."

"Kira, it's really all right. I understand."

She sighed, and he knew she couldn't hide the truth. He was grateful that her continual performances in front of the camera and in her personal life never encroached upon their relationship. He was the one person who saw the real Kira.

"Mo tells me you and Flynn spent some time together."

They both gazed down the length of Newport Boulevard at the boutiques, coffeehouses and bars. "It wasn't as horrible as I imagined. We're fine." She turned to him. "So tell me again why you're having a party at the Bullfrog *and* a reception? Won't all of the same people be at both? Isn't that a bit redundant?"

Stephen laughed. "Yes, I suppose it is, but Bear insisted that we celebrate at the bar, and since Mo couldn't stand the thought of the wedding and the reception being held anywhere but the pier—"

"We're having a party before the party. I understand."

He debated whether to mention Flynn again and realized it

was probably hopeless. He needed to let it go and focus on his own happiness and enjoy his daughter's brief visit. He imagined that she wouldn't be around often after he married.

"So, has much changed in OB since you were last here?" he asked.

"Not really. I think I recognized that panhandler at the last corner."

They both laughed, and as they approached the Bullfrog, a man stepped out on the sidewalk with his broom. At the sight of Kira, he scowled, but he didn't retreat. From the description Megan provided, Stephen assumed this was Bear, who was literally a bear of a man. He patted her on the hand and smiled, but Bear's eyes burned into hers.

"Kira," he said evenly.

She inhaled and Stephen listened as she launched into a typical acting performance. "Hello, Bear. It's been a long time. I trust the Bullfrog is doing well?"

"Yup."

"I'd like you to meet my father, Stephen Drake."

Stephen extended his hand and Bear's face morphed into sheer cordiality. "Mr. Drake, it is a pleasure." He pumped his hand up and down furiously. "I hope you know you're marrying the best damn woman in Ocean Beach, if you'll pardon my French, sir."

"No need to apologize, Bear. Mo is indeed the best woman in the whole town." Bear finally let go of him, and he wondered if his shoulder was dislocated. "I trust everything is prepared for the party tonight?"

"Got it all planned, Mr. Drake. We'll have the usual pub fare plus appetizers, and Megan's bringing the desserts by later. It's going to be the best damn party in OB. Oops." Bear slapped his hand over his mouth. "Uh, again, Mr. Drake, you'll have to forgive my language."

"It's not a problem, Bear. And please call me Stephen."

"Okay, Stephen. We'll see you tonight."

After another hard stare at her, Bear and his broom retreated into the Bullfrog. Kira gave Stephen a weary look.

"I'm sorry," he said. "I didn't realize how hard things would be for you."

She shook her head in disagreement. "Dad, I'm fine. This isn't about me. It's about you and Mo. I'm glad I'm here for you. If people can't get over the past, then that's their problem."

He listened, well aware that she was the person most encumbered by the past. OB was where she last felt the freedom to be herself, and it was also the place that shackled her to the memories of the past. They headed down the street past the market, and she craned her neck, her step slowing.

"Do you want to go inside?" he asked.

"No, I don't see Manny. You know, this shop used to belong to Mo's mother."

"Oh, that's right. I'd forgotten that." His cell phone rang. It was Mo, reminding him of several wedding details. He listened to her instructions, which were almost unintelligible, anxiety about the wedding making her accent thicker than usual. He nodded several times and finally shut the phone, unsure of anything but having agreed to everything she said.

They turned down Coast Road toward the veterinary clinic, the morning quickly fading into noon. Kira looked from side to side, studying the landscape and most likely comparing it to the past. He figured this would be one of the last times he could talk with her privately. Kira would no doubt use the marriage as an opportunity to slip further away, her visits to OB short and infrequent, and there'd be no more solo trips to Oahu for weeks at a time. Yet again he felt as though he had failed as a father, and he should have given her more direction long ago.

"What's wrong?" she asked.

He sighed. Even without words they knew each other's moods. "I was thinking about when we went to the shore for holiday. Do you remember that?"

"How could I forget? It was the only place we ever went."

"It was the only place you ever wanted to go. I guess I should have known then that you loved the ocean."

She smiled. "What made you think of our vacations?"

"I was thinking specifically of the day we flew the kite. Do you remember that?"

"I do. The farther away it flew, the more upset I got. I thought it was leaving. I cried and screamed, and I was getting rather hysterical about the whole thing since the only part I could see was the white tail waving in the wind. You finally calmed me down long enough for me to notice the stick that held the string. I realized that you had full control of the kite. It wasn't going to leave. You started pulling the string back around the stick, just enough for me to see the outline of the kite. Then I was fine."

He stopped walking and looked at her. "Exactly."

"Dad, is this your rather obvious attempt at an extended metaphor?" she asked drolly.

He hugged her to his chest and kissed the top of her head. "I just want you to know I'm always here for you. I know how much you're hurting—"

"Dad, please—"

"No, I'm going to say it. I've always felt like I failed you. I should have stood up to your mother and forced her to see what was best for you."

"And what was that?"

"Flynn."

She pulled away, her arms folded, and he saw the tears in her eyes. As she was about to comment, Kellen whipped around the corner on his bike.

"Hey!" he shouted. He stopped the bike in front of them, realizing he was intruding. "Um, sorry."

"It's fine, Kellen," Kira assured him with a smile.

Stephen noticed that with one wipe of her palm, the tears vanished and she donned her acting persona right on the sidewalk. "Where are you going?"

"To the clinic. Is that where you're going?"

"Flynn offered me a tour of the new shelter," Stephen said. "Come along with us."

They walked the last three blocks with Kellen pushing his bike beside them. Stephen noticed how easily Kira engaged Kellen in conversation, and by the time they reached the clinic door, she had elicited his opinions about school, music and girls. Stephen looked at his daughter with great affection. She would have made a wonderful parent.

Kellen started the tour without Flynn, who joined them between patients. "Hi, Mom. I was just showing Kira and Stephen the animal compounds. I guess Kira already saw them, but Stephen hasn't."

"It's really amazing, Flynn," Stephen admired. "What a wonderful project. I take it there are many neglected animals in San Diego?"

"Oh, yeah. The amount of strays and unwanted pets is unbelievable. What we're building is a no-kill shelter that will actually work to rehabilitate the animals, since so many of them are given up because they seem mean or unmanageable."

"Yeah," Kellen said. "If they're trained properly, then people will want to adopt them. That's where I come in."

"Well, you and a few other professionals," Flynn added. She motioned to the partially built lot. "This acre belongs to us, and now we're working a little at a time to get it all built. As the money comes in, we keep adding on."

"How much do you still need?" Stephen asked.

"About seven hundred thousand. That's just a rough estimate, but I think we'll be able to get it built in another year. I'm looking at some grants right now and talking with some of the leading San Diego bigwigs. I know it will happen eventually."

"How did you come up with the idea to do this yourself?" Stephen asked.

Flynn paused and looked over at Kellen, who said, "It was Luz's idea. She always said we should do something to help. She hated all the strays that she saw in Mexico."

The four of them stood quietly, looking at the skeletal facility until a large African-American woman sauntered through the back door and called to Flynn, "Dr. McFadden, Mary Greenbush is insisting that you take a look at Wylie's tail. He's scratched it silly again. She doesn't have an appointment, but you know how she is about that dog."

"I'll be right there," Flynn called. She turned to Kellen and pointed her finger. "Don't forget your chores and remember that I love you."

"I won't, and I love you, too," he said in a voice that implied everything was a chore.

Flynn's gaze shifted to Kira. "You're coming tonight, aren't you? Face the crowd at the Bullfrog?"

"Of course."

"Aren't we supposed to have some kind of a rehearsal thing?" Kellen asked.

"That would be traditional," Stephen replied, "but your grandmother won't clog up the pier for it. She's certain that an impromptu ceremony will be fine, and I'm inclined to agree with her."

"Good," Kellen said. "Sounded boring."

"It is," Flynn agreed. She looked at Kira. "Okay, well I'll see you tonight." Flynn absently included Stephen in her statement with a quick sideways glance. Kira stared at her retreating figure until she was out of sight.

A small smile tugged at his lips. Perhaps there was still hope.

Chapter Nineteen
Kira Drake

The first rule of parties was never to arrive too late or too early, and as Kira stood outside the Bullfrog alone, she peered through the windows, pleased to see the crowd as thick as the smoke. Empty glasses cluttered the tables. She stepped to the side of the building and pushed her speed dial. Robert answered on the first ring.

"Hey, darlin'. Only two more days now."

"Hello, Robert. I just wanted to check in."

"Uh-huh. What's going on?"

"Well, I'm about to attend an engagement party for my father and Mo with the entire town."

Robert laughed. "It sounds more like a good ol' Southern lynching."

"God, please don't say that. There's one friendly resident I haven't seen yet, so I'm hoping to spend the evening with him."

"What about your friend, Flynn? Did she like those dog treats you made?"

"She loved them, and more importantly, Rufus loved them. Thanks for having some of the ingredients FedExed."

"Not a problem. Have you read those scripts yet?"

"Only one, the TV movie. It won't do anything to help my career, so it's a pass. I'll read the others on the plane. I promise."

"All right. I'll hold you to that. You better get in there. Y'all have fun."

She said good-bye, steeling herself for whatever might come, and went inside. Nothing had changed about the Bullfrog in the last fifteen years. It looked exactly the same, down to the slightly off-centered caricature of a frog that hung in a corner of the bar. She wondered if Bear ever bothered to dust it. After attending hundreds of affairs, she learned never to step more than ten feet into a room without assessing who was in attendance, where and how the liquor was served and, depending on her purpose, where she could be seen and where she could hide. At the Bullfrog she definitely wanted the latter.

The overworked waitresses couldn't keep up and everyone had downed a few rounds. She ignored some of the whispers and stares that followed her across the bar. She only wanted two things: tequila and a stool near Manny. By the time she crossed the room, she'd spotted Manny waving toward her from a small corner booth, a bottle of Jose Cuervo in front of him. Good, she thought. Before she could sit down, he had poured her a shot.

"Manny!" she cried, throwing her arms around the fisherman. Even in his good clothes, Manny still smelled of the mackerel he used to catch.

"Hello, Miss Kira. I've wanted to see you."

"And I you," she said honestly. "I've thought of you so many times over the years, Manny. How are you? I hear you own the store now."

"Yep. When Gmum died, Mo didn't quite know what to do.

Flynn certainly couldn't handle it, and Megan was already gone. She sold me the store for a song, and I've never forgotten it. Working behind the register sure beats catching fish all the time."

"I assume you haven't used Gmum's bat for enforcement?"

"No, the chip rack manages to stay on the counter, but I do have more shoplifters than she ever did." He poured more tequila and eyed her carefully. "So how is your life?"

She smiled pleasantly and downed the shot in a swallow. "Fine."

"There's been a lot of talk around town since your arrival."

"I imagine there has." She refilled their glasses again, deciding that her personal goal was to finish the Cuervo in less than an hour. "I'm just here for the wedding and then I'll be gone. I hope the good people of OB can suffer my presence just a bit longer."

Manny leaned close to her. "Who took those pictures?"

She studied his face, unsure if she wanted to dig that far into the past. The Cuervo was coursing through her system, and she only hesitated a moment before answering, "Rona."

He slapped his hand on the table. "I knew it. I knew that woman was the devil."

"I wish I had. I didn't figure it out until almost six months later. She flew into a drunken rage one night when we were on location and she confessed to everything. I fired her on the spot. My agent was furious, saying it was for my own good." She reached for the bottle again. "Ancient history."

"You better slow down, a thin little thing like you."

She smirked. "I'm barely feeling it. I've always been able to hold my liquor." She raised her glass and he followed her lead. "A toast to my father and Mo. They are truly a wonderful couple."

They clinked glasses and downed their shots. "They truly are," he agreed.

"You know"—she raised eyebrow—"I always thought you

and Mo would get together."

He circled his glass on the table, avoiding her gaze. "Oh, no. That wouldn't be right. I'm already part of the family."

She was perplexed. "What do you mean?"

He shifted in his seat and looked about. "Well, I'm Kellen's father."

"What? Really?"

"Flynn and Luz asked me to be their sperm donor. I knew they would make wonderful parents, and Flynn assured me that someday she would tell Kellen. I think she will, probably when he's out of high school."

"Do you think he suspects?"

Manny shook his head. "Nope. I don't think he's ever felt a loss. He has the whole town of OB raising him. It's no accident that his dog business is so successful. Don't get me wrong. He's a great kid and really knows animals, but no one would ever think of taking their dog somewhere else."

Manny and Kira smiled at each other. He poured another drink while she scanned the room. She caught a few snickers aimed in her direction, but now that she was tucked away in a corner, most of the partygoers didn't notice her. She couldn't see her father and Mo, but she suspected they were at the center of a large group at the other end of the bar. Just then Flynn and Megan arrived, Megan's arm wrapped around a third woman's waist. It took Kira a moment to recognize Rocco, who had shed her punker image but still looked supremely cool. Megan and Flynn were engaged in a serious conversation, Megan doing most of the talking. Judging by the expression on her face, Megan was trying to convince Flynn of something, but she seemed unwilling to agree. At the same time, they both looked in Kira's direction, and she quickly sought out her drink, certain they were talking about her. She couldn't get out of OB fast enough.

"Are you okay?" Manny asked.

"Of course."

Suddenly there was a shriek above the music, and people ran to the other room. Manny jumped up to see what the uproar was about. Soon Flynn emerged carrying a bulldog covered in frosting, a distraught elderly woman following behind. She held a handkerchief to her eyes, and Kira saw Mo, holding her hand, escorting her toward the back.

As they passed the table, Mo consoled the older woman. "It's perfectly fine, Dorothy. Don't give it another thought. We'll just cut around the dog drool."

The partygoers returned to their tables and Manny sat back down.

"What happened?" she asked.

"Apparently Mrs. Tillowix's bulldog Dewey ate a good chunk of Mo and Stephen's chocolate torte. He managed to get up on his little haunches and got a piece of the pier." Mo and Stephen's torte, he explained, was decorated with a picture of the sea and the OB Café.

"Oh, no. A chocolate torte could kill a dog."

He shook his head. "Highly doubtful. That dog has had more people food than some of the homeless folk in OB. Mrs. Tillowix is not known for following Flynn's advice."

"Can we join you guys?"

Kira looked up to see Megan and Rocco hovering above their table. This should be interesting, she thought. She had always liked Rocco.

"Absolutely!" Manny agreed. He slid over to make room for the couple.

Rocco kissed Kira on the cheek and whispered in her ear, "It's been a long time. Are you surviving?"

"Barely," Kira muttered through gritted teeth. "I'm feeling a little like the offering at a pagan ceremony."

Rocco laughed and Kira decided to play host, her proper British sensibilities taking over.

"Would you like some tequila?" She held up the bottle and reached for two clean glasses from a tray at the center of the table.

She couldn't imagine why Megan would ever volunteer to sit with her and she squirmed, nervous and waiting for the inevitable verbal assault to come. She caught Manny staring at her, amusement in his eyes.

"Kira," he began, "I'd love to ask you about your costar Joyce Gilford in *Rainchild*. Is she as lovely in person as she seems to be in interviews?"

She blushed. She hadn't thought of Joyce in months, and the last image of her wasn't pleasant. She'd hurled a shoe at Kira when Kira broke off their liaison. She glanced at Megan, who was chuckling, and cleared her throat. "Joyce is a wonderful lady." Megan lowered her head and snorted. "Do you disagree, Megan?"

Megan took a deep breath and folded her hands in front of her on the table. "Kira, darling, everyone in Hollywood knows about your affair with Joyce."

Her jaw dropped. "They do?"

"What?" Manny's voice cracked in surprise.

"After you dumped her, she told everybody that worked on that TV pilot she filmed after *Rainchild*. If you think you're hiding, you're crazy." Megan leaned across the table and whispered, "Do you know how many of your exes have come into my shop, taking your name in vain?"

Dumbfounded, she slumped back in the booth, the truth an albatross. She'd always prided herself on discretion, but she had to admit that she was often surprised at the reaction of her lovers. Why couldn't they just enjoy a friendly fuck with no strings?

"I still can't believe you slept with Joyce Gilford," Manny said. "Isn't she married with children?"

"It's not the same, Manny," Megan interjected. "There are a

ton of lesbian and bi women who marry men to cover themselves. Why do you think Kira got married?"

"Megan, be nice," Rocco warned, for which Kira was grateful.

Manny pondered this thought and turned to Kira. "So, does that mean your marriage was a fake?"

She shot daggers at Megan, her and her little Cheshire Cat smile. She took a deep breath and answered him honestly. "Yes, I married Dax what's-his-name to keep my cover. It's hard for actresses to get A-level films if you're a lesbian. It wasn't my idea."

"It was that worthless agent, wasn't it?" Manny asked. "He was nothing but slime."

"He got his, though," Megan said. "Karma got that bastard."

"Glad to hear it," Manny agreed.

The four of them raised their glasses in unison and downed their shots. Manny filled the glasses again. Kira allowed herself to slip into that tipsy state where all the sharp edges disappeared and she could face the stares of the fine people of Ocean Beach. Eventually her father and Mo arrived at their table, and soon they were all laughing hysterically. Only Flynn was missing, and each time she glanced around the bar, she was disappointed. She excused herself to the restroom and Megan followed. As she crossed the linoleum, her knees buckled. She quickly caught herself, and Megan grabbed her waist.

"You're wasted."

"You are no better, deary."

They waited in the line, giggling and leaning against each other. As two women exited, one glanced at Kira hanging all over Megan and said to her friend, "Geez, she can't have one sister, so she goes after the other."

At that, Megan stuck out her foot, tripping the speaker, who nearly fell flat on her face.

"Sorry, deary," Megan said, not a touch of sympathy in her

voice. "What bitches," she said to Kira.

"Please don't make it worse, Megan. Everyone already hates me."

Megan touched her shoulder. "If it matters, I don't hate you."

"It does." She leaned her head against the wall, enjoying her Cuervo buzz. When they returned from the bathroom, she decided it was time to leave. While she would have liked to see Flynn, she'd had her fill of Ocean Beach folk for one night. She followed Megan through the crowd, determined to say her good-byes to Manny and Rocco. Driving would be a challenge, but she'd be careful. She felt a tap her on the shoulder and turned to see Flynn standing next to her.

"So have I missed the whole party?" Flynn asked.

"Hello," Kira said, a little too much excitement in her voice. "What can I do for you?" She hoped she wasn't slurring her words or slouching in some odd position.

"You're a little drunk."

"Of course not. I'm British. We don't get drunk. We get tipsy. Is the dog okay?"

"I think he'll be fine." Flynn held up two darts. "You think you're up for some darts? All or nothing. Winner gets whatever she wants."

She frowned, unable to read Flynn's eyes and wondering if this was a joke. "What could I have that you would ever want?"

Flynn grinned. "I'll think of something."

Suspicious, she narrowed her eyes, her heart pounding at Flynn's flirtation. "What are you up to?"

Flynn handed her a dart and she went to the line. In mid-throw, Bear stepped in front of her, his arms crossed. "I'm sorry, Flynn, but this woman isn't welcomed here. I'm making an exception for your mom and allowing her in the bar, but there's no way she's throwing darts. This board's for regulars only." He pointed behind him at the old board, and a few of the partygoers nodded their heads in agreement.

Megan approached and stood on the other side of Kira. Surrounded by the McFadden sisters, she suddenly felt sorry for Bear.

Megan leaned forward into Bear's face. "What are you saying, Bear? Flynn ain't a regular?"

Bear held up a hand in disagreement. "Not saying that at all, Meg. Flynn's the best person I know. It's this movie star who's not allowed. She doesn't belong."

"That's bullshit!" Megan yelled.

Bear snarled at Megan, and several people crowded around the two of them, some siding with Megan and others with Bear. Kira stepped out of the circle and found a chair in the corner. The argument grew, and soon the noise was deafening, many drunken patrons chiming in. As a good actress, she noticed the faces, the body language. So much negative energy and all of it directed at her. An aria from *Madame Butterfly* drifted through her brain and muffled the harangue of the bar patrons. Then it was as though she was watching a silent movie, focusing only on the anger, the gestures. The room was spinning and she buried her head in her hands. She felt a touch on her back, a soft stroke that calmed her.

"Let's get you out of here."

Chapter Twenty

Flynn McFadden

Shame surged through Flynn as she helped Kira stand. Tears streamed down Kira's face, and she buried her head against Flynn's shoulder. "Hey," she whispered. She lifted Kira's chin and wiped away the tears. She was lost in the gorgeous brown eyes, and the chaos around her disappeared. Kira was in her arms, the sweet-smelling chestnut hair overtaking her senses. She had not experienced this feeling for a long time, and it was intoxicating. She remembered what it felt like to want a woman.

"I just want to go home." Kira's voice was a breathy sob in her ear.

Flynn kissed the tears on her cheeks. She kissed her forehead, her eyelids and eventually her mouth. They shared a short sweet kiss, and when they parted, Kira was smiling. It was awkward, but it propelled Flynn's memory back fifteen years to their first kiss, which was also awkward but full of promise.

"God, Flynn," she whispered. "Why did you do that?"

"I wanted to. I'm over forty now. I don't wait for things anymore. Let's go," she said, but before she could take a step, her mother's voice echoed throughout the bar.

"Casper Byron Geldpepper!"

The crowd immediately parted as Mo slowly walked to Bear and pointed at him. "You are a disgrace to Ocean Beach."

He used all of his self-control with Mo, and Flynn noticed his hands were bunched into huge fists, but he kept them at his side. She had no fear for her mother. Like so many people in OB, he was like a son to her. "Why did you call me Casper?" he growled. "You know I hate that name, Mo."

"Because right now you need to be called by your Christian name. You're in trouble, young man." Although he was older than Flynn, he responded to the chastisement by hanging his head. "In fact, many of you are in trouble with me. You are treating my family with great disrespect. Look at yourselves and what you're doing. And look at my daughter and Kira."

All eyes turn to Flynn and Kira. Wrapped in each other's arms, Flynn suspected they looked more like a couple than ex-lovers.

"People in OB do not judge. We forgive. We live and let live. If you cannot do that, then do not come to my wedding and never set foot in my café again!"

Mo's eyes swept around the tavern, and most people couldn't meet her stare. She came over to Kira and Flynn, a smile on her face. She placed a hand on Kira's cheek and stroked it gently. "Welcome to the family, my girl. I hope it will get easier," she said with a wink. She strode through the silent tavern toward Stephen, who was waiting by the door with her purse. He held the door open for his intended, and she left without another word.

No one moved for several seconds, and Flynn was not sure what to do. It was Bear who took charge of the situation. He stepped toward them, cleared his throat and held up the darts. "Ms. Drake, on behalf of the Bullfrog and I guess most everyone here, I'd like to offer my humble apology."

As if the alcohol had not affected her at all, she smiled most graciously and accepted the darts from Bear's huge paw. "Thank you, Bear. Please, call me Kira."

He smiled and bowed while cheers erupted throughout the bar. *This is a movie moment*, Flynn thought. The party quickly resumed minus the guests of honor, but Flynn and Kira stayed rooted in the same spot gazing at each other. For the first time she felt totally relaxed with Kira, and it was only the self-restraint that came from growing older that kept her from pressing her lips against Kira's again—now that the entire bar was watching them.

Kira sensed her predicament and held up the darts. "Now, what was this about all or nothing?"

Liking the challenge, Flynn stepped to the line. She took aim and the dart sailed straight to the bull's eye. Kira frowned and stepped to the mark. She swayed back and forth, as if trying to make sure she didn't foul, unsure of her footing.

She looked up at the board, then turned to Flynn. "Why are there two boards up there? What are you trying to pull, Flynn?"

Flynn chuckled and moved behind Kira. She steadied Kira's throwing hand and pointed it in the direction of the board. "It's right there. Straight ahead."

"Are you sure?"

"Yup."

"You're not trying to trick me, are you?"

"Of course not. Go ahead and throw."

When Kira released the dart, it flew high above the board and to the right, landing in a wooden post above the bar and twelve inches from the top of Bear's head. He was too drunk and involved in a story to notice how close he had come to being stabbed in the ear.

"I guess you lose," Flynn said.

Kira turned to face her. "So what do you want me to do?"

"I've got a plan, but for now, let's get out of here."

The relief on Kira's face was obvious. "Please." They said their good-byes to Manny, Rocco and Megan and headed out into the night, up Newport Boulevard toward the clinic. "I should get back to La Jolla," Kira said.

"You're not going anywhere."

"How will I get home?"

"Well, since I wouldn't even trust my own driving, you're coming back to the house with me." When Kira started to protest, she took her arm and pulled her down a side street that would give them a view of the ocean as they navigated the hills toward home. She wondered what Kira was thinking as they passed the beautiful old bungalows that lined the street. "Why don't you have a girlfriend?" she asked, almost afraid of the answer.

Kira shrugged. The effects of the alcohol were lessening, but Flynn noticed she still couldn't walk a straight line. "It's complicated. I'm never around."

The answer was too pat, and Flynn suspected they both knew it. She didn't argue and as they turned into the driveway, Kira hesitated. "Where will I sleep?"

"I'll give you my room."

"I can't believe you still live here," Kira said. "Why don't you have your own place?"

Flynn shrugged. The answer was layered in various reasons—money, choices, pain. "I like my mother," she said simply. "It's not difficult."

Kira didn't respond but instead pointed to the VW bus and giggled. "Now that brings back memories."

Flynn led her up the narrow back staircase to the third floor, to the room where she had lived for her entire life. It was here she made love to Kira, lived with Luz and conceived Kellen. Kira moved about the space, touching the furniture, studying the place that she probably remembered but looked much different long ago. When Flynn catalogued all of the memories, she realized that only in the last fifteen years had anything significant occurred. Everything until that summer in OB was inconsequential. Her life changed when Kira arrived.

She shuffled her feet, conscious of Kira's presence in her room. "Well, the sheets are pretty clean and if you want a pair of boxers or a T-shirt, they're in the top drawer." She motioned to the old dresser Luz bought at a yard sale. It didn't match anything in the room, but Luz adored it.

Kira opened the drawer and withdrew a pair of her boxers. She held them up and smiled seductively. She dropped them back in the drawer and continued to rummage. Flynn said nothing, the moonlight casting a flattering shadow on Kira's body through the window. Her eyes followed the incredible curve of Kira's buttocks as they bent over the drawers, Kira hunting through each one for something she wanted to wear. Flynn opened her mouth to direct her away from the bottom drawer of the dresser, knowing it was only filled with her snow gear—mittens, long underwear and a ski bib.

"You won't find anything there . . ." The words died in her mouth as Kira pulled a slinky teddy out and waved it in the air. It was red with black lace and left little to the imagination. She dug farther and withdrew a matching pair of panties.

"Now this looks like something I would wear."

Flynn swallowed hard. Yes, it was definitely something Kira would wear because it belonged to her, and Flynn had kept it hidden in that drawer for years. Eventually, as her life with Luz took shape and her world filled with other things, she forgot it existed—until now.

"Do you want me to put it on?" Kira asked in an unmistakable tone.

Flynn instantly shook her head. "No, I think you should just lie down." She took Kira's hand, pulling her closer to the bed. Kira wrapped her arms around Flynn's neck and pressed her body against her, still holding the teddy in her hand.

"Do you want to kiss me again?"

"Yes, but not now. Not while you're drunk."

"Do you want to make love to me?"

All of the breath expelled from Flynn's body and she felt faint. She watched Kira's face—her lips open, ready to be taken. It was an invitation to a night of passion, something she had not experienced in over a year. She gently pushed her down on the bed and stepped away, ignoring her question. It seemed the safest response for the present.

Kira turned her head away. "You're room is smashing. I love this purple wall."

"Luz decorated it."

"Luz," Kira repeated. She picked up the framed headshot of Luz from the nightstand. She stretched out on the bed, the teddy draped over her body, staring at the photo. "Luz. What a beautiful name, and clearly perfect in every way. Just like that great Brit, Mary Poppins." Suddenly Kira sat up. "Flynn, could Luz fly with an umbrella?"

She realized Kira was not being funny or sarcastic. "Almost," she said.

"I can see why no one could ever compare." Kira slurred her words and fell against the bedspread. Flynn grabbed a blanket and covered her, placing a pillow under her head. She replaced the photo on the nightstand and the teddy into the bottom drawer as Kira settled into sleep. She moved to the door in the dark and gazed at Kira on her bed. The door clicked as she attempted to leave and Kira muttered something inaudible.

"What?" Flynn asked.

"I said *muirnîn*."

Flynn couldn't believe her ears. "Kira?"

"You used to call me *muirnîn*," Kira said before she drifted asleep.

Had she been able to continue the conversation, she would have told Kira that she did not need to be reminded, and in fact, she could detail the moment she had given her the name. She stood in the doorway, letting the memories overwhelm her. Kira stirred in the bed, and she contemplated joining her, tangling their legs together, burying her face in Kira's neck, where she could smell Kira's perfume and feel her curls against her cheek. She hesitated, caught between the past and present, and then decided to go downstairs.

She retreated to the kitchen. The clock read two a.m., and she knew Stephen and her mother were fast asleep, Stephen tucked away in the guestroom, far too proper to share the same bed before the wedding. With Kira asleep in her room, she was left only with the screened porch, a place she knew well. A nervous energy consumed her. Forget it, she told herself. She sat at the breakfast bar, her chin propped up in her hand. Nearby was the bag of dog treats, simply titled "For Rufus." She realized that would be a good name for a product and pondered who could mass-market such a wonderful delicacy.

Her thoughts drifted to Kira's surprising words. *Luz was perfect in every way.* Yes and no. To be honest, she was far from perfect. Many times she could be controlling, demanding and insistent. Flynn made her share of sacrifices for Luz—including getting pregnant. She told Kira that Luz couldn't have a baby because of her immigration status, but the truth was much less pleasant. Luz refused to give up surfing for months or allow her body to grow misshapen from a baby. She had indeed loved Kellen, but his existence was on Flynn's shoulders.

Flynn opened the bag of dog treats. They smelled wonderful. It only took a few minutes before her three dogs were wagging their tails in front of her, begging for a morsel. Once they were satisfied, Flynn read the ingredients, admiring Kira's angular handwriting, which reminded her of an architect's script, careful and methodical. A vision from the past exploded in her mind, and she was staring at the photo—the one of her and Kira that ruined their relationship. Flynn immediately pulled herself up from the stool and headed for bed, knowing the call for sleep would silence the past.

Chapter Twenty-one
Megan McFadden

With roughly thirty hours remaining until the wedding, Megan's to-do list was lengthy. Kellen had agreed to help her, and she was more than a little surprised to find Kira sitting at the breakfast table with him when she sailed through the front door to pick him up. Rocco should have helped her, she thought, but Rocco was still nursing her hangover from the night before. It would be at least a few hours before Rocco was ready to leave the Ocean Beach Hotel and join them on their errands.

"Hi, Aunt Megan," he called.

"Good morning," she said, her eyes glued to Kira, who nodded between sips of coffee. She poured a cup for herself and joined them. "How was your evening last night, Kellen?"

"Awesome. After Dewey ate the torte at the party, Mom called me and I went over and watched him for a few hours so Mrs. Tillowix could go back to the party with Mom. She paid me twenty bucks."

"Fabulous. It sounds like Mrs. Tillowix was really grateful for your help."

He nodded and finished his cereal. "I'm just glad Dewey's okay. Mrs. Tillowix was so glad that Mom saved Dewey she promised she wouldn't forget it. She would make it worth Mom's while."

"What do you think she means by that?"

"I think she'll make another donation to the animal shelter. I mean, the woman's loaded."

Megan snorted into her coffee. "Yeah, but don't forget, sweetie, she's also cheap. I know she gave the shelter a hundred grand, but she could have paid for the whole damn thing and didn't. She loves your mom and I'm sure she's grateful, but don't be surprised if her reward to your mother is a basket of fruit."

Kira set her coffee cup down in front of her. "That's rather cynical, don't you think?"

Megan raised an eyebrow. "I'll admit I've never personally been rich, but, Kellen, I'll tell you, as someone who caters to the rich and famous every day, there's a reason they stay rich, and it's because they keep their money close."

Kira shook her head but kept silent, perhaps unwilling to argue with her.

"I know Kira disagrees, and there are exceptions, but the rich are not always generous. I just don't want your mom to get her hopes up." Pretending the thought just occurred to her, she looked around the room. "Speaking of your mother, has she left for the clinic? Did you guys surf this morning?"

Kellen scowled and pointed at the screened porch. She craned her neck to see the top of Flynn's red head protruding off the futon. She knew this meant that there was no surfing and Kellen was unhappy. He learned long ago not to bother his mother when she slept on the porch. Whenever she fought with Luz, she inevitably wound up there. It also meant that Flynn had told Mrs. Jenkins to move all of her Friday morning appointments. Kellen rose and put his bowl in the dishwasher before heading upstairs to change.

Megan glanced at Kira, who seemed lost in her own thoughts. "So, if Flynn's on the screened porch, I take it the two of you either did not spend the night together or your passion crashed and burned."

Kira cleared her throat and looked at the table. "You would be correct in assuming the former and not the latter."

"Hmm. That's disappointing."

"Actually it proves your sister is quite upstanding. She didn't want to take advantage of me in my inebriated state."

How surprising, Megan thought. And how unfortunate. She chuckled and sipped her coffee.

"Megan, I have to ask you, why the change of heart?"

"What do you mean?"

"The other night in La Jolla you were ready to hang me in effigy, and you've suddenly become my ally, and you seem to be promoting some sort of liaison between myself and Flynn. I don't understand what changed."

Megan wasn't about to get into it. Besides, it was none of Kira's business. Her motivations were private and had as much to do with herself as with Kira or Flynn. She said simply, "Rocco brings out the best in me."

Kira nodded and seemed satisfied by the explanation. "Could you drop me by the Bullfrog so I can pick up my car?"

"Sure." They heard sounds from the porch and turned to see Flynn stumbling into the house, scratching her head and yawning. "Oh look, the princess is up," Megan said. Flynn harrumphed and went for the coffee. "I can see Kellen is rather upset that there was no surfing this morning."

She ignored the comment and dropped into a chair at the table, staring at Kira. "Hey, did you sleep okay?"

"Fine. I do have a pounding headache, though."

Megan glanced from Flynn to Kira, wondering if the restrained civility between them was due to her presence. If they were alone, she imagined they might have exchanged a more amorous greeting. Her theory was confirmed when Kira rose and let her hand sweep across Flynn's tousled curls as she went to refill her coffee cup. It was a sweet gesture, one that told Megan everything she needed to know.

"What's on your schedule for today?" Flynn asked.

"Well, I have errands to run, and I must do some work or Robert will have my head. E-mail, faxing, the usual. What did you have in mind?"

"I was hoping you could pay your debt."

Flynn peered over her coffee cup at a bewildered Kira. Megan had always enjoyed watching Flynn flirt with her lady friends, and most women found her too cute to resist. Of course, it had been years since she acted this way, and Megan realized the last time she witnessed it was at the bar—the night Flynn met Luz.

Flynn rose and joined her, leaning casually against the counter. Both of them were lost in each other's presence. "I mean, you owe me from last night."

Kira nodded in understanding. "Ah, the darts."

"Exactly. And I've decided how you can pay."

"And what would I need to do?"

"I want you to jump off the pier tonight with me and Kellen."

Kira took a step back and put up her hands in defense. "Oh, no. Not that. We already talked about that. I am *not* jumping off that pier. I'm too old and I could get hurt."

"It's not a big deal. I've done it practically every day in my life. It's perfectly safe—"

"And illegal. I'm sure Charlie Vernon would love to arrest me. I can see the headline now, 'Lesbian actress arrested in OB.' That would do wonders for my sagging career."

"Your career isn't sagging."

191

The comment clearly disarmed Kira, who sighed heavily. She offered a slight smile. "You're kind." She stepped closer to Flynn and wrapped a finger around Flynn's curls. "Look, I have a great idea. You surf with Kellen, and then later you drive up to La Jolla. I'll make you a fabulous dinner and we can continue our interesting conversation from last night." Kira could really turn on the charm, Megan thought.

Flynn allowed her to play with her hair and caress her cheek. Megan pretended to read the newspaper, enjoying the scene in front of her. They were whispering to each other, and Flynn had wrapped her arms around Kira's waist. It was much like it was years ago, when they saw only each other. Who would win this round? Megan wondered. Despite the flirtations, when it came to surfing, Flynn was not dissuaded by anything, including sex.

"Flynn, I can't," Kira whined, but Flynn was relentless.

They continued to debate the issue privately until Kellen bounded down the stairs. "I'm ready, Aunt Megan," he said. At the sound of his voice, Flynn and Kira instantly parted.

"Good morning," Flynn said on her way up the stairs. She quickly turned back to Kellen. "I'll make up the surfing with you tonight at six thirty. I'm hoping Kira will join us." She glanced back into the kitchen, her eyes dancing, before she disappeared.

Kellen grinned at Kira. "Cool. I've never seen you surf in OB. That will be awesome."

"It's not definite, Kellen. I'm not sure if I'll come, so don't get your hopes up."

Unable to contain herself any longer, Megan laughed heartily. "She's certainly persuasive, though, isn't she?"

Kira's eyes narrowed and she shook her head. "She is quite the charmer. I'm not surprised so many people are donating money to her clinic. Her feminine wiles are quite effective."

"At least on you."

Chapter Twenty-two
Flynn McFadden

The Ocean Beach Veterinary Clinic swirled in activity from the moment the doors opened at eight o'clock to the exit of the last patient, which could occur at the end of standard operating hours or much later. As the only veterinarian in the community, Flynn had the sole responsibility to be on call 24/7 for all of the animal population. It was the primary reason that the handful of other veterinarians who moved to Ocean Beach failed to establish a practice and gain the trust of the locals.

Each one drove down Newport Boulevard, fell in love with the town and, ironically, hung his shingle in the same building a mile from Flynn's office. They never understood what they were up against with Flynn McFadden, the native OB resident who had a secret weapon—the legacy of the town's previous practitioner, Dr. James McBee, D.V.M. To many he looked the part of a vet, with a lean body and the rugged appearance of a country farmer. No one understood why he never married, except for a select few, including Mo and later Flynn. Dr. McBee was gay, and his lover, an architect in San Diego, shared his secret life for more than twenty-five years until the lover died from AIDS in the late eighties. While Mo had assured Dr. McBee that his OB patients would never abandon him over his lifestyle, it was the lover who wished to remain closeted, and Dr. McBee honored that request.

Flynn worked for Dr. McBee throughout high school, college and vet school. Her name became tied to the clinic and Dr. McBee, whose great-grandfather founded OB with six others. Over the next two decades, all that would change would be the length of Flynn's lab coat, as she gained her degrees and eventually took over for Dr. McBee when he retired. She knew she filled enormous shoes, and no one ever said to her, "Well, Dr. McBee always did it this way," because indeed, she did everything Dr. McBee's way in the first place. And that included keeping the hours of an around-the-clock doctor who administered care whenever it was needed, never turned away patients without appointments, despite Mrs. Jenkins's protests, and made house calls. Every visit had follow-up phone conversations—no matter if it was Sunday, late on a Friday night or during one of Flynn's rare vacations. Most other vets couldn't or wouldn't adopt Flynn's daily regimen, but she knew nothing else, and she couldn't imagine caring for her patients or their owners any other way.

Mrs. Jenkins found Flynn in her office, scrolling through her list of appointments for the day. "You're late."

"Good morning to you, too, Georgia," she said, her eyes focused on the screen.

"That actress wouldn't have anything to do with your tardiness, would it? The two of you looked quite cozy last night at the Bullfrog. And people are still talking about that kiss."

"I don't think that's any of your business." Mrs. Jenkins was silent and Flynn reached for a pad and began making notes. "Please call the lab and check on Idgy's results. Make sure that insufferable salesman doesn't corner me today and see if we can order some of these ingredients from a store in San Diego. And most important, make sure that Mrs. Meadows brings in Anastasia before five o'clock today."

"You know, she might not come."

"Of course she'll come in. It's Friday. And tonight I'm surfing with Kellen, and I do not want to be late."

"Oh, is Kellen wearing a watch these days?"

She glanced at Mrs. Jenkins, an amused expression covering her face. "I think we're back to the part that isn't your business."

Mrs. Jenkins grabbed the paper off the desk and headed for the door.

"I'm going out to check on the shelter, and I'll be back in before Mr. Dennison arrives."

Mrs. Jenkins nodded. "Good. Larry wants to talk to you." Larry was Flynn's contractor and a former high school classmate.

She headed out the back door into the construction zone, walking carefully, looking down. She certainly didn't need to impale herself on a discarded nail or a piece of rebar sticking up from the ground. Unlike some construction sites, the shelter was not filled with dozens of workmen, all competing to make the most noise with their power tools. Usually only one or two people accompanied Larry to the shelter, a subcontractor who handled concrete or electrical, or the architect, but more often Larry was alone, as he was today.

"Hey, Flynn," he called from a corner.

"Hi, Larry." She joined him next to an enormous stack of two-by-fours. He was holding a clipboard and checking the order. He wore jeans and a Led Zeppelin T-shirt minus the sleeves, which couldn't handle his ballooning biceps and broad chest. Most folks might have thought he was a steroid user, but she knew he had acquired his rippling physique honestly, from years of hoisting concrete blocks onto backyard fences. Today a baseball cap covered his bald head and a shiny gold hoop earring dangled from his left lobe.

She avoided asking him how it was going or what his plan was for the day, for if she made that mistake, he would launch into a thirty-minute oration explaining the most miniscule points of hanging Sheetrock or fitting copper piping. While she liked to have an update on progress, she was content to leave all of the details in his capable hands. Her silence would ensure that he only gave her the information he wanted to provide.

Once he finished his count, he turned to her, a broad smile exposing his ultra-white teeth. "I've got a surprise for you. Actually it's for both of us. I got into the office and opened my messages to find this." He fished a paper from his pocket and unfolded it. She saw it was an e-mail from Richard Colson, her banker. She scanned the lines, unable to believe what she was reading. An anonymous donor had wired seven hundred and fifty thousand dollars to the shelter's bank account at eight o'clock that morning. "I'd say Mrs. Tillowix really came through," he said.

"She's paying for all of it? The whole place is covered?" She couldn't believe that Mrs. Tillowix had donated such a large sum. The woman only engaged in moderate generosity and this was quite out of character.

"Hey, you saved Dewey's life last night. That dog means everything to her. I know it's a little weird to think she'd pony up that much money, but that's probably why she wants to be anonymous. She doesn't want everyone else to find out and come begging."

"You're probably right." She shook her head and gazed at the frame of the building, waiting to be encased in walls, and the pipes that protruded from the concrete foundation that would connect to the new sinks and basins she had chosen. She thought it would take at least another year, and now thanks to Mrs.

Tillowix and Dewey, it could all be done in half that time. She turned to him, knowing that he had avoided hiring other people, trying to do most of the work himself to keep costs down. A fanatic animal lover, Larry owned six cats and five dogs that he had acquired from the San Diego animal shelter. For him the building was a labor of love—a combination of the loyalty that he felt toward her and his passionate belief in the project. She recognized how many weekends and evenings he had sacrificed to get the building this far.

"So now can you hire some help?"

He nodded, as if reading her mind. "I'll hire a few guys for some limited time, but that extra fifty thousand could be used to get a few more of the frills that you wanted."

She disagreed. "That's not as important as getting it done sooner."

He held up a hand. "Just let me deal with it, okay?"

She chuckled, unable to believe her good luck this morning. She threw her arms around him and kissed his cheek. "I'm glad you're my friend," she said.

He gently returned the hug before she headed back to the clinic through the maze of building materials. She stopped at the door and closed her eyes, picturing what was to be. She saw the beautiful renderings that her architect designed, and when she turned back in his direction and opened her eyes, it was there— the dream fulfilled.

"You okay, Mom?" Kellen asked as they made their way down to the pier.

Her son's words jarred her mind and she looked up from the road, a smile plastered on her face. "I'm fine. I'm just thinking that it's been a wonderful day."

"Because Mrs. Tillowix gave you the money?"

She nodded. "That's certainly part of it."

"Maybe we should send Mrs. Tillowix flowers or do something for her," Kellen offered. "I could mow her grass for like a year."

Flynn laughed. "No, honey. Mrs. T. wanted the donation to be anonymous, and I think we should just leave it alone. Hey, you know Kira might join us, right? Is that okay with you?"

He seemed pleased. "That would be great, Mom. I really like her. I don't know what happened with you guys before I was born, but she seems really cool. I Googled her last night. I didn't realize she was amazingly famous. And she's beautiful."

Flynn chuckled. Her son was as transparent as his grandmother, who would go to whatever measures necessary to play matchmaker. Mo let it be known she wanted them to be together again, but Flynn wasn't so sure. Since Kira had arrived, that summer was no longer a blur, and memories continued to appear in her mind. Surprisingly, the wonderful moments surfaced immediately—their first time in bed, Kira's surfing lesson, the long walks they took on the beach. She had a hazy recollection of the horrible confrontation at the hotel, but fortunately, the many years of separation and her wonderful relationship with Luz dulled much of that pain. Yet the more she saw Kira, the clearer that awful day became in her mind, to where she could now see Jonah's black eyes laughing at her.

"Earth to Mom!"

She whipped her head to the passenger's seat and met Kellen's concerned expression.

"Mom, are you okay to drive? You seem really out of it."

She nodded and focused on the road. She couldn't remember them getting into the SUV, and she decided she was either preoccupied or suffering from over-forty memory loss. As the FJ Cruiser approached the pier, she found herself hoping Kira was there, and she could barely hide her disappointment when she didn't see her waiting.

"I guess she decided not to come," Kellen said.

"I guess not."

They parked next to the café and pulled their gear out. Kellen ran inside for a bottle of water and emerged with Kira and surfboard in tow.

"Look who I found," he said. "She was inside talking to Grandma."

She smiled broadly, hoping she masked her feelings a little. "I'm glad you made it."

"I always pay my debts," Kira said. "I do wish I still didn't have this pounding headache," she quickly added.

"You won't get any sympathy from me. That's what you get for drinking with Megan and Manny."

They all advanced to the railing and gazed down at the churning sea. Kellen straddled the wooden beam and pulled his board next to him. "Let's go."

She joined him on the railing, and they both watched Kira, who stared into the water below. "What's wrong? C'mon, the waves will be great."

"How far down is it?" Kira's voice cracked. "Two or three stories?"

"Nah," she disagreed. "It's only about thirty feet. That's not far."

"It's easy," Kellen added. "You'll love it."

Kira placed her board against the wooden banister and glanced at her. "I'm scared."

She leaned toward Kira, realizing she was serious. She could smell the wonderful perfume Kira always wore, and for some reason it became important to her that Kira made this jump. "You can do this. It's exhilarating."

"It's far. Why don't I just walk around, and I'll join you guys in the water?"

"It won't be as fun. This is a great part of the experience."

Kira was not persuaded. She stepped back from the railing and shook her head.

"Come here," Flynn beckoned. Kira remained still, staring at the water below. "Come here." She held out her hand, and Kira took it. She pulled her up on the railing, and the three of them sat suspended in the air, their feet dangling over the water. She gently squeezed Kira's hand. "You can do this. We'll jump in together."

Kira looked at her, lips trembling. Flynn kissed her hand, and she nodded.

Before Kira could change her mind, Flynn tossed the boards into the sea and Kellen dove in to herd them together. She helped her to the outside of the railing and grinned. They waited until the sea was calm and pushed off, flying through the air toward the foamy blue water that would catch them. Kira's body exploded into the sea, and Flynn quickly tried to recover, anxious to see her reaction, hoping that the exhilaration of the water suffocated her fear. When Kira bobbed to the surface, a huge grin was plastered on her face, and she let out a scream of glee. Flynn and Kellen laughed in delight.

They surfed for an hour, and she watched Kira, critiquing her technique and checking out her body. It was apparent that Kira loved everything about surfing—the waves, the tubes and the barrels. She wore the ocean like a comfortable jacket. When they finally emerged from the water, Flynn marveled at Kira's skill level. "You're really good."

Kira shrugged. "It's all because of you. You're the one who turned me on to surfing."

Flynn's gaze wandered up and down Kira's body. "Just to surfing?" she asked, just out of Kellen's earshot.

Kira chuckled. "Are you flirting with me, Flynn McFadden?"

They headed back up the pier toward the café. "Hey, when's dinner?" Kellen asked automatically.

Flynn nodded, well aware that Kellen's thirteen-year-old stomach had not ingested food in nearly ninety minutes. He needed refueling or everyone around him would be sorry. "You're having dinner with your grandma in the café."

"What about you guys?"

"We're getting dinner someplace else," Flynn said, hoping to avoid a direct explanation. Kellen smiled and waved good-bye.

Kira touched her shoulder and murmured, "Your son is quite intuitive."

She sighed. "He's definitely getting older." They watched Kellen saunter into the café and immediately scurry back out to change in the cabana. No doubt Mo had chided him for coming inside all wet. She turned to her and said, "So now I'd like to collect on our bet."

Kira's jaw dropped. "What are you talking about? I've paid up. I jumped off the pier."

"No," Flynn disagreed. "That didn't count. You did that of your own volition."

"That most certainly does count. I jumped out of duress and coercion. I still can't believe I propelled myself from the pier."

She crossed her arms and leaned into Kira. "I can't make you do anything. You jumped because in your heart you've always wanted to."

"So what do you intend to have me do to settle this little wager?" Kira asked in an overly dramatic voice.

"You promised me an incredible dinner, as I recall."

She flashed a seductive smile. "That's all you want? Dinner?"

Flynn looked out on the water. "Well, we'll just need to see what comes after that."

Kira shook her head and touched Flynn's hand. "I think we may have a problem."

"What?"

"If paying this debt means that I have to do something I really don't want to do, then I doubt you'll be able to collect tonight."

"And why is that?"

She moved so close to her that their lips were almost touching. "Because right now I can't imagine anything I wouldn't do with you."

Chapter Twenty-three
Kira Drake

The furnishings in the La Jolla rental were modern, including the dome-shaped clock that sat on the nightstand. It had a projection capability that allowed Kira to press a button and illuminate the time on the ceiling—a curious feature, she thought. The huge blue digital numbers read 2:17 p.m. Her father would be married in less than three hours, and Kira had made no effort to rise from bed, except to go to the loo and locate a box of tissue for her intermittent crying spells.

Johnny Cash's "I Walk the Line" filled the room, but even Robert's distinct ring tone couldn't elicit a smile. "Yes."

"I don't know," he drawled. "You called me and left a message to call you. There weren't a lot of details."

She took a deep breath and centered herself. She was not upset with Robert, and she wouldn't make him the target of her emotions. "I'm sorry. I need you to change my flight. I want to be on a plane this evening, any time after eight o'clock. I don't care what airline."

He didn't answer immediately, and she suspected he was deciding whether or not to step into the backyard of their personal relationship and dig for details or keep the conversation professional. "Where is this plane headed?"

"It doesn't matter. I'm going to Canada for the next shoot, so I imagine north would be helpful, but frankly, if you told me the only flight was to Mexico City, I'd take it."

Again there was a long pause and she heard his fingers tapping on the computer. "I'll call you when I have the itinerary, and I'll send it to your PDA."

"Thank you," she said, grateful for his wisdom. Even a thousand miles away, he knew when to pry and when to leave a badger alone, to use one of his grandmother's analogies. She closed the phone and depressed the alarm clock's button, the time splashing across the ceiling, reminding her that two more minutes of her life had slipped away. She knew she must rise, take a shower and find some clothes.

She glanced about the room, spotting the negligee draped haphazardly over a chair, the exact place Flynn tossed it after she slid it off Kira's body. There was little more evidence to suggest their tryst ever occurred—except the small wooden box that sat next to the high-tech alarm clock. They were a pair of striking opposites, a timepiece with cutting-edge technology and the tiny chest with the simple clasp that her father built during his eighth-grade industrial education class.

She had found it years ago among his things, and he willingly parted with it, the sentimentality long ago forgotten. She kept it on a shelf in her London flat where it collected dust, only knowing that it was important because it belonged to him. But when she'd returned after her summer in OB fifteen years ago, she had filled it with several mementos and often stuffed the box inside her suitcase when she traveled for months at a time. Showing it to Flynn had been her mistake.

The night before, they had arrived at the rental, both needing to shower after surfing. Kira pointed to the downstairs loo and hustled up the steps toward the master bedroom, unsure of what would happen if Flynn followed her. She showered quickly and returned to the kitchen to prepare the dinner. When Flynn reappeared, she wore a look of sheer desire. After wrapping her arms around Kira's waist and kissing her neck, she whispered, "I had hoped you might surprise me in the shower."

"I thought about it," Kira answered honestly. "But I want our first time to be a little more conventional, if that makes sense."

Flynn chuckled and popped a carrot into her mouth. "This isn't exactly our first time."

She stopped chopping vegetables and met Flynn's gaze. "It's been fifteen years, Flynn."

Flynn nodded and they kept their clothes on through dinner and cleanup, until the final plate had been loaded into the dishwasher. After Flynn dried her hands, Kira immediately pressed against her and kissed her deeply. There was no more banter. They fumbled up the stairs, unwilling to wait another moment, their patience unable to span the distance between the kitchen and Kira's bed. At one point they tripped on a plush carpet step and fell flat on their backs, laughing hysterically. Flynn took advantage and climbed on top of her, locking their lips together and groping her breasts. She sighed as Flynn's nimble fingers worked diligently to part fabric, unhook clasps and expose her flesh to warm hands. Kira moaned when Flynn's tongue flicked over her nipples.

"Not here," she said, gently pushing her aside.

She rose and scrambled up the steps, shutting the bedroom door behind her. When Flynn knocked, she told her to wait. She had planned the evening, and when Flynn opened the door, the room was dark, lit only by ten scented candles scattered on the dresser and nightstands that surrounded the bed—the bed where Kira rested against the headboard, clad only in a short royal blue teddy and positioned in a suggestive way to show off her long legs.

Flynn sighed deeply, frozen at the end of the bed. "You're in a lot of trouble."

"Why is that?" she asked, her fingers trailing over the pale skin of her cleavage.

"Because you want it bad, and I'm going to make you wait." Flynn took off her shoes and sat down. She held Kira's right foot in her hand and caressed her toes. She kissed each one lightly, a wicked smile on her face. "It's going to be a long night."

True to her promise, Flynn spent hours possessing all of Kira's body. At first the caresses were incredibly gentle, as Flynn kissed and stroked her limbs, sending tingles throughout her body. She closed her eyes as Flynn's strong hands kneaded her muscles, melting her into the bed. Her body simmered while Flynn's touch explored her flesh until she eventually settled over her, having shed her own clothes somewhere between licking the inside of her thighs and the deep kisses that now filled her mouth.

"Make love to me," she begged.

"Not yet," Flynn said, her lips and tongue rolling across her neck. "I want to see your tattoo," she whispered as she pushed the teddy up over her buttocks until the silky fabric bunched around her abdomen. Flynn's finger traced the outline of the little surfboard, and Kira felt her heart pounding.

Flynn kissed the tattoo, and Kira inhaled deeply, knowing Flynn's lips were inches from her throbbing center. She pushed Flynn's head between her legs. "Now, please."

Flynn didn't obey but instead pulled herself up and raised the teddy over Kira's head. She threw it on the chair and gazed at her naked body before she finally honored her request. Hours passed as they rediscovered each other with a sophistication gained from experience and the wisdom of age. They were more patient and giving than Kira ever remembered.

Dawn approached and they lay tangled on the sheets. Flynn noticed the wooden box on the dresser and pointed. "What's that?"

Kira didn't hesitate to tell the truth. Surely Flynn would respect the past in light of their rekindled passion. "My father made it in school. I keep mementos inside."

Flynn sat up on one elbow, interested. "Can I see it?"

"Of course."

Flynn slid out of bed momentarily and set the box between them. Kira guessed Flynn would need no prodding or reminders about the contents, for they all related to Flynn and that summer in OB. Flynn laughed immediately at the first object she removed, a tiny black-and-white photo of them with Megan and Rocco taken in one of those instant picture booths. They all looked so young and in love. Next was a paper coaster from the Bullfrog and a ticket stub from their evening at the OB theater to see *Fried Green Tomatoes.* "Cool," she said, but her expression sobered when she saw the ring. She held it up and swallowed hard. "I assumed you threw this away."

"No."

And then Kira knew it had been a mistake to show Flynn the contents of the box, the evidence of that long-ago summer. She realized that the mementos symbolized different emotions to Flynn. She reached for the box, but by then Flynn had withdrawn the last item—a paper folded into fourths.

"I don't think this was a good idea, Flynn," she blurted, realizing there was no way to stop what would happen next. Flynn unfolded the worn and withered scrap, the check Jonah had written to her for one hundred thousand dollars—the amount he thought Flynn was worth. She stared at the check, holding it with both of her hands.

"I kept it because it always reminded me that our love was

real."

Flynn didn't respond. She let the check close back into its established folds and placed the other items in the box on top. Without looking at her, she returned the box to the dresser, quickly threw on her clothes and vanished out the bedroom door. Kira closed her eyes and listened to her feet clamor down the stairs. She knew the sounds of keys jangling followed by the front door slamming in hasty departure. She waited to cry, wanting to savor every sound that was Flynn. So it was only after the sound of the SUV's motor had faded and the chirping birds could be heard again that Kira allowed herself to weep.

Chapter Twenty-four
Flynn McFadden

"Megan!" Flynn bellowed from her room. Her sister appeared and she held out the French cuffs of her shirt. "Damn buttons. You need three hands to get these things."

Megan easily pushed the buttons through the fabric and reached for her other arm. "I've got it. Now do you want to tell me what happened between you and Kira last night?"

She avoided her gaze and pretended to watch her work the cuffs. "That's not important. This day is for Mom and Stephen, and that's all it's about, right?" She gave her a glare that could cut glass and Megan nodded, dropping the subject.

Megan stepped back and admired her. "You look fabulous."

She turned to the mirror and poked at her curly hair, demanding that some of her stray locks fall in place. The powder-blue silk shirt and black pants complemented her hair, and although she wouldn't agree with Megan's exclamation, she thought she was passable.

"Let's go, girls," Mo called, and both of them trampled down the stairs, Kellen close behind, fighting with his tie.

General commotion erupted as they all located their bags and wallets, while offering compliments to Mo, who looked amazing in her teal dress and pearls. Mo directed them to carry a variety of objects to Flynn's SUV while Stephen helped his new grandson master the art of a half Windsor. They scampered to three different vehicles, and Mo followed Flynn and Kellen.

"My, don't you look handsome." Mo beamed as Kellen climbed into the FJ Cruiser next to his mother. Mo waved at her and hurried to the driver's side before she could leave. Mo stared at her daughter seriously. "Flynn McFadden, this day is going to be long enough without me worrying about you. You've got ten seconds to tell me what's going on, or you need to let it go until either I'm totally ripped on whiskey sours or tomorrow morning after my new husband ravishes me, whichever comes first. What's it going to be?"

It would have been terribly easy to break down, but Flynn knew that of all the days in her entire life when she had cried on her mother's shoulder or sought her advice, this was the one day she couldn't have—that she had no right to claim. Her mother had waited for this day for most of her life, and she would not dampen it in any way. She owed her mother that.

"I'm fine for now, okay. I won't lie to you. I'm hurting, but I'll get through." She reached for her mother's hand with tears in her eyes. "You know how much I love you, and I am so happy for you and Stephen."

Mo laughed heartily and jumped up to kiss her through the window. "Me too."

She and Kellen laughed as Mo danced an Irish jig all the way to Stephen's new BMW convertible. She plopped next to her groom and kissed him on the cheek. Flynn realized how much of life they still had to live, and the thought comforted her.

"Let's go, Mom," Kellen said and pointed to the road.

They arrived at the pier, many of the guests already assembled. Flynn worried for a brief second about whether the pier could hold the weight of the entire town of OB plus a few vehicles. She followed all of Megan's directions about flower placement, and she and Kellen helped Manny and Bear finish assembling the rows of chairs. Stephen and Mo would be married at the end of the pier, facing the Pacific, the veterinary clinic in the distance.

In another half-hour the pier overflowed with OB's locals, and people milled about waiting for a signal to take their seats. She scanned the crowd and didn't see Kira. Stephen and Mo greeted the visitors as they arrived, but she could see the agitation in Stephen's demeanor. He checked his watch again and whispered to Mo, who nodded and patted his arm.

Megan sidled up next to her, studying her expression. "You haven't said more than ten words since we left the house." When Flynn just shook her head, not wanting to get into it, Megan said, "C'mon, Flynn. What happened last night with Kira? You two spent the night together, right?"

"Yeah. But it didn't end well. I walked out."

"Oh, well, she doesn't look too upset about it." Megan pointed to the café, where Kira had arrived and was greeting Mo and Stephen.

She was dressed in an elegant emerald green dress, and she laughed when Manny whispered something to her. Others crowded around her, and Flynn could see she was in her element—a beautiful star and her adoring fans. All of the past seemed to be forgiven, and she had made a brilliant return to Ocean Beach.

Kira and Stephen slowly drifted toward the front, politely conversing with everyone who crossed their path, wishing Stephen well and reminding Kira that she had a fabulous father. Flynn couldn't take her eyes from Kira, who had pulled her hair away from her face into a loose bun, the sunlight catching all of the beautiful highlights. She never met her gaze, even when they stood across from each other, watching Mo walk down the aisle and join Stephen in front of the minister.

"God, Mom looks fabulous," Megan murmured in her ear.

"Yeah."

She looked over at Kellen, sitting next to Manny and Rocco, a wide grin plastered on his face. He was the best part of her life, she realized. It was time to move on. Maybe they could find their own place, a small bungalow near the clinic. It could be *their* new beginning, just like Stephen's and Mo's.

The happy couple exchanged vows, the gentle hum of the ocean providing a supportive background. As the minister directed the kiss, everyone applauded. Kira quickly followed the crowd to the café for the reception, while Flynn lingered behind. Kira was clearly avoiding her and perhaps it was for the best.

Once the guests retreated, she let the sea fill her ears. She leaned against the railing, looking out at the water, now the home of Luz's spirit. They had cremated her and scattered her ashes off the pier when Charlie Vernon wasn't looking. She stared at the blue foam, watching the surf beat against the pillars supporting the pier. Music and laughter burst from the café, and she hurried in that direction, knowing her mother would be looking for her soon. She wormed her way through the wall-to-wall crowd, exchanging endless hugs and kisses with all of the locals who had known her family forever. Bear sobbed on her shoulder, and she wondered if he secretly harbored some sort of crush on Mo. She approached the wedding party's table, but Manny took her arm and pulled her into a corner.

He waved a knowing finger in her face. "What's going on, Flynn? You and Kira are not yourselves. You're acting like it's the saddest day of your life, and Kira's so happy you'd think someone handed her another Oscar."

She winced at the observation. "Am I really that obvious?"

He raised an eyebrow and she told herself she must try harder. She patted him on the shoulder. "Thanks."

She propelled herself across the café toward her mother and Stephen before the emotion could fizzle away. They were already on their second round of whiskey sours, and their happy expressions were contagious. She found herself smiling in spite of feeling lousy. The noise was deafening, and after three trips to the dance floor with Stephen, Kellen and Bear, she retreated to the restroom for a few minutes of privacy that didn't require her to be cordial and friendly. She hid in a stall and caught her breath, enjoying the moment alone.

Another burst of applause coaxed her out of the bathroom. She turned toward the door and almost ran into Kira.

"Hi."

Kira's shocked face quickly shifted to the broad smile she had served up all afternoon. "Hello, Flynn. Isn't this a marvelous party?"

"Yeah." She looked around, assuring herself that they were alone. "Kira, I just wanted to apologize for this morning, for running out like that. It's just when I saw that check—"

Kira took her arm. "Flynn, there's no need to explain." She leaned close to her, as if she were about to dish Hollywood gossip. "It was just sex. I mean, it was great sex, but we don't need to get all emotionally involved in it."

Two women walked in and Kira laughed at nothing in particular. She immediately started chatting with them about their outfits and Flynn darted out the door. Stephen, Mo, Rocco and Megan were all engaged in a singalong with Mrs. Tillowix on piano, and the whole café joined in on the choruses. She crossed to the exit and headed out to the pier. She promised to give her mother this day, and now she wasn't sure she could make it. A few of the guests huddled over the railing smoking their cigarettes and enjoying the view of the sea. She spotted her banker, Richard Colson, coming toward her.

"Hello, Flynn," he said with a wave.

"Hi, Richard."

Richard Colson looked the part of a banker, with a bow tie and a serious disposition. People trusted him with their money because he found nothing humorous about his job or his life. Mo had tried unsuccessfully for years to make him laugh every time he lunched at the café. Flynn was sure the thick jowl lines that surrounded his mouth were the result of years of frowning, and she once suggested that he get a pet. A dog or cat, she thought, would help him find his heart, since he lived life in a constant flat-line pattern. Today, however, she was almost jealous, wishing she could control her emotions or deny them completely.

"Very fortunate windfall you experienced the other day. I'd say Larry could finish in three months if he hires the right crew."

At the mention of the money, she smiled slightly. "Yeah, I was shocked. I can't believe Mrs. Tillowix came through for us like that."

Colson's eyes narrowed and he pursed his lips. "I don't follow. I'm not talking about Mrs. Tillowix's donation. That was helpful, but I'm speaking of the seven hundred and fifty thousand dollars that was deposited two afternoons ago?" He sounded as though she was unaware of the generous contribution and he was the first person to inform her.

She was confused. "Wait, Richard. I thought Mrs. Tillowix donated that money, you know, since I saved Dewey during the engagement party."

He folded his hands in front of him and shook his head. "Flynn, you know Mrs. Tillowix would never make that kind of contribution, not even for her beloved dog. She is not your primary donor."

Flynn scratched her head, puzzled. "Well, if it's not her, then who is it?"

He sighed. "Flynn, I thought you were brighter than this. I know the donation was to be anonymous, but think about it. You only know one person capable of giving you that much money and only one person who would ever *want* to give you that much." Their eyes met, and for the first time in her life, Richard Colson made a joke. "That is, unless you know *another* rich movie actress?" The corners of his lips turned up ever so slightly. He was clearly amused by his own humor. He continued past her without further explanation to the other end of the pier.

The facts were a jumble, and Flynn quickly assembled the pieces in her mind. She raked a hand through her curls and went back to the café. She needed to confront Kira. She could barely get through the door without running into pockets of well-wishers, most of whom were extremely inebriated. She felt like a pinball in the crowd, searching for the emerald green dress. Unable to see anything clearly, she climbed on a chair for a better view. At the sight of her, there was a roar of approval.

"Three cheers for Flynn!" Charlie Vernon cried.

Flynn waved off the applause and found the bride and groom at the banquet table. Mo sat on Stephen's lap feeding him wedding cake while Rocco and Megan cuddled nearby, sipping Champagne and engaging in an overt public display of affection. She rushed the table and stood over all of them. "Where's Kira?"

They looked baffled. "She left just a minute ago," Stephen offered. "Something about catching a plane, of course." The disdain in his voice was obvious.

Mo patted his hand sympathetically and looked at her daughter with concerned eyes. "Flynn, darlin', is something wrong? She didn't say good-bye to you?"

"I need to talk with her right now."

She pushed her way back through the crowd toward the door. When the café finally spewed her out the exit, she gazed down the long pier and saw Kira's vibrant dress in the distance. Her shoulders sagged in defeat. There was no way she could catch the woman, even if she ran. She turned back to go inside and nearly stepped on Rufus.

An idea hit her. The little dog sat at attention, his brown eyes staring at Flynn and his tail sweeping back and forth across the wooden pier. She bent down and clapped her hands. "Who wants a treat?" Rufus barked and jumped up. She pulled one of Kira's soft cookies from her pocket and fed it to her happy pooch. "Want more?" He yipped, and she pointed to the end of the pier. "Go to Kira! Get a treat!"

He turned and took off, his little legs flipping in the air with each stride. She was amazed how fast the old dog could run when he was motivated. She followed behind at a brisk pace, her eyes glued to the brilliant green dress and the chestnut hair. He overtook her in less than five seconds and she greeted him with a big smile. Flynn watched as she stopped and bent over to pet the hysterical animal. Rufus would not let her proceed, determined to obtain a biscuit. Flynn knew if Rufus was anything, he was stubborn. Twice Kira tried to pass him, but he jumped in her path, and her kind heart wouldn't allow her to ignore the little dog when he was so persistent.

He saw Flynn approaching and offered a bark.

Kira turned around, a look of panic in her eyes. "Flynn, what's going on with Rufus?"

"He just wants a treat." She reached in her pocket and flipped the mutt another biscuit. He devoured it and she gave him one more before pointing back at the café. "Go."

"Hmm," Kira said. "Why do I think I've been played?"

"Why didn't you say good-bye to me?"

She laughed nervously and looked away. "I couldn't find you, and I do need to go."

"I thought you weren't leaving until tomorrow."

"My flight changed. I need to head out tonight to Canada."

She watched Kira's eyes for the slightest hint that she was lying. "What's in Canada?"

"I'm due in Vancouver to start a picture."

She leaned against the railing casually. "What's it about?"

"I really can't remember. It's either a mother losing her son or a comedy about two women riding across the United States in a Camaro."

"And they'd film that in Canada?"

"Believe it or not, most Americans couldn't tell the difference, I guess." She glanced at her watch and moved toward the pier stairs. "Now, I really need to leave. Do take care." She started to walk away, her heels clicking against the wood.

Flynn quickly stepped in front of her, blocking her path. She reached for Kira's hand and held it in her own. "Wait. Am I going to see you again, or will you avoid me for the next fifteen years?" Kira said nothing and averted her gaze. Flynn stroked the back of Kira's palm with her thumb and stepped close, until she could smell the scent of her shampoo. "Do you really believe that there was nothing between us last night?"

Kira stared at the pier. They said nothing for a long while, until Kira suddenly looked up with great sincerity. "What do you want from me, Flynn? We went to bed. It was nice, but there were no promises. We owe each other nothing." She paused, her eyes unwavering. "Look, I have sex with lots of women. It's just natural for me. No strings and no emotions. There doesn't have to be commitment behind every romp in the sack. Don't make more out of it than it was."

It was a slap in the face. Flynn dropped Kira's hand. Apparently satisfied that she had explained herself, Kira put on her sunglasses and started down the pier. Flynn closed her eyes. Kira's words hit hard, just as they had fifteen years ago when she told her it could never work. There was a ring of familiarity to Kira's speech and it took her a few seconds to realize why. Once everything clicked into place, she ran to Kira and grabbed her arm roughly.

"Don't you dare do this to me again. It's not going to work this time. Jonah's not here to rush in and save you."

At the mention of Jonah's name, Kira whirled around and met

Flynn's eyes. "What are you talking about?"

"You're acting. Practically that whole speech is from *The Autumn Months*. You know, where Cecile leaves Victor? Did you think I wouldn't notice? I saw that movie a dozen times." Kira stared at the ground but didn't flee. "Where the hell is Kira Drake? Where's the woman I slept with last night?"

Suddenly Kira's eyes were blazing. "You ran out on her."

"No, I ran out on the past. You showed me all that stuff that you've saved, especially that awful check from Jonah, and I didn't know what to think. Was last night about how you feel now, or is it some old memory?"

"I'm not sure," Kira whispered, and Flynn sensed she was being honest. "My feelings for you were so strong then—and now . . ."

Flynn wrapped her arms around Kira's waist. "What about now?"

Her eyes filled with tears. "I admire you so much, Flynn. Your life is so rich, and you've filled it with such purpose. Kellen is amazing, and the clinic, and the shelter. You've done so many wonderful things with your life. I guess I'm a little jealous."

Flynn shook her head. "Why would you be?"

"Let me see if I can explain it. At the risk of bringing up the past, if we could go back in time to that moment in the hotel and change the result, would you want that? Knowing how it all turns out?"

"No," Flynn admitted. "And honestly, I remember so little of that day. It's a bad memory that I've blocked out. I let it go. That's how you move on and search for happiness."

"Personal happiness," Kira said wistfully. "I stopped looking for that a long time ago. I decided I was never going to hurt anyone again the way that I hurt you."

"But you have to be hurt, Kira. You can't avoid pain. I would never trade what I had with Luz, despite the outcome."

"I don't know. It's not that easy for me."

"It's just choices, Kira. You had that awful man and your mother controlling your life for so long. Let go of Jonah and your mother. Your father did."

At the mention of Stephen, tears filled her eyes and Flynn embraced her tightly. "Oh, God, Flynn. I've wasted so much time."

"It's okay. It's not too late."

"What would you ever want with me?"

"You mean besides the fact that you contributed three-quarters of a million dollars to the shelter?"

Kira scowled. "That was supposed to be anonymous."

Flynn laughed and wiped the tears from her cheeks. "Honey, there's no such thing as anonymous in OB." They both laughed and Flynn stroked her beautiful hair. "Kira, I think you're smart, and beautiful, and you're an incredible surfer. But I'm probably not the best judge, since I'm blinded by your celebrity."

She mustered a slight smile. "You really think I'm a good surfer?"

Chapter Twenty-five

Mo McFadden

The entire wedding party and their guests crowded around the back windows of the café, watching Flynn chase after Kira. Megan grabbed the binoculars Mo kept under the counter and adjusted the lenses.

Kellen tapped Mo on the shoulder, a worried look on his face. "Grandma, isn't this spying?"

"Of course not, darlin'. This is family."

"Give us the play-by-play, Meg. We can't see hardly anything," Manny said.

"Okay. Flynn's stepped in front of Kira and she's stopped running away. She's holding her in her arms."

The crowd sighed. "Poor Kira," Bear exclaimed.

"She'll be all right," Mo said.

"You know, Mo," Charlie Vernon interrupted, "technically you could be violating the Peeping Tom laws."

She glared at him and the entire crowd voiced their displeasure with grunts and comments of their own. Mo pointed a finger at him. "Do you want Flynn to be alone for the rest of her life?"

"Of course not."

She reached over and unclipped his badge from his shirt. He had come to the wedding straight from work, wearing his uniform. "There, you're off duty. Now shut up and be a good friend."

Kellen cocked his head to one side. "Why are we watching them, Grandma? They're just talking."

"No, my darlin', they're dancing."

"What do you mean?"

"They've been apart for a long time and they have to relearn the steps."

"They're starting over," Stephen added.

"Oh." Megan gasped. "Kira's crying on Flynn's shoulder."

The entire café sighed and Bear sniffled. "It's okay to cry." Mo patted him on the arm, and he blew his nose into his handkerchief.

"They're getting close. Flynn's touching her hair. She's caressing her cheek."

"She needs to kiss her," Rocco stated.

"You are exactly right," Mo agreed.

"Who? Mom?" Kellen asked.

"No, Kira!" all of the adults exclaimed in unison.

"She needs to be the one to kiss your mother," Mo explained to him. "It can't be the other way around. Kira must forgive herself for what happened. C'mon, my girl, you want to. I know you do."

Megan stamped her feet in excitement. "Kira's going in. And we have a kiss on the cheek."

The entire café broke into cheers and applause. Mo reached for Stephen and planted a friendly kiss on his mouth. When they parted, he smiled. "Maureen, my love, I see where your daughter gets her passion."

Megan pulled the binoculars from her eyes and whirled around. "Quick. Everyone back to the party. They're coming this way."

The reception resumed, but Kellen remained at the window, his hands in his pockets. Mo slid her arm around his shoulder. "Kellen, what's bothering you?"

"Do you think Mom will forget Luz?"

She smiled. "Not at all, my boy. Your mother will always have Luz in her heart. I know this is hard to understand, but Luz would want your mother to be happy. She would want your mother to be with Kira."

"Why?"

"Because Kira loves your mother. I think she's always loved her, and it's finally their time to be together."

Kellen pondered her words. "Is it like you and Stephen?"

"Yes. Love must happen in its time."

They both watched Kira and Flynn approach, talking and laughing. "Does a kiss on the cheek count?" Kellen asked suddenly.

She squeezed his arm. "It most certainly does. It's a beginning."

Chapter Twenty-six
Kira Drake

For two months Kira and Flynn subsisted on daily phone calls, e-mails and the occasional handwritten letter. At first their communications seemed stilted, as they worked to find their voices, focusing on easy topics such as family and the animal shelter construction. Much had changed during her absence. They were already thinking of plans for a dog bakery next to the shelter, and more importantly, Mo and her father had moved out of the house on Narragansett and into a La Jolla condo that overlooked the ocean. According to Flynn's e-mails, Mo had insisted she no longer wanted to deal with such a big place, and frankly, as a newlywed, she wanted a cozy love nest just for her and Stephen. Kira also suspected Mo was making room for her, even with Kellen down the hall.

As their separation grew into weeks, they talked of their feelings, using bolder words, risking their hearts and eventually flirting shamelessly. Kira knew that although a thousand miles separated them, they were closer than they had ever been. They were now true friends—friends who recognized the lingering sparks of the past and the finite opportunities presented for happiness. Her return to OB would bring their relationship full circle.

Since it was an August Saturday at dusk, she knew exactly where to find Flynn. Kira had arrived home a day early and wanted to surprise her. As she crossed Abbott Avenue toward the ocean, she saw Flynn catching a wave, her body leaning hard to the side, daring the sea to wipe her out. A tourist stopped near her and gazed out at the surfers.

"Wow, that one's good."

She smiled at the comment. "That's Flynn, and yes, she's a great surfer." Among other things, Kira thought.

The man studied her. "Don't I know you?"

"I don't think so. I'm just a local." She swung her legs over the seawall and trotted down to the shore before the tourist could recognize her. She stood at the water's edge until Flynn caught sight of her. The result was a maddening paddling effort on Flynn's part as she attempted to close the distance between them.

When she finally crawled out of the ocean, dripping wet, Kira threw her arms around Flynn's neck. "God, I've missed you."

"I've missed you," Flynn murmured into her ear. "I'm so glad you're back." She looked into her eyes. "I'm glad you wanted to come back." She picked up her board and grabbed her backpack from the sand. She hugged Kira again, and they headed up the stairs to the café.

"I can't wait to see the shelter," she said. "It sounds like it's really coming along."

"We're about three-fourths of the way through, and Larry's done an amazing job."

"It's so exciting." She took Flynn's arm and squeezed.

They glanced at each other and smiled with genuine affection. "From everything you wrote, it sounds like the movie went well. Are you pleased?"

"It was a wonderful experience, and I thought I really nailed my character. I loved it, and I can't wait for you to see it."

"I'm looking forward to it. And I'm glad you had a great time. Loving your work is important."

"And that's the point. It's been a long time since I've enjoyed making a movie."

"I hope our e-mails and phone calls helped."

Kira nodded, but she was still troubled.

Flynn's eyes narrowed. "Is something wrong?"

"You didn't answer my last letter. I was thinking what I wrote to you may have been too strong."

Flynn chuckled. "No, it wasn't too strong, and I did write you a letter back, but by the time I finished it, I knew you were coming home in a couple days, and I didn't want just anybody to open it." She cleared her throat. "My response was a bit graphic."

"Would it have offended my proper British sensibilities?"

Flynn laughed heartily. "Definitely."

Secretly pleased, Kira said, "Then I must read it."

"Actually, I was planning on reading it to you tonight, when we're alone." Her expression sobered. "Of course, there may be a problem."

"What?"

"Our friend Rufus probably won't want to share you with anyone." Flynn paused. "Do you know what I'd really like to do tonight?"

Kira shook her head. "No, darling."

"Watch your movie *Beach Town*. I never saw it."

"I wonder why," Kira said dryly. "I mean, it is certainly worth seeing, as it is one of my better performances. You know, I was head over heels in love during that shoot. I suppose I could sit through it, as long as there's popcorn."

"Deal."

"There is one more thing I wanted to ask you." She stopped walking and took Flynn's hand. Flynn glanced around the pier, and she saw Flynn had noticed the fishermen and tourists enjoying the Southern California weather. "Flynn, I want to come out."

Flynn's eyes widened. "What? Won't that destroy your career?"

She shook her head and smiled. "I think I'm too old and too famous to be destroyed. Besides, I've learned that my personal happiness is much more important than public opinion, although I really don't think the public will care. As a matter of fact, why don't we test it?" She pulled Flynn against her for a deep kiss. When they separated, they looked around at the other people on the pier, all minding their own business—except for a little boy who stared at them and pointed. His father scolded him for pointing, saw Kira and Flynn and offered a wave. They waved back, laughing.

Flynn touched her cheek. "I so admire you. When will you really do it?"

"Well, next month my friend Carla has a film coming out. Would you be my date to the L.A. opening?"

"I think I'm free."

They kissed again and again, lost in each other's lips. A breeze drifted across the pier, like a gentle caress, telling Kira this was where she belonged. In her last letter she'd declared her love for Flynn, and she was almost positive Flynn would do the same tonight when they were alone. A series of coughs interrupted them.

They parted and saw Charlie Vernon nearby, his arms folded across his chest. "Flynn, Kira. What are you doing?"

Flynn nuzzled her cheek. "Kissing."

He glanced down at the pier. "I can see that. Don't you think this place is a bit too public?"

Kira touched his shoulder. "Officer Vernon, I do apologize. It's my fault. Flynn only kissed me because I asked her to. I'm actually planning to come out and tell the world that I'm a lesbian. What do you think of that?"

"Oh," he said, his face turning crimson. "Well, it's nice to see you again, Kira. Welcome back." He strolled down the pier without another word.

They laughed hysterically, and she led Flynn into the café, which was busy with the Saturday crowd. Kellen and Stephen sat at a table playing chess, while Mo served several customers at the counter. At the sight of them, the three family members rushed to welcome her back. The rest of the crowd smiled and waved but then quickly returned to dinner. There was no great fanfare for the movie queen, no stampede for autographs and no requests for photos, because this was, after all, Ocean Beach.

Publications from
Bella Books, Inc.
The best in contemporary lesbian fiction

P.O. Box 10543, Tallahassee, FL 32302
Phone: 800-729-4992
www.bellabooks.com

WITHOUT WARNING: Book one in the Shaken series by KG MacGregor. Without Warning is the story of their courageous journey through adversity, and their promise of steadfast love.
ISBN: 978-1-59493-120-8
$13.95

THE CANDIDATE by Tracey Richardson. Presidential Candidate Jane Kincaid had always expected the road to the White House would exact a high personal toll. She just never knew how high until forced to choose between her heart and her political destiny.
ISBN: 978-1-59493-133-8
$13.95

TALL IN THE SADDLE by Karin Kallmaker, Barbara Johnson, Therese Szymanski and Julia Watts. The playful quartet that penned the acclaimed Once Upon A Dyke and Stake Through the Heart are back are now turning to the Wild (and Very Hot) West to bring you another collection of erotically charged, action-packed, tales.
ISBN: 978-1-59493-106-2
$15.95

IN THE NAME OF THE FATHER by Gerri Hill. In this highly anticipated sequel to Hunter's Way, Dallas Homicide Detectives Tori Hunter and Samantha Kennedy investigate the murder of a Catholic priest who is found naked and strangled to death.
ISBN: 978-1-59493-108-6 $13.95

IT'S ALL SMOKE AND MIRRORS: The First Chronicles of Shawn Donnelly by Therese Szymanski. Join Therese Szymanski as she takes a walk on the sillier side of the gritty crime scene detective novel and introduces readers to her newest alternate personality—Shawn Donnelly.
ISBN: 978-1-59493-117-8
$13.95

THE ROAD HOME by Frankie J. Jones. As Lynn finds herself in one adventure after another, she discovers that true wealth may have very little to do with money after all.
ISBN: 978-1-59493-110-9
$13.95

IN DEEP WATERS: CRUISING THE SEAS by Karin Kallmaker and Radclyffe. Book passage on a deliciously sensual Mediterranean cruise with tour guides Radclyffe and Karin Kallmaker.
ISBN: 978-1-59493-111-6
$15.95

ALL THAT GLITTERS by Peggy J. Herring. Life is good for retired Army Colonel Marcel Robicheaux. Marcel is unprepared for the turn her life will take. She soon finds herself in the pursuit of a lifetime—searching for her missing mother and lover.
ISBN: 978-1-59493-107-9 $13.95

OUT OF LOVE by KG MacGregor. For Carmen Delallo and Judith O'Shea, falling in love proves to be the easy part.
ISBN: 978-1-59493-105-5
$13.95

BORDERLINE by Terri Breneman. Assistant Prosecuting attorney Toni Barston returns in the sequel to Anticipation.
ISBN: 978-1-59493-99-7
$13.95